The Officer's Wife

The Officer's Wife

A Chief Tobias Mystery

B. Sidney Smith

*S*mith
*S*tudios

Smith Studios is an imprint of Platonic Realms
235 Dabney Lane, Pamplin VA 23958, USA.

Printed in the United States of America
10 9 8 7 6 5 4 3 2 1

Smith, Becker Sidney. *The Officer's Wife.*
ISBN: 978-0-9636847-1-4

This book is a work of fiction. Short stories featuring Chief Tobias may be found on the author's website, www.bsidneysmith.com.

Cover art by the author.

for WHS

Chapters

The varieties of physical evidence, the motives of the culprit, and the efforts which he will make to evade detection combine to give this crime an interest, both academic and dramatic, that can be found nowhere else in the whole catalogue of the penal law.

* * * * *

In order, however, to provide a basis for a logical discussion of investigation as an applied art, it is necessary to create for ourselves the fiction that it is a science, complete with general principles and special theorems....

John E. O'Hara,
*The Fundamentals of
Criminal Investigation*

1 ...In a Military Manner

Woods Barracks, Nürnberg, West Germany,
Friday, 27 June 198-, 0730 hrs.

"**G**uard-force! UH-tin-*shun!*" Our dozen and a half heels snapped together in unison. Sergeant Carson pulled back the toe of his right boot, dug it into the cobblestones, and made a sharp about-face by spinning on his left heel and snapping his right heel loudly against it. The lieutenant, a West Point graduate, boyish and disciplined, took carefully measured paces from the side to the front of the formation, executed a facing movement, and stood with his nose only six inches away from, and two inches higher than, Sergeant Carson's. When the latter jerked his right hand up to salute I had a ridiculous notion he was going to throw a punch and knock the lieutenant sprawling. Of course he didn't. It was just a salute.

"Guard-force formed for inspection, sir!"

I hate inspections, and I *loathe* guard-mount inspections. My fault for being in a military intelligence battalion, I suppose, but I had a particular grudge that morning: until late the night before I'd expected to have the day off. While the lieutenant strutted and turned his way down the line of stiffly standing soldiers I cursed myself again for being idiot enough to answer the phone. It was what we called a "hey you!" event—a man scheduled for the 24-

1

hour guard detail was sick, or something, and I was the first person in his platoon to be reached. My wife had planted herself in front of the television with pursed lips after I hung up, and was jabbing the needle fiercely into her cross stitch when I went to bed.

The lieutenant was neither imaginative, nor subtle. To the man next to me he said, after a cursory glance at his uniform and boots, "What's your first General Order?" An obvious question. There are only three General Orders (laid down by Eisenhower, or some such demigod) and every soldier memorizes them in boot camp under the threat of increased "physical training"—torturous exercises performed to the accompaniment of staccato taunts from the drill instructor—until they can recite their General Orders in their sleep, and sometimes do.

Satisfied with his answer, the lieutenant performed a left face, took a thirty-inch step, performed a right face, and stared hard at my name-tag.

"Good morning, Pfc Smith," he said.

"Good morning, sir," I said seriously.

A pause while he studied my boots.

"What's your second General Order?"

"Sir," I said, my eyes fixed on a point behind his head. Then that unaccountable hesitation which strikes me at such moments set in, and it was an awkward three seconds before I finally blurted, in a single breath, "I will obey my special orders, and perform all my duties in a military manner, *sir!*"

He turned smartly to address the next soldier, but it was an interview to which I didn't listen; my awareness freakishly focused on the sensation of a bead of sweat which had formed in the hollow of my upper lip. After a few moments focused in this way, my body a plank and my gaze unwaveringly fixed in the air a few feet

from my face, I began to wonder if I was onto the secret of yoga—
if there wasn't after all some connection between unnatural, rigidly
sustained body positions and some kind of altered consciousness.

My trance was broken by the sound of Sergeant Carson calling my name. He had rejoined the formation, conferred with the
lieutenant, and saluted him on his way, back to whatever it is lieutenants do. I was so surprised at his call that I looked over my
shoulder to check the name of the soldier behind me.

"Pfc Smith?" he called again.

I stepped forward.

"Pfc Smith, you are chosen for Colonel's Orderly. Report to
the Staff Duty desk at oh-eight-hundred."

"Yes sergeant," I said, and stepped hesitantly aside. Me? He
had chosen me? I *never* get picked for Colonel's Orderly!

But that was great, I figured, suddenly sensible, because after
my "interview" with the Battalion Commander I'd be released, almost certainly, and could spend the day with my family after all.
I could fix the TV antenna for my wife. She would be pleased. I
might even take her to dinner. She'd really be pleased. Always
press your victories home, I remembered reading somewhere.

This will all make more sense if I explain that I enlisted late in
life—in my mid-twenties—and then I met and married Maggie, a
deal which included a half-grown daughter at no extra charge. My
wife tolerated but never pretended to understand my being in the
Army, and truthfully I find it increasingly hard to explain even to
myself. My official job title is "Intelligence Analyst," which is an
impressive sounding occupation—it sounded downright thrilling
when the recruiter broached it to me after reviewing my scores
on the Army's entrance exam—and I had signed my enlistment
contract in a fever of anticipation. The reality was obviously less

appealing. As a private in the Army I was, regardless of job title, basically a warm body, which, kept fed and in uniform, could be placed wherever a warm body was needed. In my section, when they weren't buffing floors, pulling guard duty, or running mindless errands, warm bodies were needed primarily to baby-sit equipment in the motor pool. My greatest achievement as an intelligence analyst had been learning to break track on our armored personnel-carrier cum tactical intelligence vehicle, and maintain its suspension. To my deathbed I will carry an abhorrence of the cloying scent of GAA (Grease, Automotive and Artillery).

Hence my pleasure at the turn this day had taken. I doubt I was much more disappointed with Army life than the average run of young soldiers, but unlike many I had a real home to go to when released from duty, and a real wife and family who, coarse jokes aside, bore no resemblance to the NCO's who dictated life's realities on base.

When I not-quite-bounced into Battalion Headquarters and announced the reason for my presence, the bleary-eyed NCO whose 24-hour tour of duty was coming to an end stared at me distantly, then nodded at a chair in the hall.

"Have a seat."

I sat.

"Got a book?" he said after seeming to forget my presence for a few minutes and then to remember it again.

"Uh, no," I said. "Sergeant," I added.

"Too bad."

"Where's the Commander?" I asked.

"Gone to Division."

"Oh." Division. That was in Katterbach, fifty-five kilometers away. An hour there and an hour back, given German traffic, plus whatever time he spent there.. . .

"Did he say when he'd be back?" I asked.

"Nope."

"What time did he leave?" I was being almost insubordinately inquisitive, and added, "Sergeant," by way of compensation and also as a prompt; his eyes and the slackness of his face suggested he might lapse into a coma. He frowned deeply, though whether in displeasure with me or in the effort to recall I'll never know, because just then the phone rang.

While he answered it Sergeant Carson strode in, having briefed his guards and posted the first relief. He plopped his gear on the desk and lit up a Marlboro.

"Afraid you're gonna have a wait," he said with cheerful brusqueness, "the CO and sergeant major just left for Division."

"Oh hell," I said inwardly. And then I said worse things. I looked bleakly ahead at a morning with nothing to occupy my time and attention but the self-absorbed comings and goings of the MP's on duty, and the crackle of the radio when the gate guards checked in from their posts. As had been pointed out, I didn't even have anything to read, unless one included under the heading "reading material" a copy of Soldier Magazine from the stack that was maintained on the staff duty desk, but I considered it propaganda, and the thought that I might be driven to peruse its colorful accolades for high-tech, well-heeled violence out of sheer boredom was depressing beyond words.

So I sat. The minute hand chased the hour, caught it, chased it again.

I began to nod.

"Hey, Smitty," Sergeant Carson broke in, snapping me out of a shallow dream. "I can't let you sleep. How 'bout goin' down to the snack bar and gettin' us each a soda? It oughta be open," he consulted his watch, "b'now."

Good idea, I thought, and I can pick up a Stars & Stripes newspaper. Though not exactly the New York Times, it would be an infinite improvement over nothing at all.

I took the change that he dug from his pocket and stepped out into the startling brightness of a Bavarian summer's day. Clover and dandelions sprouted among the cobblestones at the edge of the road, and the high sun cast into stark relief the ancient buildings that housed our modern army, as they had housed the armies of Hitler and the Kaiser before us. Traffic sounds drifted across the wall that separated our camp from the bustle of Nürnberg outside. It was named Woods Barracks, after a noted World War II general (American), but people mostly just called it the *kaserne*, using the German word for any military compound.

I bought two large Cokes, the newspaper, and, in a sequence of perverse impulses, a burrito, an egg-roll, and a cherry turnover.

When I reentered our headquarters I was arrested in my movements by a heated conversation coming from my immediate left, through the door of the MP's duty office.

"Look, young man, if you think I've got time to listen to excuses—"

"I am a lieutenant in the United States Army, *Mister*."

"All right, *Lieutenant*—"

"That's *sir* to you."

"Look, Lieutenant, sir, I don't want one of your damned vans with some teenaged traffic cop behind the wheel, and I don't want to stand here arguing with a butter-bar fresh outa Corn State U! I just want the keys to my vehicle, and a driver, a good driver, a mature driver, preferably, with something better on his mind than scaring an old man to death by trying to keep ahead of Hermann on the *autobahn*!"

The voice was deep and rich with anger, and I wondered that any young lieutenant could stand fast in the face of it. Yet, I also couldn't help feeling that the anger was too convincing—too practiced—to be very serious, and I guessed that beneath it lay a great deal of humor. These thoughts came all in an instant as I stepped quietly through the hall, straining to hear that remarkable voice again. It was the lieutenant who spoke next, however.

"Here," he said, "here's your damned keys. Find your own driver."

"Oh, but *sir....*" The voice had become deeper, if possible, and almost broken, as if by stones churning together in the throat, but now it was the voice of a pitiable old man. "Surely you have someone you can spare for an hour or two?"

"I won't have anyone," the lieutenant said peevishly, " 'til this afternoon."

The other voice broke into a chuckle at that, a chuckle that made me smile. "Right," it said.

Then its owner came into the hallway, a large, husky man in tattered jeans, a grungy blue t-shirt, and sneakers. He had dark, bushy hair that was streaked with gray, and an enormous salt-and-pepper mustache. The only thing about him that didn't look unkempt was his heavy pair of tinted eyeglasses. These were two slabs of curved glass stretching from eyebrow to cheekbone, held together and to the face by slender gold fittings. They flashed in reflection of the sunlight that was streaming through the door as his gaze wandered up and down the hall—he looked as though he expected to see someone with "driver" stamped on the forehead and standing ready by the door. He had his hands on his hips, tanned, fleshy, work-worn hands, and he rocked agitatedly up and back on the balls of his feet.

Intent on studying him, I paid too little attention to setting our refreshments on the table, and one of the drinks toppled sideways. Fizzy brown soda burst from the paper cup and splashed across the desk. The man's head snapped toward the sound, then he raised a finger and pointed it forcefully at me.

"You!"

I froze.

"What are you doing?" he demanded, striding up to the desk.

"He's spillin' my Coke's what he's doin', God dammit!" Sergeant Carson rushed to push papers away from the spreading liquid.

But the stranger's attention was fixed on me and he didn't wait for an answer, which was just as well.

"Do you have a military driver's license?"

I nodded.

"Sergeant, you don't need this man here, do you?" His hands were back on his hips. "All he does is make a mess, anyway."

Sergeant Carson looked at the stranger, then at me. "Go on," he said. "I don't know what Chief's up to, but it'll keep you outa my hair 'til the CO gets back."

The stranger turned abruptly and strode back down the hall.

"I'll tell him where you've gone," Sergeant Carson said, mopping up the mess with Kleenex. I hesitated. "Well, go on soldier— Chief don't wait for privates!"

I snatched up my hat, forgot my Coke and snacks, and trotted out the door. "Chief" was halfway down the street and walking fast. I maintained my trot to catch up with him, a little impressed at his absolute confidence that I would be hurrying along behind.

A hundred yards from the motor pool gate he stopped and tossed me a set of keys.

"Olive-green VW hatchback, license plate NB1058," he said, pointing at the motor pool. "I'll be right here." He turned and unlocked the door of a powder blue Toyota and began to rummage in the back seat.

I found the car. In contrast to the Toyota it looked chaste and well cared for, with its flat green paint and black vinyl interior. At the motor pool gate a guard signaled me to stop and sauntered over to the driver's side window.

"I gotta see yer dispatch."

"Uh," I said, looking under the seat and opening the glove box, "doesn't look like I've got one."

"Can't let you go without a dispatch."

"Call Sergeant Carson on your radio," I said. "He knows what I'm doing."

The guard hesitated, then walked back to his shack. For reasons I can't well explain—except to say that the stranger, in the force of his personality, had taken my will and made it his own—I stomped on the gas, left two short rubber streaks on the pavement, and swung out onto the road.

"Hey!" the guard yelled, but I didn't look back. "Chief" was waiting by his car and flung open the passenger door before I had fully stopped. He threw what was unmistakably a revolver under the seat, got in, and slammed the door.

"Let's go," he said.

At the gate to post the guard didn't check our papers, fortunately, seeing as we had none, and my passenger directed me to head straight for the north-south *autobahn*.

At last I said, "Are you in the Army?"

He smiled. "I'm sorry, haven't introduced myself. Chief Warrant Officer 2nd Class Tobias. And you are...?

"Pfc Smith," I said. "I work in intelligence."

"Ah! That's hopeful. Maybe you'll have some."

I stole a glance at his shaggy hair and mustache. "Have you been on leave?"

"Supposed to be," he said.

That explains it, I thought.

"Since yesterday," he added.

No, it didn't. He'd have to have been on leave for quite a while to grow a mustache like that one. The regulations governing mustaches were pretty strict.

"You're thinking I don't look much like a warrant officer in Uncle Sam's army."

"Um... yes, sir."

"Don't call me 'sir', it confuses me. 'Chief' is okay."

"Okay, Chief."

He stretched and put his hands behind his head. "I've probably got the only job in the Army," he said, "where grooming to military standards can get you into trouble." He grinned at me, then frowned a little. "No, I guess the counterintelligence goons have it much the same, only more so."

"What do you do?" I asked, somewhat tense.

"I'm a detective with CID," he said.

I tightened my grip on the wheel, keeping my eyes fixed on the center-line of the road. Criminal Investigation Division. The *real* cops. I thought of the revolver under the seat with sudden alarm, and a keener excitement.

"Are we going after criminals now, Chief?"

He caught the tone in my voice and laughed. "We'll have to get you a gun of your own, just in case."

I know when I'm blushing, because my cheeks get hot.

"Actually," he said, "today we get a treat. A real treat. Are you squeamish?" he asked, giving me a sudden glance.

"Not especially," I said cautiously.

"I'm sure you'll do fine." After a moment he said, "Do you know anyone named Merrick?"

I shook my head.

"Good. The body will be that of a stranger to you then."

I didn't notice the drift of the car until it was too late to correct it except by a violent lurch to the left. The *body*?

"You mean there's been a murder?"

"I have no idea," he said with a shrug, but then added brightly, "We can certainly hope so."

2 *Corpus Delicti*

Matson Barracks, Erlangen, West Germany,
Friday, 27 June 198-, 1220 hrs.

He directed me to leave the highway at a sign that indicated Erlangen, a university town of about 50,000, plus the students. Beneath the sign was a white plaque with an American flag, an arrow, and the words "U.S. Military Facility: Matson Barracks." This was the home of an armored brigade, and the post was alternately abuzz with activity or abandoned to wives and children, depending on the training schedule that took the units to their maneuver areas close to the Czechoslovakian border.

This was one of the quiet, abandoned periods, I would come to find out, but such things were far from my mind as I struggled through swarms of bicycling students in the heart of town.

I wanted to know what was going on.

"Shouldn't we have some MP's with us?" I wondered aloud.

"Already there," he said, "although I'm sure more will be coming when word gets back to Battalion that a body's been found."

I didn't understand, and my face showed it.

"We're not quite official yet," he explained. "I did a favor once for the brigade commander and his wife, a little matter regarding their eldest daughter that we needn't go into." He paused. "Anyway, she was there, or nearby, or something, the wife that is, when the body was found, and she called the colonel and had him call me. Got me out of bed, in fact." He looked thoughtful as we turned into the housing area. "I guess I'm flattered."

The U.S. government housing area on Matson *kaserne* was a loosely ordered block of three-story, stuccoed apartments interspersed with playgrounds, lawns, asphalt parking areas, and young trees. In front of one of the buildings was a knot of people, mostly women in light summer dress, plus two or three men in uniform. They stared at us as we pulled in and parked in front of the door.

Chief looked at them and winced. "I told the Colonel to keep everybody the hell out, but you know how it is. The fundamental human instinct," he proclaimed, "is nosiness." He sighed and took off his glasses to wipe them with his shirt. "I just hope they haven't mucked it all about."

For the first time I had a chance to study his eyes. They lay in fleshy nests of astonishingly fine wrinkles, and wore a frank, sad expression. In contrast to the earthy tones of his skin, the irises were blue. I would come to see those eyes express every human emotion, from hilarity to surprise to withering anger, but the longer I knew him the more convinced I became that this was the foundation of his face, and therefore of his personality: a large-eyed and mellow sadness, complemented, enhanced even, by a rose-hued bunching of the cheeks and upturned set of the mouth that betrayed an aptitude for joy.

The next moment the glasses were back on and he was bounding out of the car. Ignoring our small audience, he snatched the keys from me and opened the hatch-back, and lifted the black carpeted lid of the storage space. Beneath it were several small aluminum cases with handles, like suitcases, each neatly stenciled with a black number on the top and "CW2 Tobias, CID," neatly lettered beneath. He opened "No. 7" and drew out a green, spiral notepad and a black, felt-tip pen. He handed me the pad, then hesitated.

"You got a pen?" he said.

I fumbled in my pocket and showed him my U.S. Government ballpoint with a hint of pride—it was an inspectable item.

"Yeech! Use this." He handed me his. "Now then," he said. "Open to the first page and write what I tell you—neatly mind. Uh, 'Call received Colonel Crick 1045 hours. Message: Wife of Captain Merrick discovered dead in quarters, cause of death unknown. Husband in field with unit. Arrived Erlangen'—say, what time is it?"

I told him.

" 'Arrived Erlangen 1220 hours.' Oh, put the date at the top of the page, my name, and then yours."

He watched me studiously while I did this.

"Now, listen carefully." His voice dropped to a near-whisper. "This is, until proven otherwise, a murder investigation. Your job as the assistant detective—don't blush!—is to do exactly what I tell you and to use your brains. The main job of any detective is to notice things. It can be any kind of thing, so long as it might have a bearing on the crime or the people involved in it. When you notice things, write them down in that book. When I notice things, I'll tell you to write them down. *Alles klar?*"

I nodded, then grinned. "*Ja!*"

"Good. You can begin by noting the composition of our welcoming committee." He nodded at the group by the door. "Then grab numbers one and two, lock up, and follow me." He pulled cases 3 and 5 out of the car, tucked No. 7 under his arm, and marched past the staring crowd without a word. He paused for a moment to study the mailboxes, then stomped up the stairwell. I, scribbling furiously, counted spectators and fumbled for concise descriptions. Then I grabbed the cases and ran.

When I reached Chief he was just being let into an apartment on the second floor. On the door was a small, cross stitch plaque such as are sold at the innumerable bazaars organized by officer's wive's clubs at each *kaserne*, and which are serviced by local craftspeople who live by churning out knickknacks sodden with local color. "Cpt Merrick & Family" it said, and was set about with a tracery of small, pastel flowers. I wondered if they had children, and how many.

Inside the apartment a small group rose from chairs and a sofa as we entered and, as the MP who had opened the door shut it behind us and resumed his post, a large, ugly man in BDU's (camoflage fatigues) stepped forward to shake Chief's hand. It was Colonel Crick, the brigade commander.

"Chief Tobias," he said, something like a smile breaking his heavily seamed face, "good of you to come."

"How are you, sir?" Chief said deferentially.

The colonel ignored the question. "Mrs. Crick and I," he said, glancing at an obese, nervous-looking woman who hesitated behind his elbow, "seem to be always putting ourselves in your, ah, in your debt."

"Not at all, sir."

"This time, though," the colonel continued, "we may have been, ah, a little hasty. Natural causes, didn't you say, Doctor?" He turned and cued with his other arm a major, also in fatigues, who wore the insignia of the Medical Corps on his collar.

"Looks it," the latter chimed in.

"Chief," the Colonel said, finally releasing his grasp on Chief's hand, "let me introduce Major Suarez, our brigade surgeon."

"Pleasure," Chief said shaking hands, this time very briefly.

"Anyway," said Colonel Crick, "I'm sorry to have called you back from leave, ah," and here his eyes scanned Chief's bushy hair and tattered clothes, "unnecessarily." Immediately I classed the colonel as the kind of leader who commands, not by simple and direct instruction to his subordinates, but by the unstated pressure of his will and official power. He was the kind of man I would have loathed to work for, and I assumed Chief would just nod his head, pick up his cases, and head for the door. Instead he took off his glasses and began slowly to wipe them with the hem of his t-shirt. Then he fixed the colonel with a bright, humorous gaze.

"I'll just have a look then, shall I?"

"Of course, of course," the colonel said, smiling broadly, "you can confirm our conclusions!"

"Who found the body, by the way?" Chief asked.

"The housekeeper," Mrs. Crick broke in; "one of our enlisted wives—Mercy Blickwell. She's upstairs at the Worms's quarters, poor woman. Nancy Worms is giving her tea." She glanced at her husband out of what I took to be habit. "And a little brandy," she added.

"Well, this shouldn't take long," Chief said, as though making light of some small but unpleasant chore. "Shall I call you, sir, a little later? At your office?"

Like a skillful sailor tacking against the wind, Chief persuaded Colonel Crick to leave, and Mrs. Crick to go upstairs and keep Mercy Blickwell company until he could come up and speak with her. That left Major Suarez and the MP. The latter was posted outside the door with orders that no one was to be admitted.

"No one," Chief intoned seriously. "I don't care if he outranks the President, the Pope, and your mother put together." Then he turned to me. "What are you doing?" he demanded, for the second time that day. I had been standing discreetly out of the way, properly intimidated and respectful, I thought, in the presence of a full-bird colonel. But Chief, again, gave me no time to answer. "You should be taking notes like mad—what the hell's the matter with you?"

I flipped open my notebook and began taking notes like mad.

He turned slowly on his heels, scanning the room. It was a very large room, serving as both living room and dining room, and separated from the kitchen only by a low counter. Like other family quarters I had been in, this one had a depressing effect on the senses, being a forced hodgepodge of private belongings and government issue furnishings. Unlike families in the real world who could gradually accumulate belongings to fit their home, circumstances, and individual tastes, Army families had to fit what they had into wherever they were sent as best they could, and make up any shortcomings from the local warehouse. This explained the multi-colored, ragweed rug keeping company with lacy white curtains, and the presence of an impressive, black leather divan side by side with rust-colored, tweedy chairs. There were fashionable prints on the walls and a modest collection of porcelain figures and bric-a-brac.

"I wonder if she did her cleaning before she found the body?" Chief muttered. "Looks like it. Damn." He turned to Major Suarez. "Body's in the bedroom, I guess?"

"Yep," Major Suarez said. He led the way and I followed behind Chief, feeling a little giddy. The door to the bedroom was shut, and we gathered around it. There was an exchange of glances, then the doctor opened the door and we all went in.

The heat in the room was tangible, the more so that it was accompanied by a sweetish, sticky smell that I felt I had experienced before but couldn't place. The room was also very dark, with heavy curtains drawn across the only window. Major Suarez reached for the light switch, but Chief grabbed his hand. Smiling apologetically, he levered up the switch with his thumbnail.

The body was on the bed, covered by a white sheet. Chief drew the back of his hand across his forehead.

"My lord!" he said. "Was the heat on when you—?"

"Everything's exactly as we found it." Major Suarez said. "Except for the sheet. I thought it best to... you know."

"Yes," said Chief, "Nothing less decent than a corpse." He walked around the bed and lifted a corner of the sheet. "Oh," he said, his face curiously blank. He laid the sheet back down, then frowned. Reaching across, he gently lifted the top of the sheet and folded it back about 10 inches, then folded it back again, and so on down the length of the bed. When he had gotten it past the feet he lifted the sheet clear and folded it into a neat bundle.

I had expected to be nervous in the presence of a corpse, nauseous, repelled, even frightened. Instead I was very, very embarrassed. Mrs. Merrick had dressed for her death in a garter belt, black silk stockings, a lacy, bra-like affair that lifted her breasts without covering them, a black felt "dog collar" choker clasped with mother-of-pearl, and nothing else. Nothing, that is, unless you counted the fur coat, but it was open and she lay on it more than in it—it covered only her arms. Her mouth and her eyes were limply, expressionlessly open, and her essentially naked body lay spread-eagled on its back, like a brutal parody of the lingerie section in a soft porn magazine. An open and nearly empty 2-liter bottle of vodka was propped at her left side, in the hollow of her waist above the hip.

Being dead had not entirely robbed her of considerable beauty. Her body was lean but generous in form. Long, reddish hair permed to a Botticelli wave cascaded onto the bed, framing a delicately featured face. The eyes were large and seemed greenish, but it was difficult to be sure because they were dry and cloudy. The pupils, too, looked odd, as though they had somehow lost their shape. She had just the right sprinkle of freckles across the bridge of her nose and on her shoulders to the slope of her breasts, but these were subdued by a deep, even tan. Apart from the lifeless chaos of her eyes, her appearance was marred only by a slight pastiness of the skin and a drool on her cheek that had dried to crustiness.

And she was dead. My throat constricted and I must have made some sort of noise, because Chief glanced at me sharply. He shoved the sheet into my arms.

"Go get a drink of water," he said, "and leave this on the couch, or something."

I left the room, grateful to be out of the heat and the strange smell, yet vaguely anxious to get back lest I miss something or fail in my job. But for a moment I just stood in the hall and stared at nothing in particular. Then Chief called out to me.

"Bring back number two!" he yelled.

Case number 2 turned out to contain an elaborate camera kit, and it was only after Chief had taken at least a dozen photographs of the body that he broached the subject of the examination with Major Suarez. The brigade surgeon, for his part, had begun with detached interest in the proceedings, but with the photo session this had degenerated quickly into consternation, and by the time Chief asked, "What's this about 'natural causes'?" he was visibly annoyed.

"I think it's pretty obvious," he said shortly.

"What's obvious?" Chief asked mildly. He took the notebook from my hands and handed me the camera.

"Well, look at her!"

We looked. Then Chief returned to studying my notes while I put the camera back in its case.

"Perhaps you didn't know," the doctor continued, "that alcohol is a poison? That people die from alcohol toxicity—an overdose of booze—every day?"

"Not bad, Smitty," Chief said to me. "But you didn't note the brand of the vodka." He handed the notebook back and I hurriedly entered the data in. Then he turned to Major Suarez and took off his glasses. "Yes, sir, I'm aware of it. Lost a friend that way years ago." He paused. "Are you a forensic expert, doctor?"

"I'm authorized to give a certificate, if that's what you mean."

Chief didn't answer, but neither did he release the Major's gaze.

"No, I'm not," Major Suarez admitted, "and you won't find one this side of Frankfurt. Call it accidental death, if you prefer, but the woman died of drink, and I'm ready to sign my name to it." The medical officer thrust his hands in his pockets and glared at the corpse. "What the hell's all the hocus-pocus?"

"All right sir, if you can just help me out with a couple of details." Chief motioned for the doctor to join him at the bedside. "Tell me about the rigor."

"Fairly advanced."

"Completely advanced?"

"No...," Major Suarez gripped Mrs. Merrick's chin and pushed it firmly back and forth, a movement which rocked her upper body gently. "Neck and face rigid, arms stiff down to the wrist"—his hands moved methodically down—"torso rigid, abdomen getting hard, the hips and knees will flex slightly, ankles still malleable." He sighed. "Rigor still setting in," he concluded. "Probably last a day or two."

"Time of death?"

"Impossible to say with any precision, as I'm sure you know. With the heat in this room it might have come on more slowly than usual—say not less than six or seven hours ago, and not more than fourteen."

"Take a stab at it," Chief urged him.

"I'd guess eight or nine hours, with the heat. That's only a guess—"

"All right, now," Chief said, "anything out of place? Has she been moved since death?"

"Definitely not. Here—" and he lifted her onto her side. "Look at this, and this." He pointed to places where the skin was blotchy and purplish. "Lividity quite pronounced in the buttocks, the backs of the calves, the shoulders, and down the spine. She died right here; the blood settled precisely where the mattress is most depressed."

"Excellent! You're all right, Doc. Anything else catch your eye?"

Major Suarez laid the body down and straightened. "She died of drink, Mister Tobias."

"Oh, sir," Chief said, "we haven't finished—"

"Look. A young woman, ignorant, decides for whatever reason to tie one on. Not knowing any better, she chugs a bottle of

100 proof spirits. It doesn't take long, you know. Coma. Death."

"Why didn't she throw up?"

"They don't, always. On an empty stomach.... " Major Suarez shrugged his shoulders.

Chief dropped his chin to his chest, and frowned. "You're probably right, of course," he said. Major Suarez picked up his bag as though the matter were settled. I felt relieved; the argument made me feel awkward, and I couldn't fathom why Chief was being contentious. Not only was there the vodka bottle, but I had begun to decipher the smell and realized that it was mostly a smell of alcohol, together with the odors of urine and stale perspiration.

"Tell me sir," he said quietly, "Is it normal for habitual drug abusers to be ignorant of the effects of alcohol?"

"No. Why? Do you see needle marks on her arms? I don't, and I looked."

"I wouldn't expect to," Chief countered. He unhooked a stocking from the garter and began to roll it down her left leg. "You've been out of school too long, Major. All the uptown users make their injections right... here!" Gently he spread apart the toes of her left foot.

Major Suarez, reluctantly it seemed, stooped to examine the exposed skin between the toes. His eyebrows shot up. "How did you know?" he asked.

Chief smiled and put his hand on the other's shoulder. "Little hints."

"I guess I—"

"Listen, Doc. You'll be registering the body at Nürnberg Army Hospital, right? When you get to the morgue, tell them to set her aside where she'll keep for a couple of days. Get a little blood and aspirate the stomach. Nobody could object to that—it's routine, and it will tell us how drunk she was. While you're at it, aspirate the bladder. We may as well learn what we're dealing with."

"I guess, under the circumstances...." Major Suarez began. He looked worried. "They don't like scandal here. Not among officers. The colonel—"

"You're a doctor," Chief cut in. "Just between you and me and the lab tech, okay?" He steered him to the door. "Tell the ambulance drivers they can have her in a few minutes, will you? Thanks for your help, sir. We'll have this wrapped up in no time."

He shut the door and grabbed me by the elbow.

"Quick!" he said. "I'll dictate. Come over here by the body, so we won't be overheard."

He pulled off her other stocking and started with the toes again, spreading them one by one.

"I make it not less than twenty punctures. Hard to say—the marks overlap. Nothing on the ankles. The dorsal pedis veins were spared, then. Wait a minute. Well, that could be anything. Call it 'single unidentified mark on left ankle.' Okay. Fingers of both hands curled. Palms slightly livid. Red, even. I hate to say it, Smitty, but the lady was puttin' away some juice. Yeah, capillary blemishes on the neck ... she's been dippin' pretty heavy. A good six-month binge, anyway." He stood and put his hands on his head.

"Tell me something," he said. "What do you make of that tan?"

"Um," I said, looking hard, "it seems ... pretty thorough."

"Too thorough. No lines is one thing, but Smitty, there are some places it's just too awkward to get a tan. It may be trivial, but why get your tan from a bottle in the middle of June?"

I shrugged. Fear of cancer?

"Okay," Chief said. "This lingerie didn't come from the post exchange...."

We found the labels. They were from a German manufacturer and looked expensive. I jotted down the information. Next he produced a large magnifying glass from No. 3 and examined her face, then the rest of her body meticulously. Then he took a handful of small, numbered vials and a pair of tweezers from the case, and proceeded to take samples while I documented them from his dictation: "Bottle number one, hair from scalp; bottle number two, fibers from bra; number three, fibers from garter; number four, scrapings from fingernails, right hand; number five, left hand ditto; number six, hair from pubic region—uh-oh!"

I looked away hurriedly.

"Remind me to have the lab type the contents of samples six and seven. It might be our best clue to who she was last with, before she died."

Finally, after twenty-two bottles, he stopped and wiped his brow.

"That reminds me—" He opened a small box which contained several different types of thermometers. He put one, a digital thermometer in a little stand, on the mantle, and then took a second, an ordinary rectal thermometer, over to the body.

"How you holding up, Smitty?"

"Oh...." I was saved from answering by a knock at the door. It was the ambulance drivers. Chief met them in the hall and convinced them to wait outside. When he returned he stood over the body, his arms crossed, staring at the late Mrs. Merrick almost as if he expected her to sit up and tell us in her own words why she was dead.

"You know," he said at last, "she probably died of alcohol poisoning, after all." He sighed unhappily. "What do you think?"

"If that bottle was full when she started, Chief, and assuming she drank it, then I guess she must've."

"Assuming," he echoed. "Oh, room temperature eighty-three-point-two degrees fahrenheit, rectal temp eighty-six-point-eight. Note the current time, too."

"You can tell from what's in her stomach, right?" I asked while copying this data.

"Maybe," he said, "but unfortunately, maybe not. Unless she had just eaten, her stomach is probably empty, with the alcohol having been absorbed into her tissues and the water, what there was of it, passed into the intestines. Her blood and tissues will give us a pretty clear idea of how drunk she was, but not how she got that way."

"You mean there's no way to tell?"

"Unless there's some just lying in her esophagus we won't be able to get a sample, and unfortunately vodka doesn't have any distinctive smell. It's practically pure ethanol." He leaned over and smelled her mouth. "Wait a minute...." He sniffed again. "Smitty, come here!"

I went and stood opposite him by the bed.

"Smell her mouth."

I braced myself and leaned over her. I couldn't smell anything but the alcohol smell, and shook my head.

"Here, wait a minute." He made a fist with one hand and wrapped his other hand around it, then thrust violently into Mrs. Merrick's abdomen. There was a slight gurgling sound, and we both sniffed at her mouth again. It was a smell I was familiar with, although I don't care for the stuff personally.

"Scotch," I said.

"Bingo."

While the ambulance drivers removed Mrs. Merrick's body

Chief went upstairs to the Worms's quarters to make some calls and check on his witness. I stayed behind to arrange his various kits on the dining room table, which he had designated as our temporary headquarters.

When he returned he gathered up a tape measure, ruler, pencils, and a large tablet of graph paper, and led the way back into the bedroom. There we sketched and diagrammed the entire room, tediously noting the distance of everything to everything else, and from there to where different parts of Mrs. Merrick's body had lain. All the while Chief admonished me not to disturb anything as I contorted to reach over and around the various pieces of furniture. Then he took another dozen photographs.

We returned to the dining room; this time to get the fingerprint kit from No. 5. There were actually two complete kits, and Chief took a few minutes to instruct me in their use. I was then set to dusting the bedroom door and walls—the large, flat surfaces—while he tackled the furniture and an assortment of toiletries atop the dresser and vanity desk. The door was covered with prints, but except for a palm-print and some fingertips, the walls were disappointing.

"Nice palm," he said, looking over my shoulder.

"Thanks," I said, wiping sweat from my upper lip. "Can we turn the heat off yet?"

"Soon as we get these prints. Come look at this." He led me to the vanity table. "All these articles," he said, indicating make-up kits, hair spray and perfume bottles, hair brushes, and mirrors, "show the same set of prints. Hers, no doubt. Except for this mirror." He held up an oval mirror with a brass frame and handle. "This," he said pointedly, "has no fingerprints at all. None." He looked at me. "Doesn't that just make you *itch?*"

"Um...," I said.

"I challenge you to give me one good reason why this should appear untouched by human hands."

"Well," I said, "maybe it needed to be cleaned."

"Humph. Would you wear gloves to wipe off a mirror? Now, come look at this." We approached the bed. "This headboard is littered with prints; at least three sets in my opinion. That," he said glancing at me sidelong, "you may properly consider suggestive. But it's nothing to the foot board, which, like the mirror, has no prints at all!"

"Gosh," I said.

"Gosh indeed. And the icing on our mystery cake is the thermostat control knob on the space heater, which—let me see if you can guess."

"No prints?" I offered.

"You're a detective," he beamed. "I congratulate you!"

"Wait a minute," I said excitedly, "why didn't they wipe off the doorknob? It's loaded with prints!"

"You mean the doorknob that you, and Major Suarez, and Mercy Blickwell, and God knows who else have been using all day?"

"Oh, yeah," I said, abashed at my ready stupidity.

"You've got a point, though. I'll be very interested if there are any prints of Mrs. Merrick's there, or of anyone else we can't account for. Let's lift them and let the lab boys tell us."

Lifting the fingerprints was an exhausting process. It was done with clear tape, and every specimen had to be placed in a special notebook with all the information about where it was found neatly lettered next to it. Then yet another notebook was selected, and I was detailed to make a complete inventory of the room's contents while Chief went meticulously through each drawer, the closet, across the floor, the window sills, the wall.. . .

"Bored yet?" he said finally.

"No. My hand is a little crampy."

"Mmm." He stood in the center of the room and turned slowly around. "You should be, there's nothing here." He pulled up the bedding in a perfunctory way, and looked between the mattresses. "In fact, there's simply not enough here."

"How do you mean?"

"Did you notice the nicotine stains on her fingers? Yes, of course you did; I saw you write it down, and that she was right handed. That was good work, by the way." He sat on the bare mattress and leaned back on his elbows. "Anyway, why does Mrs. Merrick dress—or undress—in X-rated lingerie, sit down to a bottle of vodka, and ostensibly drink herself to death without smoking any cigarettes? Not normal behavior for a heavy smoker."

I looked at the large glass ashtray on the nightstand and nodded my head. It was clean.

"Maybe she smoked in the living room, and came in here just before she died," I conjectured.

"I suppose that's possible. We'll check with the housekeeper about the condition of the ashtrays. But there's another problem: where's her purse?"

"Hunh? Well, there's lots of purses in the closet."

"Yes, but they're all empty. You married, Smitty? Ever look in your wife's purse?"

"I try not to," I admitted with a grin.

"Full of junk, right? So, I ask you again, where's her purse?"

"Maybe in one of the other rooms."

"Maybe so. Let's not forget to look." He leaned down and

looked under the bed. "What a knot-head I am," he said, and dragged out a large, flat, cardboard box. He cocked his brow at me and wagged his finger. "Always check under the bed!" he scolded, and lifted the lid. He whistled. The box was full of lingerie, of a kind with what she had been wearing. "Now, why is she keeping Frederick's of Hollywood under the bed?"

We inventoried it. All of French, German, or Swedish manufacture.

"Next question. Why a fur coat? Some kind of fantasy? Had she gone out dressed like that? Or was she entertaining in? She wasn't wearing any shoes, and none of the shoes in the closet were damp or soiled."

"The weather's been dry for a couple of weeks," I offered.

"True."

"Maybe she took her shoes off."

"And maybe she never went out," he concluded. "It boggles my mind, at least, to imagine her out and about in that outfit." He jumped to his feet and put his hands on his hips. "The great and final question," he growled, and glared at me fiercely, "is why she had a bottle of vodka propped at her side when the last thing she had to drink was scotch?"

"Well," I began, "maybe she was going to drink the vodka next, but died before—"

"Bullshit." He put his hand on my shoulder and smiled. "What do you really think?"

"I think somebody else was here."

"Good man. I think so too. Let's go do the other rooms."

My heart sank. "Do we have to sketch them too? And inventory everything?"

"No. We'll settle for a determined clue-hunt."

After dusting the phone, light switches, doorknobs, furniture, and bathroom and kitchen fixtures (confirming that the house-keeper had managed to complete most of her job), Chief began going through cupboards.

"Here's the liquor cabinet," he said, "and here's the scotch! Pricey stuff, too—I don't think they sell this in the States. Hmm. Mercy's duties don't extend to dusting the booze, I see. If this bottle's been handled in the last month, I'll resign my commission. Take a look."

The bottle had an undisturbed layer of dust; thick on the shoulder of the glass, thinner on the neck and sides.

"It's never been opened," I said. "Maybe she had another bottle."

Chief looked at me with a good-natured frown.

"I like you, Smitty. You keep me honest. Well, what else have we got here? Bacardi (the clear variety—how chaste), peach brandy, cherry brandy, Kahlua, creme d'menthe, Tanqueray gin, Triple Sec, Irish cream ... damned near all you could ask for in a home bar, if you aren't too exotic a 'tender, and all of it dusty and most of it never opened. Except the rum—it's dusty but recently handled, and only half-full. Only one thing missing...."

He paused.

"That's your cue, Smitty!"

"Oh!" I dithered. "Uh...."

"The vodka."

"Of course."

"Go fetch it here a minute."

I went to the table and picked up the zip-lock plastic bag that held the vodka bottle. The vodka itself occupied a plastic jar, sealed and labeled.

"What do you notice?" he said.

"It's clean," I realized.

"Right, with only her prints, and damned few of those. Now tell me she washed the bottle before opening it! And something else—fetch the flashlight from number eleven. Now, see the dust on the shelf? See any places without dust?"

I nodded; there was one clean spot.

"What shape is it?" he asked.

"Rectangular."

"Hand me the bottle." He carefully took it out of the bag and set it on the shelf. The base of the bottle was rectangular. It was a perfect fit. Then he handed the bottle back to me with a delicate smile.

"Mind you," he said, "I don't consider your 'second bottle' theory completely blown, but if there was another bottle we should be able to find it."

He hopped up. I noted that as clues began to accumulate he became increasingly animated.

"Is the trash kept under the sink? Nope, next to the refrigerator. And it's full! This will be fun."

We dumped the plastic can on the kitchen floor and squatted down together to go through it.

"No scotch bottle," Chief murmured, "but here's the cap to the vodka bottle. I count three cigarette butts, all menthol."

I got out my notebook and started listing contents.

"Pretty boring stuff," he continued. "Lots of microwave dinners, a few eggshells, banana peel—you know what?"

"What?" I said.

"There's something wrong with this garbage. Smell it."

I smelled it, shook my head.

"Look at this banana peel. Black. And these eggshells. See what I mean?"

I chewed on my pen. "I get it!" I said. "It's all dried up. Old."

"You got potential, Smitty, you really do. We need to talk to Mercy, and also find out how long Captain Merrick's been in the field. You ask me, Mrs. Merrick hasn't been home much... whoops! What's this? Somebody missed the basket." He reached down between the refrigerator and the stove, into the small space where the trash had been kept. "Shame on Mercy for forgetting to sweep back here!"

He held up a paper towel. "It's almost still damp, unlike the rest, and a little grimy. Ah! What do you make of this red stain?"

"I took the scrap of towel and stared at it. There was a thin red smear, about two inches long across one corner, and another smaller one near the middle. I shrugged my shoulders.

"If your eyes won't tell you, try your nose," he suggested.

I did, and immediately held it away. "GAA," I said.

"Gee-hay-what?"

"G-A-A. Grease."

"Fascinating. Ever seen red grease before?"

"Unh-uh. The stuff we use in the motor pool is kind of tan-colored."

"Hmm. I've seen blue, black, and brown, but red is new to me." He cupped his hands over his mouth and nose, and creased his brow furiously. Then he dropped his hands and gave me a keen glance. "You know, this is getting interesting."

3 Interviews

Matson Barracks, Erlangen, West Germany,
Friday, 27 June 198-, 1500 hrs.

Chief decided to interview his witnesses in the Merrick living room, since it would enable him to conduct the interviews in privacy, and because, as he put it, its "proximity to the death chamber" would "encourage a sober earnestness in the testimony."

It had come to light that six people had witnessed the body before us; Mercy Blickwell, Mrs. Crick, two other neighbors who had answered Mercy's distress calls (screaming on the lawn as one put it), and of course the colonel and Major Suarez. So the house-keeper was to be interviewed first, while the Colonel's wife was detailed to ring up the other two neighbors and detain them in the upstairs apartment.

"And we may as well talk to the Worms woman, while we're at it," Chief said.

I was provided with a new notebook, and with a small tape recorder that fit in my breast pocket and could be turned on and off through the cloth. "Put it in the right-side pocket," Chief said; "I don't want to have to listen to your heartbeat for hours later—and for God's sake don't fidget."

Mercy Blickwell was a short, plump woman with a flat face and brown hair that looked as though it had been cut at home.

She wore a pink cotton blouse, white polyester pants that were too small, and tennis shoes. Chief sat her on the divan, where she perched on the edge with her knees together, clutching a small purse. She'd been crying, and the red streaks on her face punctuated her tense, frightened manner.

"You must be from Arkansas, Mrs. Blickwell," Chief said in a voice like your favorite grandfather. He sat lazily in a tweed chair and stretched out his legs.

"Why—*yes!*" She didn't cease to be tense, but Chief had captured her interest and for a moment her attention was distracted from herself. "Actually I'm from Oklahoma—that's where I was born—but we grew up in Little Rock. How'd you know that?"

"Would you like to smoke?" he asked, magically extending a pack of Marlboro's, the top flipped up.

"*Yes!*" Relief expressed itself through every limb. "That horrible Mrs. Worms won't let anyone smoke in her house, and they wouldn't let me go home...." She lit her cigarette, took an enormous puff, and blew a stream of silvery smoke that spanned the room and spread along the opposite wall. "Are you really a policeman?" she asked suddenly.

Chief dug in his wallet and handed her his CID identification. It took her a full twelve seconds to comprehend it, then she handed it back and stared at him. Her face slowly puckered.

"Am I in trouble...?" A tear worked loose and streaked a well-worn trough down her cheek.

"Goodness, no!" Chief said firmly. "We just need to ask you a few questions, about Mrs. Merrick."

"Oh that poor woman," Mercy said, and shook her head sadly. Then, in a dramatic whisper, "I was so scared."

"It's a terrible thing," Chief agreed. "Have you been doing her apartment for very long?"

"Since right after they moved in," Mercy said. "She put a ad up in the PX—I remember it was right about Easter last year."

"Do you clean for lots of the ladies?"

"Oh yes. I do Paddington's, and Rickter's, and Benson's that's right above us (he's only a staff sergeant but she works both her jobs), and Franklin's, which is my husband's platoon sergeant, and Hernandez' place, and, let's see...."

"I guess the Merrick's was pretty easy?" Chief cut in.

"Not at first it wasn't. I never knew a worse woman for house-keeping! I swear she never washed a dish. But lately," she said, suddenly vague, "they don't seem to be home much."

"Where do they go?"

"I don't know." Mercy's gaze shifted to the floor. "She was stayin' with friends, I think, when Captain Merrick's gone to the field. He's a company commander since Christmas, and they been in the field a terrible lot."

"Did she say what friends she was staying with?"

"Unh-uh."

"Other officer's wives, perhaps?"

"I don't think so...." She stubbed out her cigarette.

"Is there something you're afraid you shouldn't say?" Chief prompted gently.

"No, it's just that—"

Chief offered her another cigarette, which, after an infinitesimal hesitation, she accepted eagerly.

"People been sayin' terrible things about her." She lit it, took a long drag, and spoke with the smoke in her lungs; "That she spent a lot of time with Germans."

"With Germans?"

Mercy leaned close to Chief, her eyes bright, and said in a low voice, "That she had German *boyfriends*."

"Now listen carefully, Mercy," Chief said, echoing her confidential tone, "I need you to tell me exactly what happened today, starting with when you got here."

"Well—"

Chief had to prompt her for each detail, but slowly it emerged that Mercy Blickwell had arrived at 8:15 that morning to find the apartment virtually unchanged from the previous Tuesday. There was some dried mud on the carpeting, and the kitchen and bathroom sinks had been used. The toilet paper on the roll had been used up—or so she supposed, it was gone anyway—which was odd because she'd put a new one out last time.

When she arrived she checked the bedroom. The door, she said, was open just a crack, and all she could see was that the curtains were drawn and that someone was on the bed. Sleeping, she thought.

"You didn't go in?" Chief asked.

"Oh, no!" Mercy said. She explained that Mrs. Merrick usually slept late, and that she'd been warned never to wake her up, even though the sound of the vacuum cleaner always woke her anyway, and she would come out in her robe and fix a pot of coffee while Mercy did the bedroom.

"But this time she didn't wake up," Chief said.

"No.…" Mercy's eyes misted.

How long had she spent cleaning, Chief wanted to know. She said there'd been very little to do; she'd vacuumed and dusted, and then, feeling she needed to earn her money, she'd done the windows.

"Did you clean the ashtrays?"

"Just the one in the kitchen."

"What else did you do?"

"Well," Mercy said, tightening her grip on her purse and staring at her knees, "I wasn't sure if I should leave, or what to do. Mrs. Merrick always liked me to do the bedroom especially, but I couldn't just go in.. . . ."

Mercy began to cry.

"Get Mercy a glass of water, would you Smitty?" Chief said to me. I rose and went to the kitchen.

"I'm sorry," Mercy whined when I handed her the glass.

"That's all right," Chief said. "I expect you must've been a little worried about her when she didn't come out."

Mercy nodded vigorously, gulping water.

"And you just wanted to check—?"

Mercy set her glass on the coffee table and looked at Chief, her tears turned off as easily as a spigot.

"She was *hard*," she said wonderingly.

Chief gave her another cigarette.

"I swear on the baby Jesus I won't never forget the way she was starin', just starin' and starin'—and dead like that!" She blushed. Then she hung her head and grinned, stealing sidelong glances at each of us from under swollen lids. "I hope whenever I have to die, I'm rightly dressed."

"I hope so too," Chief said. "Did you touch anything else in the bedroom?"

"No! I just ran right out. I was that scared."

"Just one other thing," Chief said, "and we'll let you get home. When you unlocked the apartment this morning, how many times did you have to turn the key?"

"Well I—now let me see." She mimed turning a key with her

left hand. "I'm pretty sure it was all the way locked," she said finally.

"Then you had to turn it twice?"

"I think so." She didn't sound convinced.

"You're certain, at least," Chief said, "that the bolt was bolted?"

"Oh yes. I think so. It usually is, 'cause she's always careful about that. She tells me to bolt it when I'm cleaning, 'cause of she said there might be rapists—" She shot her hand to her mouth and her eyes grew round. "Oh holy Jesus! Do you think one of them rapists...?"

"No," Chief said. "I'm absolutely positive there was no rapist."

"Wouldn't that be terrible!"

"Mercy, may I look at your key?"

"Hunh?"

"Your key. To the apartment."

"Oh." She opened her purse. "Wouldn't that be terrible," she repeated, handing Chief a large, silvery key. "She always said to me, 'Mercy, make sure you lock the door always. I'd hate for a rapist to come in and get you.' And now she's—"

"Mercy," Chief insisted, "there was no rapist."

Mercy pressed her lips together.

"You won't need this key any more, I shouldn't think—I'll give it to Captain Merrick when I see him."

"Oh that poor man," she said, but I heard a little note of pleasure beneath the sorrow in her voice. The drama taking shape in her mind's eye appealed to her. This is the sort of woman, I thought, who keeps in business those weekly papers that sport headlines about two-headed babies, and Elvis returning from the dead.

When she was gone Chief spent a few minutes locking and unlocking the front door with her key. He looked lost in thought, with his brows drawn together and his tongue sneaking in and out through his teeth at the side of his mouth. It was an odd, self-forgetful gesture.

The door was of the German security type. It had a fixed knob on one side and an L-shaped handle on the other, with a key hole on each side sharing the same barrel and bolt assembly. It could be bolted or unbolted only with the key, and even unbolted it required a key to open it from the outside.

"Go get those keys out of the evidence box, the ones that we found in her coat," he said finally. I brought them; little Tupperware container, cotton wadding, and all. He didn't take them out, but found the apartment key and held Mercy's next to it.

"As I thought," he said. "This key of Mercy's isn't one that came with the lock, which means it probably wasn't issued to the Merricks when they occupied these quarters."

"You're not supposed to make copies," I said knowingly.

I labeled a new container for Mercy's key while he called upstairs on the phone to invite the next witness down. Then he quickly cleaned out the ashtray and opened a window. He also took the glass Mercy had used, handling it gently with a piece of tissue, put it in a plastic bag, and dropped it in the evidence box. When the doorbell rang I took up my station, notebook in hand.

Mrs. Sabrina Grason was a petite woman whose ready warmth and artless beauty were the sort to make other people feel somewhat self-conscious in her presence. She wore a clingy white sweater, a skirt that hugged her waist and hips before flaring in wide pleats to the tops of her calves, and high-heeled sandals. Her hair was an explosion of tight brown curls that danced like springs on her shoulders, but which were pinned back at the temples to reveal a round face, straight nose, expressive mouth, and large chestnut eyes.

"You must be the one they call Mister Chief," she said, politely extending her hand.

"Chief Warrant Officer Tobias," Chief corrected, "but please call me Mister Tobias."

"Oh, I'm sorry." She ducked her head with a grin. "My husband—Lieutenant Grason?—tried to teach me the different ranks, but I just can't make them all stick, somehow."

"It's quite all right. Won't you sit down?" Again he indicated the divan, and sat in the other chair. It was evident that we were not to be introduced, but as she sat down Mrs. Grason gave me a friendly glance and a smile. I was consoled.

"I understand you were one of those who answered Mrs. Blickwell's cries, and who found Mrs. Merrick in the bedroom?"

"Yes," she said, suddenly very serious.

"What do you think might have happened to Mrs. Merrick?"

She looked plainly puzzled. "I thought—didn't she drink too much? That's what Mrs. Crick said."

"That's what it looks like. I just thought you might have an idea of your own."

Mrs. Grason shook her head slowly.

"How many of you came into the apartment?"

"Just myself and Mrs. Crick, and Mrs. . . . uh . . . "

"Mrs. Bradley?"

"Yes."

"Did you all go into the bedroom?"

"No, just Mrs. Crick. Mrs. Bradley stayed in here, with Mrs. —with Mercy."

"And what did you do?"

"I went as far as the bedroom door." Mrs. Grason's gaze drifted to the window as her attention focused inwardly back to the scene.

"What did you make of it?"

"I don't know," she said softly.

"Were you surprised at how Mrs. Merrick was dressed?"

"I guess so."

"Did Mrs. Crick turn the light on?"

"Um ..." She put her fingers to her temple as though the effort to remember threatened to give her headache. "No, I did—I turned the light on." She looked up then and put her hands on her knees, facing Chief with a bland, cooperative expression.

"Do you smoke, Mrs. Grason?" Chief asked pleasantly.

She didn't answer immediately; a faint smile touched her lips. "Sometimes."

"Smitty, get us an ashtray, would you? And bring Mrs. Grason a glass of water." I went to the kitchen while Chief asked if she had known Mrs. Merrick well.

"No," she said. I set the ashtray and water in front of her, but she ignored them and did not smoke. "You see, Michael and I have only been here a few months."

"Are he and Captain Merrick in the same battalion?"

"No, he's in staff. 'S' something."

"In what battalion?"

"First of the Twenty-Eighth."

"But that's Captain Merrick's battalion."

"Oh."

"Do you work, Mrs. Grason?"

"Yes, but some people don't think it's work, really. I mean, not like a job."

Chief waited with a patient smile.

"I do some modeling, sometimes."

"For an American firm?"

"No—yes!" She grinned and huffed with impatience at herself. "You see, I did work back home—catalogs and stuff mostly—but not since Michael and I got married and we came here." She twirled one of her locks around a finger. "He doesn't like me doing it. He's a little jealous."

"Then you don't model anymore?"

Bland cooperativeness returned to her face; she didn't take her eyes off of Chief's as she shook her head and said, "Unh-uh."

"Thank you, Mrs. Grason," Chief said abruptly. "Smitty, would you note down her phone number? We may want to speak to her later." He rose and went to the phone, and in a moment was telling someone to send the next witness down.

Mrs. Grason, giving me her phone number on a slip of paper, leaned close.

"I don't think he likes me," she said.

Mrs. Georgette Bradley had strong features, with a Dixieland smoothness of skin, auburn hair, and gray eyes. She was brief, and very frank.

"My children are hungry, you know," she said coming in the door, and preempted niceties by plopping on the couch.

Chief took his cue and wasted no time.

"Did you know the deceased?"

No, Mrs. Bradley did not know Mrs. Merrick, and had never cared to; she had thought her to be vain, petty, and a waste of time. When asked what she had done when she was in the Merrick apartment that afternoon:

"I hardly came in at all. Blickwell was a mess—it was all I could do to get her to stop wailing. I took her upstairs almost immediately."

"Did you go into the bedroom?"

"No. I never saw the body," she allowed herself a dry smile, "such as it was."

"Do you know Mercy well?"

"No. I keep my own house. Anything else?"

Chief sighed. "Perhaps another time."

When she had gone he sank into his chair, took off his glasses, and rubbed his eyes.

"Let's go upstairs," he said. "I need a change of scene."

We were out the door when the phone rang. Chief and I looked at each other, and then he went back in and picked it up.

"Hello?" he said. After a moment he put the receiver back in its cradle.

"They hung up," he said.

Mrs. Crick opened the door to our knock. A greasy smell and a clattering of pans from the kitchen suggested that Mrs. Worms was keeping busy. She emerged, wiping her hands on a towel, and pointed to the couch.

"Sit down," she demanded. She turned on her heels and stalked back to the kitchen, yelling over her shoulder; "Is Coke all right, or do you want beer?"

Chief and I stared at one another.

"Nothing, thanks," Chief said.

We walked into the dining area, which, like the one in the downstairs apartment, was separated from the kitchen only by a low counter. Mrs. Worms had opened the fridge and was rummaging in the lower shelves.

"I don't mind, really," she bawled; "looks like I've got ginger-ale." She stood and snatched the lid off of a Tupperware pitcher. "And I've got some juice left. The girls drank all the coffee, but I could make a fresh pot, or if you like tea—"

"Please," Chief said, "Pfc Smith and I have got to be going. If you could just answer one or two questions for us before we go?"

She was a tall woman with striking features that were not pretty, but strong and handsomely formed. She had a rich shock of ebony hair gathered in a long ponytail, and her skin was the hue that is sometimes called olive. She closed the fridge and wiped her hands on the towel again, then looked at Chief with an inexplicable air of defiance, her dark eyes flashing.

"Well?" she said.

"May we sit down?"

"Of course."

Chief didn't move. She dropped her hands rigidly to her sides and stomped to the couch, a behavior which reminded me very much of my daughter; a pre-teen, she does the same thing when sent to clean her room. We filed into the living room behind her, myself last, surreptitiously (I hoped) clicking on the tape recorder through the heavy cloth of my fatigues.

"Did you know Mrs. Merrick?" Chief asked.

"Yes."

"Well?"

"Hardly."

Chief waited.

"She was not popular," Mrs. Worms snapped. "Most of the wives are nice people, and not accustomed to—her sort."

"What sort was that?"

"I'm sure the other women must have told you."

"Mrs. Worms, let me make myself clear. My job—my military duty—is to find out why she died, and whether any crime was involved. Can you understand that? Just a job, like banker or bricklayer. Now, will you help me? Think of me as a bank teller or something, and just tell me what I need to know, ok?"

Under Chief's patient, intelligent gaze she dropped her defiant air, and for a moment I thought she might be going to apologize. She stared at the coffee table. "What do you need to know?" she asked in a low voice.

"Do you think anyone might have wanted to kill her?"

"I don't know. I could have."

"I beg your pardon?"

The room was very still, and Mrs. Crick murmured "Oh dear!" under her breath.

"She was a bitch," Mrs. Worms said. Her voice was a monotone.

"Mrs. Worms, where were you last night?"

"With John." She took a deep breath. "We went to dinner at the club, and then came home."

"John is your husband?"

"Yes." Mrs. Worms began unaccountably to cry. They were big tears that gathered on her lip and formed drips at the end of her nose.

"Mrs. Worms—"

"Please leave," she said. "My God, please."

I was spellbound, having never witnessed such a scene before. Chief appraised the woman for what seemed a long time before speaking.

"Of course," he said, not unkindly, and rose to go.

We were locking up the Merrick's apartment when Mrs. Crick came down the stairs. "She asked me to leave, too," she said anxiously. Her face was set in a concerned frown and she moved in nervous fits and starts, starting down the stairs ahead of us, then stopping and turning back, beginning to speak, changing her mind, and then, just as we stopped on the step above her to listen to the thought that was brewing on her face, shaking her head and fidgeting her way down the stairs again. Finally, at the door, she stopped and grabbed hold of Chief's arm.

"She said she was sorry," Mrs. Crick said. "For, well, for being... rude." She looked so concerned that I almost protested myself, but my fledgling thought was preempted by Chief's ready courtesy.

"You mustn't think of it. I am sure the day has been very stressful for her. How soon is she expecting her baby?"

Mrs. Crick opened her mouth to speak, shut it again. Chief held the door for her and we emerged blinking into the late afternoon sun. Colonel Crick was striding up the sidewalk with another officer at his side, and waved to us, quickening his pace. Mrs. Crick looked alarmed, and grabbed Chief's arm again.

"Nobody knows about that yet," she said. She looked a fierce question, and I was sure she would have said more, but the colonel was upon us, and the moment was gone.

Colonel Crick introduced the man at his side as his executive officer, but to no apparent purpose.

"Rachel," he said to his wife, obviously dismissing her, "I'll be a little late getting home—don't wait supper for me."

I almost thought she would say "Yes sir." Instead she nodded and then shook her head worriedly. "Poor Captain Merrick," she said, and walked away in a kind of crouch. Her husband took a deep breath, and his eyes passed meaningfully over the space in which I was standing.

"Smitty," Chief said, "how's about stowing these cases?" I went and busied myself, but I was not out of earshot.

"I decided I better call and introduce myself to your boss—a Lieutenant Colonel Bragg?" Crick began.

"Ah," Chief said.

"He was surprised to hear from me; says he didn't know anything was going on here. I know I probably shouldn't have called you directly, uh, this morning, but then I expected you would inform your superiors yourself...?"

"Of course," Chief said lightly. "He'll be receiving my full report in an hour or so."

Colonel Crick was silent for a moment, and I stole a glance; he was frowning, as if in thought, and digging at the pine needles on the sidewalk with the toe of his boot.

"Died of drink, then, did she?" he said at last.

Chief shrugged his shoulders. "On the face of it, that's the best explanation. The lab people should be able to let us know before long."

"You mean you've ordered an autopsy?"

"I don't think you understand, sir," Chief began, but he was interrupted.

"I don't want a lot of damned upset over this thing, you get me, Warrant Officer Tobias?"

"Not so fast, Colonel."

Crick straightened like a man insulted.

"Sir," Chief said, in a tone of voice that just missed being deferential, "a military dependent has died from unknown causes, and there will be an autopsy. I can point out the chapter and paragraph of the regulation that says so if you'd care to study it. Meanwhile, I shall naturally have to make my report, and carry out whatever orders I'm given. I want to thank you for calling me, and if there's anything I can do for you, anytime, I hope you won't hesitate to call again."

There was a pause. Chief's tone could hardly be construed as disrespectful, yet he had given up nothing the colonel evidently wanted. After waiting a decent interval for a reply, Chief came to attention and snapped his arm up in salute.

"Thank you again, sir!"

The colonel returned the salute and we hit the road.

4 Rumors and Ruminations

Woods Barracks, Nürnberg, West Germany,
Friday, 27 June 198-, 1630 hrs.

"**P**rick."

We had entered the highway, and this was the first Chief had spoken.

"He doesn't quite seem to know what he wants," I offered.

"Exactly." A few minutes later he said, " 'If you pick up a starving dog and make him prosperous, he will not bite you.' " He took off his glasses and began to wipe them with his shirt, then looked at me with a humorous gaze and raised brows. " 'And that's the principal difference between a man and a dog.' "

"Mark Twain," I said, smiling.

"Well, I'll be damned." He put his glasses back on. "Smitty, who's your boss?"

"Um, well, Staff Sergeant Williams, mostly."

"That's right, you're in intel. Like it?"

"It's kind of boring."

"Yeah." He stared out the window the rest of the ride.

When we got to base an off-duty guard who was loitering in front of battalion headquarters followed us with his eyes as we parked and then ducked into the door. I had a notion he'd been told to watch for us, and this was confirmed when we went in and the

MP lieutenant, the one with whom Chief had argued that morning, stood outside his door and smirked at us as we came through the hall. Sergeant Carson gazed at us and sucked his teeth.

"The CO wants to see you," he said, looking at Chief.

At that moment the gaunt figure of Lieutenant Colonel Bragg appeared in an adjacent hallway. "Get in here, Toby," he said crossly.

"Yes, sir," Chief nodded, and then turned to me. "Take the boxes along to the evidence room. The clerk will show you what to do."

Chief and I separated down different hallways, but Sergeant Carson called me back in a stage whisper.

"What's up?" he asked.

I hesitated. A vague sense that the matter should be confidential, plus my own perplexity regarding where I stood with respect to it, overcame my natural impulse to gossip. I shook my head and turned away.

Turning in evidence was a tiresome process. The purpose, I gathered, was to maintain a demonstrable chain of custody. Each item had to be carefully described and numbered on a receipt, and each receipt signed and countersigned, and stamped of course. The evidence was then reverently laid in trays, and the whole works locked in its own cage. The clerk was very efficient, never interrupting the process with extraneous remarks like, "Golly, what's that?" as I would have done.

When I returned Chief was still closeted with the commander. There was a chair by the door of his office, which I had no sooner sat down in than the door was flung open and both men came out and stared at me. I sprang up and came to attention.

"This him?"

"Yes sir."

"Who's your commander, son?" the Colonel asked.

"Captain Richards, sir."

"Hmm. Understand you made 'the man' today?"

"Yes, sir."

"Well, you're released."

"Yes, sir." And before I could turn to go he was back in his office. Chief gave me a quick wink, and followed him.

I was unnerved. Was I in trouble too? I wanted more than anything to stay and talk to Chief, but released means released— means get outa here. Why make matters worse by risking disobedience? I couldn't even park the car in the motor pool, and linger that way, because Chief had the keys.

"You gonna tell me what's goin' on?" Sergeant Carson asked as I passed by.

"I've been released."

"Oh ... so?"

I shrugged my shoulders. I didn't want to talk.

"What are you doing home?!?" My wife, who is a beautician, had her hands steeped in some orange goop which she was massaging into a woman's scalp in the living room.

"Daddy!" My son tackled my shins, and I lifted him into the crook of my arm.

"You been a good boy?" I asked, snatching a kiss from my wife over the poor woman's head.

"Light—hhhot!" he said, pointing and nodding his head vigorously, and then he twisted my nose. He would be two years old in a month.

"Sorry to be inconvenient," I said. "Made the man today."

"So you're off?"

"Yep."

"Wonderful! Honey, meet Cathy."

"How do you do," I said.

"Hi," she managed, somewhat plaintively.

"Sorry to catch you at a disadvantage. Maggie being good to you?"

"I hope so. Everyone says she's the best."

"It's true."

"Giving her a mohawk," Maggie said.

"Oh ... please don't—"

"An orange one?" I asked.

"Yeah!"

Cathy looked worried. My wife teases her clients almost cruelly, but they invariably become devoted to her after the first visit. It was no accident that her informal little business had blossomed, in only a few months in Germany, into a nearly full-time occupation, and that by word-of-mouth alone. Back home in Seattle she had a commanding reputation, and it was rumored that her clients put a price on my head when they learned I was taking her away. Nobody here seemed to mind that she worked in her living room, and it was understood that there were no fees for her services; ladies were allowed to give her any gift they liked—checks accepted.

"So, if you 'made the man,' where've you been all day?" she asked.

"You won't believe me," I said, bouncing a jumble of giggles on my knee.

"Uh-oh. *Who* is she?"

"Funny you should ask that." I set the giggles down and began to unlace my boots. I was aware that I should be discreet, but....

"Do you know a Mrs. Merrick?"

Maggie shook her head, but Cathy became animated.

"Kimberly Merrick? Matson Barracks?"

"Yes," I nodded.

"She's famous!"

Jackpot. All I had to do now was listen.

"Famous?" Maggie prodded.

"Oh, my dear, you've no idea!"

"Queen of the ball? Loved by all?"

"Hated, more like it. The woman's an *absolute* slut."

"No!"

"Yes! Her husband's the laughing stock of the Division."

"Like, give me an example."

"Well, I don't know the details, but when he's gone to the field, it's said, she invites men, right into their quarters—"

"Really?"

"Anne McGillicutty said she told her they were just friends, but she dresses like a hooker in furs—"

"Who's Anne McGillicutty?" I interjected.

"The brigade chaplain's wife on Matson *kaserne*. She's very nice."

"Hmm."

"She wears furs?" Maggie said, keeping the conversation on track.

"Yes, her father's rich, or something."

"So does her husband know?"

"He must. They're never seen anywhere together, except maybe the 'must attend' affairs, like the Brigade Ball, and then she's a little clam, never says boo, and treats the other wives like they're dirt and she's royalty—except then she makes eyes at their husbands."

"I wonder how long they've been *married*."

"Practically newlyweds!"

Maggie looked at her watch. "Time for rinse," she said. They trooped off to the bathroom.

I had no real ache to drop the news of Kimberly Merrick's death into things. I found my daughter in her bedroom and contrived to help her with her homework until Cathy was done and gone.

When we emerged, victorious, from our struggle with fractions, Maggie was stirring noodles in the kitchen. After giving her a proper greeting (to the inevitable accompaniment of "Ugh, you guys!" from my daughter) my wife grabbed me by the ears and gave me a stern look.

"While you set the table, you can tell me about Merrick."

"Yes ma'am." I grabbed the plates from the rack.

"Well?"

"Susan," I said to the ten-year-old, all ears at my elbow, "set the table. Here's the plates."

"But she told you to do it!"

"Susan," I repeated, deadpan, "set the table. Here's the plates."

"Yes, *sir*."

I waited 'til she was out of earshot.

"She's dead."

Maggie gave me a blank stare. I kissed her on the nose.

"Tell you about it later."

"Now, that's not fair!" She put her hands on her hips and, mocking me with my Army nick-name, threatened, "Pay-backs are a bitch, Smitty!"

"I know. I'll just have to risk it."

We said grace. Maggie played 'maybe-I'll-eat-it-and-maybe-I-won't' with the monster in the high-chair. Susan stated flatly that she expected to be taken shopping at the Post Exchange tomorrow. I was responding to this while pretending to have nothing much on my mind. Our table was a portrait of limited success; a kind of parody of Norman Rockwell.

"What about the zoo?" I attempted. "There's a good zoo here that we've never—"

"You mean after we go to the PX?"

"I haven't said yet we could go shopping."

"But—"

"There's more to living in Germany than shopping at the Post Exchange. We have an opportunity here that most people only dream—oh hell!"

The phone was ringing. Maggie answered it.

"Hello? Oh. Just a minute." She looked at me and I shook my head. "He's not here. What? Just a minute." She set the receiver down and came back up the hall.

"He says he wants to talk to you whether you're here or not. Says his name's Chief."

I ran to the phone.

"Chief?"

"That the wife?"

"Yeah."

"I want to meet her—she's a remarkable woman."

"I know."

"How many kids?"

"Two. A girl and a—"

"Good man! Can you come over?"

"Uh...." I covered the mouthpiece and looked down the hall at Maggie, who was standing in the arch of the hallway with her arms crossed. "Now?" I asked.

"You a detective or aren't you?"

I grinned. "Yeah!"

"Grab a pencil. Ready? Mozart Strasse 21, by the tracks. You turn left off the SudRing at the sign that says Spielzug Museum. Twenty minutes?"

"Um, yeah. Okay."

He hung up.

Marriage may be justly described, at its most prosaic, as a careful balance of personal debts. Maggie accepted my sincere (but unexplained) IOU with stalwart silence, and let me kiss her goodbye.

Chief's building was three storeys of ancient red brick, capped by a steep roof with little Art Nouveau dormers poking out from the moss-green, ceramic shingles. I decided it must be a turn-of-the-century structure. This made it quite a rarity in central Nürnberg, as anyone who has seen photos or films of the devastation wrought upon the city by the war can attest; historically important buildings were restored, but modern ones were simply replaced. More interestingly, and very unusually in this well kept town, it was derelict. I had no trouble telling the number over the door—it was carved into the stone—but the door itself hung loose and disheveled, like a drunk on his last bottle. The entryway was dark, and stank. I found a timed switch for the stairwell light. Germans are a progressive and practical people, and even in private

homes the hallway lights are often worked by a switch that shuts
off automatically after a few minutes. However, my situation was
little improved by the murky glare from the low-wattage bulb that
hung by its wires overhead. The intercom and buzzer system for
the several apartments was heavily vandalized, and most of the
nameplates were bare. Next to the top button had been painted in
red—nail polish?—"TOBIAS #3A."

I pushed the button and waited. I pushed it again. A pair of
moths had found the light, but apart from the random tink-tink of
their bodies against the bulb, there was utter silence. With some
unease I peered up the narrow stairs, then began to ascend. The
first landing had three doors, on one of which could just be read,
"1B." On the next were "2A" and "2C." This meant Chief must live
in the attic.

I was halfway up the last flight when of course the lights went
out. I decided it was safest to backtrack; there had been bottles
and other trash on the stairs below, and heaven knew what traps
lay ahead. Accordingly I made my way down in the darkness and
felt for a button, pushing the first one that I found. A primitive,
angry buzzer sounded. After a pause I continued searching with
my fingers, practicing *"ein entshuldigen"* (beg pardon) under my
breath, but no one came to a door. At last I found the switch.

At the pinnacle of my steep climb was a little landing, no more
than a meter square, and a wooden door unencumbered with orna-
ment save for the characters "3A" painted on it in rough, slender
strokes of the same iridescent crimson. I rang the bell, and almost
instantly Chief's disembodied voice sounded in the air behind my
left ear, scaring me nearly out of my boots.

"That you, Smitty?"

"Yeah!"

The door clicked and swung noiselessly inward on a dimly lit hall.

"I'm in the study," he called. "Down the hall on the left. Shut the door!"

The apartment seemed to consist of a single, very long hallway, with doors pairing off on each side at regular intervals. The floor of the hall was bare, but the plain white walls were relieved here and there by nondescript artwork in small wooden frames. Chief told me later that the rooms making up his apartment had been servants' quarters. Each servant was given a small room with a half-sloped ceiling and single dormer window, and the hallway originally connected with all three of the building's stairwells.

The study was the only room larger than ten feet on a side. Chief explained that three of the rooms had been knocked together, making a long, open room segmented by two broad arches. It was really a study, library, and—I suppose one must say "parlor" even though the word isn't current; "living room" simply isn't descriptive. In any event, one end was given over to comfy chairs and little side tables, and included a small bar. At the end opposite the bar was a complex of desks and work tables, dominated by two personal computers wired together in some fashion, with two or three printers and other devices that were strange to me. A potted vine hung in each of the three dormers. Also, there was a very long, narrow table running down the center of the room, the top of which was littered with diverse objects: books and maps, a drawing pad, a compass and other instruments, a microscope, a half dozen geometric shapes made out of wood, a brass figurine of a many-armed pagan goddess, a candle in a small wrought iron stand, the skeleton of a human hand and forearm, a ceramic bowl filled with marbles, and other miscellany whose nature or purpose

I could not identify. Every wall in this remarkable room was blanketed with books. The books were neatly arranged, but not a single square foot of space was available for anything else.

I forgot to make an important exception: On one wall, in a space between the shelves, was a large aquarium. It was about four feet long and contained some sand, a large piece of driftwood that jutted several inches above the glass, and an enormous iguana that sunned itself on the branch under a strong lamp, its green and metallic-blue scales flashing brilliantly in the bright light.

Chief was hunched on a stool in front of one of the computer monitors, and was typing furiously. He spun about and greeted me with a broad smile.

"Smitty! Glad you could come."

I said nothing, but stood with my garrison cap in my hands and turned slowly on my heels, taking it all in.

"My study. Like it?"

"You're like a character in a novel, Chief."

"Oh." His smile faded uncertainly, and I realized that it genuinely mattered to him that I like him.

"I mean," I began, and then shut and opened my mouth twice. I was abashed by this frank appeal from someone with whom I was almost, after only a single day, involved in a kind of hero-worship. I blushed, as usual, then grinned and threw my hands up.

"It's great!" I exclaimed. "It's really great."

"Good." He came and put his arm around my shoulders, leading me toward the bar. "Thirsty? Like a beer?"

"That'd be great."

"That's Nietzsche, by the way." He pointed to the lizard. "I tell my German friends his name's Bertrand Russell, so as not to offend 'em—either way, I can argue circles around him. Cop a seat."

I sank into a chair. He opened a small fridge, popped the cap off a bottle of the local pilsner, and handed it to me with a tall glass. He hadn't changed his clothes since the afternoon, I noticed, and the apartment had an odor that—well, it wasn't unpleasant, wasn't stale, but it was a little musky. A hazard of bachelorhood, I decided. It was certainly better than the troop billets, which smelled of socks.

He poured his own beer, and sat facing me.

I summoned myself. "No doubt I'm wondering why you've asked me here," I said.

He savored the phrase for several seconds, then giggled, which was the oddest thing I'd yet seen. He sat back and chewed on the stem of his glasses.

"You ought to be a writer, Smitty."

"Sometime I'll invite you over, Chief, and show you my rejection slip collection."

"No kidding?"

"Yep. I'm hoping to get enough to paper the bathroom when we get back to the world."

"Hmm."

We sat and sipped at our beer in comfortable silence for a few minutes. I noticed that it was difficult to be tense around Chief, perhaps because he was so ponderous and concentrated—it was like sitting down to share a conversation with a mountain.

"Had any thoughts about today?" he said at last.

I had, but I hadn't had time for any thoughts about the thoughts, so it took me a moment to phrase them. "I'm pretty sure that someone was there when Mrs. Merrick died," I said slowly, "and that the person didn't want anyone to know they were there.

But if she was murdered, it must have been poison, or smothering with one of the pillows, or something like that."

"Not bad. Those are reasonable conclusions. Except that she wasn't smothered—that's easy to detect, and none of the signs were there."

"Like for instance?"

"Oh, blueness around the lips and nose, things like that."

"Poison, then."

"Perhaps," he said. He sipped his beer. "But there are problems. There were no positive signs of someone else's presence, only negative ones. If she had been entertaining, either we or Mercy should have been able to note the fact. The bed hadn't been slept in, dishes hadn't been dirtied, and—very telling—the ashtrays hadn't been used, except for the one in the kitchen. And that one only had three butts in it, from what we found in the garbage. Additionally, there were no likely poisons in the house. No sleeping pills in the medicine cabinet, or other drugs—nothing that wouldn't have caused a violent reaction or left a tell-tale sign."

"Alcohol—" I began.

"But what kind? The last thing she had to drink was Scotch—where did it come from? And who did it come from? Her husband was in the field. Had she been out for a fling in nothing but her skin and a fur coat? As you say, whoever it was wished to remain anonymous. Why, unless the death was unnatural? If the woman you're with suddenly drops unconscious, do you carefully array her on the bed with false evidence and wipe the prints, or do you call an ambulance and hope for the best?" He took a long swallow of beer and belched discreetly. "What's it all about, Smitty?"

"I give up."

"I hope you don't," he said seriously, "because I want your

help. That's why I asked you here."

I waited, uncertain of his meaning and suppressing the excitement I felt. Being an enlisted soldier in the Army is much like being a peasant in a feudal society, and the prospect of being lifted from drudgery to a position of challenge and interest by some sympathetic lord is every peasant's dream.

"I had a chat with the light bird today," he said, meaning Colonel Bragg. "He doesn't altogether see it our way, if you know what I mean. Colonel Crick shook him up a little, perhaps, or maybe not, but in any event he's not keen on treating this as a homicide. In fact, he ordered me to go back on leave—after dressing me down in good old military fashion for responding to Crick's call without going through him first."

Chief made a sour face, and took a largish swallow of beer.

"I didn't exactly lick his boots," he said, "but it was a tug-of-war, and in the end he would only agree to have the apartment sealed for a few days pending a little quiet investigation—to be conducted strictly on my own time—and if I can show him some solid evidence of foul play, fine. If not, case closed. Meanwhile, I get none of the battalion's resources to help me out. I'm on my own—with one exception." He smiled at me strangely. "How would you like a change of duties, Smitty?"

I think I gasped.

"It seems your section is over-strength at the moment," he continued, "or so the colonel thinks. I won't deny I helped him think it, but anyway—so what? Well, what do you say?"

"Um, sure! I think it'd be great if, I mean, if you mean, that is—" I was hopeless.

"Okay. If it's all right with you, you're going to work for me for a while. Prost!" He held up his glass, and I clinked mine against it with a smile that spoke clearly. He banged his on the table and, raising it to his lips, took several ounces at a gulp. Then he closed his left eye and fixed me with his right. "If we can prove we've got the goods on this case," he said, "—maybe for quite a while."

5 The Lab and Other Diversions

Nürnberg, West Germany,
Saturday, 28th June 198-, 0615 hrs.

The excitement occasioned in me by my sudden change in circumstances was obsessive—the sort that bubbles and perks in the brain with a will of its own. I found myself early Saturday next to my still sleeping wife, staring out the window at the emerging blue of the sky in a state of complete wakefulness. Some, saddled with an energy that could not immediately be matched to its object, might have gone for a long walk, or exercised, or even anesthetized themselves with TV. I am a family man; I cooked breakfast. By the time Maggie appeared in the doorway, looking puffy and bleary eyed and beautiful, I had bacon sizzling on the stove, pancakes warming in the oven, and juice on the table. I squeezed her and gave her her coffee.

"How would you like your eggs, sweetheart?"

"This isn't fair...."

"Hunh?"

"Every time," she said, "that I finally figure out that I'm better off alone, without some S-O-B messing up my life, you go and do something like this." She gave me the warmest smile in the western hemisphere, and a kiss that did justice to the smile. "It isn't fair."

We lingered over our toast while the kids watched cartoons, and I did my best to fill her in. I could see she was doing some powerful digesting.

"So, let me get this straight. This 'chief' just grabbed you, and took you gallivanting around to look at a dead woman, and suddenly you're working for him instead of Sergeant Williams? Starting today?"

"Well, today he just wants to visit the lab. Monday is when I transfer to his section."

"And he's going to meet you here?"

"At ten," I nodded. "More coffee?"

"I guess I could take Susan shopping," she said tonelessly. "The house is a mess."

"Oh, well," I said. "Can't burn it down—we're on the third floor." She gave me a look. "We could burn Susan down...."

"That's true. Hey, Susan!"

"Forget it," Susan said without taking her eyes off the screen.

By the time the doorbell rang I had vacuumed, Maggie had subdued the kitchen, and Susan had been set to cleaning her room. Chief came in smelling of roses—that is, he carried a small bouquet of them, pink and yellow.

"You must be Maggie," he said to the wife; "These are for you."

"Oh!" she said. "I... thank you!"

"Peace offering," he explained. "Wanted to do something to make up for my selfishness in stealing your husband on a Saturday."

"Oh."

We settled in the living room while Maggie conjured up coffee with cheerful efficiency. She hadn't been completely won by

Chief's gesture, but if it was only his opening gambit then the campaign was going well.

My daughter appeared in the doorway. That is, part of her did: one staring eye, one foot, and a bit of the skirt.

"Come in, Susan!" I called. "Chief, this is Susan. Susan, meet Mister Tobias."

Chief rose like an old fashioned gentleman and said, "How do you do, Susan?"

"How do you do?" she managed admirably.

Chief sat back down, and the two of them stared at one another for a few moments.

"My dad says you're a policeman."

"I'm afraid it's true."

"I stole something once."

"No!"

"I took some candy from a grocery store, but my mom made me take it back, and apologize."

"Ah. The same thing happened to me once," he said. "Only, it wasn't candy, it was ... well, never mind about that—my mom did the same thing. It was very embarrassing."

Maggie brought in the coffee, with my youngest at her heels doing his clumsy best to remain hidden behind her legs. I set him in my lap.

"Mikey, can you say hello to Mister Tobias?"

"Light, hhhot!" he said courageously.

Chief examined him as one might examine any benign oddity, and smiled. After a decent interval I banished them both to their rooms.

"It was very kind of you to bring roses," Maggie said sociably. "Tell me, where are you from originally?"

"Utah, originally."

"Oh, are you a Mormon?"

"No, couldn't stick it. Had an ancestor, though, who was Brigham Young's barber, name of Pyper; he was also an opera singer, I believe. The rest of the family is not remarkable, unless you count my great aunt Cordelia. She ran a cathouse in Reno between the wars."

Maggie tripped over a swallow of coffee, and coughed for several seconds.

"You do hair, I believe?" Chief asked.

Maggie nodded and cleared her throat.

"Officers' wives, mostly, or enlisted?"

"Officers'—they, um, they pay better."

"Naturally. Did you know Mrs. Merrick?"

"No—my husband knows that."

Chief's face went blank, and Maggie related the previous afternoon's gossip. She warmed to the subject considerably once she got started, and Chief told me to get a pen and paper.

"I'm surprised at you," he added, "holding out on me like this. Make note of Cathy's last name, too. You were planning on telling me sometime, weren't you?"

"I hope not!" Maggie said. We both stared at her. "It's just, I mean—" She seemed suddenly nervous. "Oh, never mind. I don't know how to explain it."

"Of course," Chief said. "And I've been very rude. I'm sorry."

"Oh, no!" Maggie said. "I didn't mean—"

Chief held his hand up. "When I was eight or nine," he said, "my father began taking me with him to the barbershop. He was not a talkative man, you know, but I heard him tell the barber things that stunned me, and I wouldn't dare to repeat some of them even now for fear some relative or other might be listening. It's a sacred bond between barber and customer. Old Tom the barber was the next thing to a saint, I believe, considering the burdens of others' souls he bore safely with him to the grave." Chief took a deep breath and stared pensively into his coffee. "He died in '73, and I haven't found a decent barber since."

"I'd be happy to cut your hair," Maggie offered with rich sincerity. "I do my husband's—"

Chief laughed. "Oh, no!" he said. I'm not so easy. You'd get all my darkest secrets, and then Smitty'd find out and have no respect for me anymore."

"It's true," I said. "I would."

"Huh!" she teased, "Think I tell him everything?"

"I should hope not," he said. "Men are fragile creatures."

"Don't I know it!"

"Now, wait a minute—" But I was ignored.

"Tell you what Maggie. Let's make a deal. Smitty and I are pretty sure somebody killed this woman. Frankly, we haven't got the faintest idea who, or how, or why, but we think so anyway just to be ornery. Now, I know better than to ask you to compromise any future confidences, but just in case—just in case, mind you—someone tells you something useful, will you help us out any way you can?"

Maggie smiled an almost wicked little smile, and beamed at Chief. "Sure," she said.

Chief's conquest, I felt, was really too easy.

"You get to meet another character today, Smitty, if we're lucky."

"Yes?" I enquired. I was enjoying the scenery, and I was fascinated by Chief's driving. He seemed completely unconscious of the activity, yet there was a placid style to his movements that was engaging—and surprising, as driving in Europe is, for most Americans, a harassing experience at the best of times.

"The guy who runs the lab on morning shift during the weekends is a Brit, from London. His name's Cuthbert, if you can believe it, George Cuthbert, and his wife and friends call him Ginger."

"Why is a Brit working for the Americans in Germany?"

"Good question. I don't know. His wife's from Belize."

"South America?"

"Central. It's a good guess the reasons are pretty prosaic—jobs are tight in England. You'll find if you get out and about that there are clubs and restaurants that cater to the British and Irish immigrants, just as there are for the American soldiers.

"Anyway, he's a character, and he seems to like me, and that's two points in his favor right there. And he's a hell of a biochemist and a fine amateur forensic scientist to boot. The clincher is, he has no more respect for military rules and 'regs' than he absolutely needs, to work in an Army hospital, and that makes him mighty useful occasionally. Let's hope he isn't on vacation, or something."

Ginger wasn't on vacation, and greeted Chief with a loud "Whoo-up!" and a fierce hug. He was six-foot-five and no bigger than my hat size east to west, giving him approximately the proportions of a large floor lamp. The top of his head was bald and shiny, but around the back of it at the level of his ears was a kinky orange frieze that stood out from his scalp about two inches. The nose was narrow and highly arched, the chin pointed, the mouth thin as a pencil line and wider, almost, than his very jaws. Eyes the color of the sea swam behind thick, round spectacles. He wore a long white lab coat, and black Nikes.

"I was just saying to the lab assistant," he exclaimed, "If Chief Toby don't show today, I'll eat my specimens—and here you are! Now, tell me I don't know a thing or two about karma!"

"It's uncanny," Chief agreed. "Ginger, meet Smitty." Ginger looked at me with a critical frown. "He's a detective," Chief added.

"Really! A detective, you don't say!" He took my hand in both of his and pumped it like a shriner at a convention. "Come, come, both of you, and be edified: I've something to show you!"

He led the way at a harried pace down the back corridors of the hospital, to a small room that was all stainless steel fixtures and bright lights. There was a sinister symbol on the door with the words "BIOLOGICAL HAZARD" blazoned beneath, and "Authorized Personnel Only" lettered below those. The room was a battleground of warring odors, in which the sharp aroma of formaldehyde seemed to be losing ground to something more organic and distinctly unpleasant. I guessed the source of the conflict might be located among the jars of nameless things that were neatly arrayed on the profusion of glass-enclosed shelving at every side, until Ginger spoke again.

"Look at this!" he cried, indicating a small tray on one of the dissecting tables.

"Yuck," Chief said for both of us.

"Now, now, steady on! 'Tis only a heart—a heart of darkness, you might say; the owner decided he didn't want it anymore."

"I thought you weren't allowed to do autopsies here," Chief said.

"We're not, and I didn't, you insufferable bore. The *Bundes* boobs did the dirty work, and forwarded the remains of their butchery here when they found they'd got hold of an American. He was run over by a train, you see, and they hadn't much to go by—his face was history, and he hadn't been considerate enough to carry an ID. Matching his fingerprints to those of a missing GI was all that kept him from an unmarked German grave. Well, that and his underwear."

"So what's the edifying bit?"

Ginger looked at each of us in turn and adjusted his glasses. "Along with the remains was found an enormous hypo, the sort one uses to give Dumbo his vitamin shots. It was empty. Now, what do you suppose—?"

We were silent for a few moments, and the wheels turned.

"Was he stabbed with it?" I asked.

"Hardly," he said witheringly.

"It was a drug overdose, then," I tried, showing I was not to be intimidated.

Ginger glared. "I said it was empty. Clean! Spotless! Unsullied—"

"You wish us to infer," Chief said smoothly, "that he did not die when he was hit by the train—"

"Yes?" Ginger became animated.

"—but that he was already dead—"

"Yes, yes?"

"—of an embolism."

"Yes!! Excellent!! You astound me—I bow!" And he did.

"What's an embolism?" I asked in a small voice.

"I'll show you!" Ginger slid the tray between us and picked up a scalpel.

"It's a blood clot," Chief explained, "caused in this case by—"

"I said I'd show him, didn't I?" Ginger said irritably.

Chief shrugged and put his fingers over his mouth.

"Now, look here," Ginger said to me. "You know that the heart is essentially a pump, yes?"

"Yes."

"And what happens if you let air into a pump?"

"Ah!" I said, light dawning. I had an uncle who lived on a boat, and he was constantly cursing his bilge pump for getting leaks and letting air into the system. "Simple, it stops working because—"

"Precisely. Now suppose you took a large, empty hypodermic, and pumped twenty or thirty cc's of air into your veins?"

"It would travel up the vein," I said, "until it reached the heart, and then—gosh! It wouldn't take long, would it?"

"No," Chief inserted gravely.

"You'd be out like a jack in the box," said Ginger. "Nevertheless, it would be dashed unpleasant, I should think, for a few moments."

"And you can tell because there's air in the heart?" I asked.

"Well, perhaps not, at this late date. But let me ask you another question. What happens when blood comes into contact with air?"

"Uh, it scabs. I mean, clots."

"Quite so. And if our inferences are correct, we should find something rather goopy right about here, in the right auricle . . . and so we have!" He probed with the scalpel, and came up with a glistening red mass. His smile was something to behold.

"But, look here," Chief said. "How do you know it was suicide, and not murder?"

"He left a note," Ginger said simply, "and it was *his* syringe."

"Oh."

"His girl jilted him—the old song."

"But why the train?" I asked.

Ginger shrugged, pulled off his gloves, and set to washing his hands. It was clear the matter held no further interest for him.

"Well, Ginger, old friend—" Chief said.

"You need a favor."

"So to speak. You got a cadaver in yesterday, from Erlangen. Female, twentyish, name of Merrick."

"Oh!" Ginger brightened. "Is she yours?"

"So to speak."

"Say on! You want my opinion, I suppose?"

"Ye-es...."

"Uh oh. Out with it! Your not asking me to dissect her, I hope—as you so helpfully pointed out a few moments ago, that's a bit above my echelon."

"I'm not talking about a complete autopsy—"

"Lord!" Ginger cried. "Make me grateful for small blessings!"

"—but if you could see your way to checking for one or two things—"

"My shift is over."

"—I'd be very grateful."

"As it happens, I've already run the standard tests, plus one or two the doctor johnnie asked for, but I suppose I could be persuaded...." He hesitated.

"Yes?"

"It's going to cost you." Honestly, he had a wolfish sort of smile that was positively frightening.

"What, then?"

"Lunch!"

We went in Chief's blue Toyota, me curled like a broken spring in the back seat. Ginger directed us to a dark, timbered cellar that smelled of beer and mustard, and promptly ordered for all of us in loud, barking German. Over the tops of liter mugs of frothy *hell* (German for light—meaning not dark—beer), and plates of steaming sausages and kraut, we discussed the case. Actually, that's a slight distortion; they discussed, I took notes.

Our chemist saw no reason to disagree with Major Suarez's ("the doctor johnnie's") opinion that she died of liquor. Her blood alcohol was right off the chart, but there was nothing else about her fluids that was in any way remarkable. No suggestion of asphyxiation, nothing broken, none of the distress associated with cardiac arrest—in short, a pretty peaceful way to go, in his opinion.

"Did you check for drugs?" Chief asked.

"THC positive, coke positive—but not much."

"What about narcotics?"

Ginger shook his head.

"Amphetamines? Heroin? LSD? I want you to run the gamut."

"I'm telling you, I did. She was having a spot of the Sherlock Holmes between the toes, and smoking dope. That's it."

"Damn."

Ginger didn't understand Chief's consternation, and said so.

Chief sighed heavily and began from the beginning: The woman's apparel, the discrepancy of liquor bottles, the wiping of prints, the works.

"I was unconvinced," Ginger said slowly, when he had done, "until you mentioned about the ashtrays. That woman was a smoker. Either that or, to judge from the state of her teeth, her brand of gum was Wrigley's bituminous coal."

"Exactly. The whole appearance of the thing's out of character."

Ginger drained his mug, banged it on the table, and stared at his distended stomach. "Actually, if you hadn't put in all that bit about being an officer's wife, and what not, I'd have said the death was *highly* characteristic."

"What? How so?"

"I haven't always worked in the pristine hallways of Uncle Sam," he said. "When I was a young lad, just out of school, I worked at a large National Health institution in London's East End. Our most frequent customers were common derelicts, dead of exposure and the loss of their livers to cirrhosis. But the next most frequent, and incomparably most wrenching to have to work on, were the young kids, girls from fifteen to twenty for the most part, who'd just gotten lost somehow—already dead to society— and lived by whoring and stealing, and died of overdose, eventually, or at the hands of some murdering scoundrel; or maybe, some of them, from just living too hot, too hard, and burning up inside." He signaled to the waitress and tapped his empty beer mug meaningfully.

"Anyhow," he continued after a reflective pause, "that's what 'Merrick, K.' reminds me of—not as dissolute as most of those were, of course—but essentially the same. And from what you've just told me, I guess there are probably a couple things you don't know, even yet."

"Such as?" Chief prodded.

"There were vaginal fluids."

"I know."

"I tried typing them.   Couldn't be done—the sample was mixed."

"I didn't know," Chief said quietly.

"Then you probably don't know who it was hit her—?"

"Say again?"

"Somebody hit her. You must have seen it! A big bruise on her left cheek?"

Chief and I looked at each other and shook our heads.

"Are we talking about the same woman?" Ginger cried, exasperated.

"Slow down, old son. We'll have a look, later. Drink your beer."

The waitress had dropped off another round. On impulse I grabbed mine and lifted it high.

"Prost!" I said.

"Prost!" they echoed, and we clinked our mugs over our heads and banged them on the table before taking a long draught.

"Righto!" Ginger said. "I'd best offer up the old 'cherished opinion' before I get too drunk."

"That's the spirit!"

"She died of drink."

"Ginger... my man..."

"Okay, okay. I tell you, she had enough booze in her to kill two seasoned drunks, but if she didn't die of that—then it was an aneurysm, a blown fuse, burst vessel, what you like, in the old noggin. I didn't check for aspirin or such that can do that readily in the presence of alcohol, but I shall. I'll not carve into her skull, so if that's what happened you'll have to wait for the autopsy to find out."

"Get an x ray."

"Fine."

"And if it wasn't an aneurysm?"

"Act of God...?"

"What about air in the vein, like your love sick GI?"

"Very unlikely. Was there a syringe in the room?"

"No, but there wasn't a suicide note, either. Will you check?"

"Really, you know, it takes at least a modicum of skill. The GI was a medic—"

"But will you check?"

"Oh, hell!" Ginger looked pretty uncomfortable with the idea.

"Look, Ginger...," Chief's voice was like old brandy—it burned into you and insinuated warmth into your very bones. "Nobody but us three believes in this thing. They'll get it termed an accidental death, and you know what that means. It will take a week just to get the body to the forensics lab at Landstuhl. Then they'll cry 'work overload,' and sit on it for a month before they even get her on the table. Then the paperwork drill begins, and the results will be confidential. My office might get the report by Christmas, and then it'll just be a telex with "natural causes" buried somewhere in a page of meaningless, technical bullshit. Meanwhile, our perpetrator is decorating his tree—"

"Blast you! You'll have me weeping, next." Ginger fumed silently and wouldn't take his eyes off his beer. "You owe me, mister bleeding Chief Tobias."

"My first born is yours. How long will it take?"

"I won't even think about it 'til my next shift. Call me in the morning."

"That'll be great. Drink up, Ginger, and we'll take you home."

It happened that Ginger lived in a small town north of Erlangen, so after depositing him with his wife and kids we naturally thought of spinning by Matson *kaserne* on the way back. Chief said he didn't have anything clearly in mind. Although Captain

Merrick had returned from the field the previous evening and Chief was eager to interview him, he was staying at the Crick's and Chief had been warned off trying to see him before Sunday. It made him gnaw his teeth, but there was nothing he could do about it.

We pulled into the housing area, and parked in front of the Merricks' building. Chief stood in the middle of the parking lot and gazed up at the windows. The parking area occupied the center of a broad stretch of ground that separated the Merricks' building from one parallel to it, and Chief was turning in a circle, looking at all the windows in turn. He mumbled something.

"What's that, Chief?"

"A platoon," he said. "See all those windows? Behind any one of them might be the witness who could tell us who was here Thursday night; the one who watches, the busybody, the snoop, the one who sees all—every neighborhood has one, and I would usually assign a platoon, as I was saying, of door knocking, interviewing MP's to find out who it is."

I looked from one building to the other, up and down. "How about that one," I said, and pointed. There was a face at a window, just peeking around the edge of a lace curtain, but as Chief looked it withdrew. He caught the movement of the curtain, however.

"I keep forgetting," he said, and slapped me on the back. "I don't need a platoon—I've got Smitty!"

I believe I stood pretty straight.

"Still," he went on, "we'll have to do the old door-to-door, and it's gonna be a bitch. We'll start tomorrow; that is, if Maggie can spare you."

"Oh, certainly," I lied. After a moment's thought I added, "She may demand you for dinner."

"Oh?"

"It's possible."

"Well. Are you sure it's really necessary? I mean, I'd be delighted of course, it's just that I ... uh ... "

"It's a question of balancing accounts."

"Ah."

We trooped upstairs in a sober mood. It wasn't clear what it was we were to do in the Merricks' apartment, and I was on the verge of asking several times, but Chief began to look very occupied with his thoughts and before long I gathered the question might not have any very clear answer. He went here and there, lifting cushions and opening cupboards, with his tongue sneaking thoughtlessly in and out between his teeth. Taking my cue from Chief I wandered about and looked at things. I started by lifting pictures away from the wall and looking behind them, with the result that I nearly destroyed a framed pencil sketch of some cathedral (Rheims, I think) by letting it slip through my fingers to the floor. Catastrophe was averted by the intervention of the toes of my right foot. Chief just looked at me and cleared his throat pointedly.

The picture frames being something of a washout, and dangerous to boot, I had a go at the bedroom closet.

The male partner was not much of a dresser, I deduced—there were actually very few articles of men's clothing. What there was of his attire tended to denim, mostly, and (yuck) polyester. The female was another proposition entirely. She didn't "tend" to anything—she plunged. The closet was one of those wall-to-wall affairs with sliding doors, and nine of it's twelve feet in length was given over to her impressive collection of silk blouses, wool skirts, and shimmering one piece what-you-may-call-ems. She was fondest of fire engine red, especially in the one piece items, with ivory and midnight blue running close seconds. A little pull-out contraption was loaded with several pounds of silk scarves, and the shelf above was stacked tight to the ceiling with shoes. Not a hat person, I noticed. There were shoes on the floor also, and several on a kind of rack. Spiked heels were the mainstream in her footwear, and summoning the image of that compact, finely proportioned figure that had lain on the bed behind me just the day before, I reflected that not only had she possessed the natural endowments—to turn the heads of the opposite sex and thus arouse the jealousy of fellow females—but she had collected all the right accessories, too.

At last I wandered out, and discovered Chief sitting in the middle of the living room floor. Next to him was a large ammunition can, for 18 millimeter shells I guessed, though I confess not very knowledgeably; at any rate it was about eight inches by eighteen, and fifteen high. It had been painted olive drab and had a large, black cross on the side. He was pawing through its contents, which he had dumped out on the floor.

"What's up?" I said.

"Kit, first aid, economy size, one each. Look at this!" He stood up and unfolded an enormous bandage in a cellophane wrap. It stretched from his shoulders to his ankles and was marked 'Pad, Sterile, X Large.' "What do you suppose this is for?"

"Not a paper cut," I observed.

"No."

"Where'd you find it?"

"In the utility closet, under a pile of blankets."

"Interesting."

"Just as you say. It says 'Cpt Merrick, Combat Lifesaver' on the lid—Hi! Don't touch it, I haven't dusted!"

"Dusted?"

"For prints!"

Oops.

"I doubt it's any use to us, but still...." He put the contents back in carefully, and closed the lid, using a handkerchief. "There's an I.V. set and a full saline bag, but no syringes and no drugs."

He put it away, flopped on the couch, and proceeded to wipe his glasses. I stood at the window and stared at the dying colors of the sky through the lace curtains.

"We're being watched out that same window again, Chief."

"Really? Good. Make a note of which window and we'll hit there first thing tomorrow."

"Right."

"Y'know what, Smitty? This is not a material case. We got clues, but they don't tell. It's going to be a people case, I can tell. I hate people cases."

"How come? I mean, what's a people case?"

"Well...," He paused. "Sometimes when someone is murdered the material clues tell the whole picture, if you know how to read them. You've got the lead pipe and the victim in the library, and it all points right to Professor Plum. Then you just lean on Plum, and build your case. Other times it's just random—the mugging victim in the park, say—and you either find the needle in the haystack or you don't, but in any case the whole thing is more or less accidental from start to finish. The victim could have been anybody walking in the park in that time and place, and it could have been any thug."

"I'm with you so far."

"Okay. Once in a while you get a case that is clearly not a random act of violence, and at the same time it is not a simple game of Clue where the evidence speaks for itself. That's what we have here. Somebody either killed that woman, or else just let her die and scrammed. Now, I'll lay you a hundred to one that Captain Merrick's got a hundred witnesses to swear he was a hundred miles away—which he probably was. So where does that leave us? This is a closed community, where everybody knows everybody, yet her neighbors hate her unanimously, and are also unanimous in their ignorance of where she went and what she did with her time. So either one or more of them is lying for some reason (which, incidentally, I think likely) or we're stuck with finding a mysterious German boyfriend, or boyfriends, on our own, in a country of 60 million Germans. That's what I mean by a 'people case.' The solution will come, if it does, by breaking down social façades and getting someone to speak; or at least to point in the general direction of the boyfriend."

"Maybe he drove a blue Mercedes," I said. "Look!"

A car had parked below the window, a blue Mercedes with German plates. A silver haired gentleman had gotten out and was leaning on the hood in a lazy way, smoking a cigarette.

"Looks like he's waiting for someone," Chief said. We stood side by side in the window and studied him. "I wonder—uh-oh!"

He'd seen us. He gazed up at the window for several seconds, and then tossed away his cigarette and got back in his car.

"Get the number!" Chief yelled, and ran out the door.

The Mercedes pulled away and disappeared around the corner of the building just as Chief hit the street. I didn't credit his chances, but he jumped in the Toyota and sped after him. I turned out the lights and locked up before going down to wait by the street. I didn't wait long.

"Lost him," Chief said when he pulled up. "Did you get his

plate number?"

"Well," I said unhappily, "some of it."

"Some?"

"The letters and one number."

"Oh. Oh, well."

"He smokes a filterless cigarette," I said, holding up the butt.

I got in, and he drove me home in a somber silence.

"Well, Chief," I said when he stopped before my door, "what time in the morning?"

"Noonish?"

I nodded.

"We'll meet at battalion—we'll want the kits for these interviews. Oh, and Smitty?"

"Yeah?"

"Cheer up. Probably Ginger will have something. I like that air-in-the-veins idea. It reminds me of a Dorothy Sayers novel I read once. Ever read Dorothy Sayers?"

I said I hadn't.

"We'll have to fix that—Peter Wimsey is the best. In one of the novels the murderer was going about giving people embolisms, and it took Peter the devil of a time to think of it. I'll bring the book tomorrow, if you'd like."

"Okay, Chief," I said. "Good night. Be prepared for a dinner invite."

"Right."

6 Day of Labor

Matson Barracks, Erlangen West Germany,
Sunday, 29 June 198-, 1200 hrs.

It may as well be said at once that there was no embolism, and x-rays of the head revealed nothing. Ginger struck out.

This news was delivered by Chief on the steps of our battalion headquarters, where he met me at noon. We drove to Erlangen in the "scarab" (Chief's term for our olive-drab Army Volkswagon), and along the way he filled me in on the day's plan of attack. He'd arranged to meet Captain Merrick at the Crick's at 3:00 o'clock, and meanwhile we were to knock on doors and get to know the neighborhood. Chief had purposely timed this activity for after church-going hours, and we would just take potluck of whoever was home in the early afternoon. Despite the talk about the "watcher at the window" the previous evening, Chief decided to start at the ground floor of the Merricks' building and work each stairwell methodically.

The first door we knocked on was opened by a handsome black whose unshaven face and loose fitting jeans and t-shirt made clear he was enjoying a day off. This was Captain Williamson, the occupant of the quarters directly beneath the Merricks'. After introductions and a brief explanation of our purpose he became very friendly, invited us in, and offered us beer, which Chief politely

84

refused.

"Coffee then?"

"That sounds good. Smitty?"

"It sounds great."

"So, you're investigating Kimberly's death?" The configuration of the living room, dining room, and kitchen made it possible for him to make coffee and carry on a conversation at the same time.

"That's right," Chief said. "Did you know Mrs. Merrick well, sir?"

"Just to speak to." He grinned; "And to look at, of course. By the way, my name is Henry—unless you're under my command my rank comes off with my uniform. Not supposed to, I know, but it does."

"Fine with me. What did you think of her?"

"Oh, well, I think she was a mistake—Andrew Merrick's mistake. I knew Andy from butter-bar days. We weren't great buddies, but we were friendly enough, and I knew when I met her he'd gone and done something he'd regret."

"Why was that?"

"Because she was a little high-society bitch," he said, cheerfully brutal; "pretty as a picture, and poisonous as a snake. I wouldn't be surprised to learn she married him just to get back at somebody else, or on a bet or something. My wife heard she'd gotten kicked out of college one too many times and ticked off her rich papa, and Andy Merrick was just a safe port in the storm."

"Who did she hear that from?"

"Beats me." He shrugged his shoulders.

"Was she friendly with Mrs. Merrick?"

"My man, nobody around here was 'friendly' with that girl.

I've seen her about with one or two of the lieutenants' young wives, but that's about it."

"Who, for instance?"

"I don't know. There's a pretty one, uh... her name is Caisson, or something—I've seen her with Kimberly once or twice. Just on the stairwell, but they seemed to be on good terms."

"What did she look like?"

"Pretty. Curly brown hair, natty dresser, petite. Real cute."

"Grason? Sabrina Grason?"

"Could be. I really don't know."

I tried to catch Chief's eye for an exchange of meaningful glances, but he ignored me.

"Well," he continued, as if reading from a dull script, "uh, Henry, were you home Thursday night?"

"Yes. Got home around six, ate, watched TV."

"Hear anything unusual upstairs?"

"Nope." He poured the coffee.

"*Ever* hear anything unusual upstairs?"

"Used to—they used to fight quite a bit."

"But not recently?"

"Not for months. By the way, the death was accidental, wasn't it? That's what my wife said."

"Well, we don't really know."

He motioned us to the couch, and we all sat down. He seemed to grow tense, and there was a silence while he and Chief studied one another.

"Somebody killed her," he said at last.

"Again, we don't know. That's why we're here, sir."

"Okay," he said. "I'll play the game."

Chief paused to wipe his glasses. I was impressed with his knack for not sounding like Joe Friday, while still placing his questions in a tone that seemed to compel candor. I have since learned that interviewing witnesses is an art, one that is mastered through years of study and practice, and that mastery in this more than anything else separates the Sherlocks from the gumshoes.

"I've gotten the impression," Chief said finally, "that Mrs. Merrick wasn't home much lately, is that true?"

"I've heard it said."

"Heard what said?"

"Heard that she—" He stopped for a second. "Look, they weren't doing well. If you ask enough folks on post you'll soon hear all the stories about her you can stomach—and maybe some of them are true. I don't know, and it's none of my business."

"What kind of stories? That she was having an affair?"

"Like I said, it's none of my business."

"Okay. You said you knew Captain Merrick before?"

"Met him at ROTC camp, Ft. Lewis. Um, summer of '84."

"What's he like?"

He reflected for a moment. "John Wayne's kid brother— always was. The name tells you everything: Andrew Jackson Merrick. He always had to stand a little straighter than everybody else. He's all right, though. A little stiff with troops, I think, but he's a successful officer. The NCO's respect him."

Captain Williamson, having undergone this strange metamorphosis from genial confidant to cautious colleague, would tell us little else, and after a few minutes we moved on.

"Let's get some of those stories he promised, Smitty," Chief said, and we knocked on the next door.

Two hours later, bloated with coffee, tea, and diet soda, we leaned against the scarab to catch our breath. We had found a half dozen wives and/or husbands at home, and I was appreciating Chief's lament the day before about the work involved in canvassing witnesses. Few had anything to offer. None had seen anything useful Thursday night, and only two related any gossip of substance, both wives who were home alone, without the modifying influence of their husbands to temper their eloquence. The reason for their solitude was simple: they were spouses of soldiers in Captain Merrick's battalion (the unit currently in the field) and hence, by serendipity, the very ones best disposed to wax knowledgeable regarding the deceased.

The first, a homely but personable woman of about thirty-five and the wife of another battalion staff officer, was quietly reticent in tone but voluble in detail. She related that there were several rumors regarding Mrs. Merrick: that she was having an affair with another officer; that she was having several affairs with several officers—and civilians; that she was a reformed prostitute; that she was an unreformed prostitute; that she was a drug user; that she was a model for pornographers; even that she was homosexual. The last was perhaps the least creditable, though the witness (a Mrs. Baker) made it clear that she didn't credit any of them. She didn't know Kimberly well, she said, but although it was clear she had been a disturbed young lady, Mrs. Baker didn't doubt that she was mostly just misunderstood, and unhappy, as who wasn't? Chief said nothing to reveal our certainty that one at least of these rumors was true. He did his best to elicit the name of one of the rumored lovers or consorts, but she was unable or unwilling to provide any such clues.

The second woman was both more fervent in her assessment of the victim and considerably more concrete. She was the "watcher at the window," an enlisted man's wife who lived in what are called "temps," for temporary quarters, on the top floor. There being a general shortage of housing in the community, especially for lower paid soldiers with large families, the worst hard luck cases were often billeted in the attics of the officers' quarters until more suitable arrangements could be found, and it was thus that Mrs. Greta Hernandez was placed in command of such a strategically located window.

A young German national only recently married to a hispanic soldier, she was still too alienated by her new milieu to be taken up in its society, but she was curious about her new neighbors and studied them with fascinated interest from her perch on the top floor. Once Chief was able to make clear the purpose of our visit she became very serious. She had lived in the apartment, she said, since February. She recognized Kimberly Merrick immediately from Chief's description but, although she had watched the proceedings on the sidewalk below on the previous Friday, she had not known what it was about, and it was news to her that Kimberly was dead. She evinced that it was no real surprise.

"She was always like a hooker dressing! *Immer* with the red dress and shoes with long heels—she made her husband go away, I know it! A bad, bad woman. So, somebody killed her? I believe it."

She said that Kimberly rarely left her apartment during the day, but had recently left it at dusk or shortly after almost every night, and sometimes seemed to stay away for days at a time. She didn't think Captain Merrick had really lived there since April, although he came now and then for an hour or two. Kimberly had never driven herself when she left. Usually she took a taxi, and sometimes she was picked up by a German man. Asked to describe him, she said he was an older man and drove a blue Mercedes, a late model sedan.

"And when she returned?" Chief asked.

Mrs. Hernandez had never seen her return but once, on a night several weeks ago when she'd been unable to sleep. It had been at two in the morning, and Kimberly was dropped off by the same blue Mercedes. She hadn't seen who was driving the car.

"And what about Thursday night? Did she leave with the same man?"

Mrs. Hernandez shrugged. "I am not seeing Mrs. Merrick since Tuesday."

The Cricks lived in the only free standing house on the *kaserne*, a split level, wood frame affair looking like a lonesome transplant from midwest American suburbia. Mrs. Crick opened the door and showed us into a living room that was decorated to a fault in early New England furnishings and appointments, right down to the maple chairs and scrimshaw bric-a-brac. She left us after making introductions.

Captain Merrick looked well scrubbed and very composed when we entered, and my first and lasting impression was of a man whose personal world was narrowly defined and largely disassociated from the actual world around him. He was dressed in crisp blue jeans, a western style shirt with mother of pearl snaps, and snub-toed boots. His face seemed to have been sculpted with large tools—one had an eerie sense that it lacked detail. He was built on the same frame as Clint Eastwood in the days of his early fame, and his hair, brown I suppose, was clipped so close to his head as to be nearly invisible. He rose from the couch when we entered and shook Chief's hand perfunctorily, but his long, angular face was very still, if not sorrowful, and it was not quite in a monotone that he offered us something to drink. We declined, and when we were all sitting Chief took a deep breath.

"I'm sorry to have to trouble you," he said. "I'm sure this is a very difficult time." He paused, but Captain Merrick said nothing. "Any time a military member—or a dependent—dies overseas," Chief continued, "the Army is required to make a thorough investigation of the death, and most of what I have to ask you is just routine." Captain Merrick was motionless. "You with me so far?" The man nodded slowly. "Okay, uh, has anyone spoken with you concerning the circumstances of Kimberly's death?"

"Just Colonel Crick."

"And what did he tell you?"

"That she drank too much."

"Did that surprise you?"

"No. I don't know."

"Was she depressed?"

"I couldn't say," he said, and there was an odd tone of contempt in his voice.

I had been taking notes, as usual, but Chief suddenly reached over and stopped my pen.

"I don't think that'll be necessary this time, Smitty."

He took the note pad from me, glanced at it, and snapped it shut. He leaned forward and looked at Captain Merrick with a challenging air.

"You don't think I should be here, do you, Captain?"

"Nobody does."

"Why not?"

"Because—" Captain Merrick stopped and his face flushed a

bright red. He jumped to his feet and turned away with his hands in his pockets. "Because my wife's dead, God dammit!"

Chief removed his glasses and began to wipe them with his shirt. "And...?" he said quietly.

The other man seemed to collect himself a little. He walked to the window and stared out in silence.

"I think Kimberly was murdered," Chief said evenly.

"Bullshit."

"Why weren't you two living together any more?"

"None of your damned business."

"And who was her German boyfriend?"

"I don't know about any boyfriend," he said after a pause.

"How long had you been separated?"

"I told you, it's—"

"—none of my damned business, I know. You don't give a shit about your wife do you?"

Captain Merrick spun on his heels and gaped at Chief. "How dare you—"

"Kimberly's been murdered, and you don't give a rat's ass about it. Glad she's gone?"

"Get the fuck out!"

Chief didn't move. "I only know what you tell me, Captain Merrick. Did you murder your wife?"

"I—" he paused. "No."

"You could've."

"Sounds like I need a lawyer."

"Do you?"

"I was in the field."

"Grafenwöhr is only an hour and a half away. Did you have your car with you?"

"No."

"Someone else's car then."

Colonel Crick's voice, like a muffled avalanche, cut in: "I can answer that."

We turned. He stood in the doorway with his hands on his hips.

"No POV's are allowed when a unit is in the field. Now get out."

"I don't think that's wise, sir."

"I don't give a damn what you think. You're not going to harass this man in my house. The door's over here."

We rose to go. Chief stopped with his hand on the knob.

"Colonel Crick, somebody was there when Kimberly Merrick died. It may not be official yet, but when it is—"

"When it is, Chief Tobias, I'm sure someone with authority will let me know."

We stood on the sidewalk. Chief was gazing at the sky as if in thought, but I could tell that he was very angry. I didn't understand why he had handled the interview the way he had, but it was clear to me that, whatever his reasons may have been, it didn't turn out like he wanted. He dug in his pocket and fished out some change.

"Smitty, why don't you walk down to the snack bar and pick up a paper. It's only a couple blocks. I'll wait in the car."

While there I ran into Mrs. Crick.

"Done already?" she enquired.

"Yes, ma'am," I nodded.

"Andrew's been in such a fidget," she said, "the poor man. Kimberly's father is coming tomorrow, and his own mother can't make it until Tuesday morning, the day of the funeral service."

I made a sympathetic face.

"I'm glad he's got someplace to stay, at least," she said nervously. "A man doesn't like to have to live day and night under the same roof with his commanding officer."

"Oh, I thought—where is he staying?"

"I don't know the address. He probably told that "Chief" man. Now that's a man I'd want on my side. So courteous."

When I came back Chief was leaning on the trunk of the VW with a smile on his face.

"Smitty, did we ever check the Merrick's mailbox?"

"Huh?"

"I count on you to think of these things."

"Sorry Chief. But don't you think Captain Merrick would have checked it?"

"Probably, but maybe not. If there's something good in it, it might put me in a mood to forgive you forgetting it before now. C'mon."

We stood before a bank of mailboxes in the Merrick's stairwell and scratched our heads. We didn't have the key.

"Hold up your hand," Chief said. I did, and he held his next to mine. "Yours are longer, and skinnier," he said. "Go for it."

I stuck my hand through the flap and dug around.

"I think I've got something!" I said, and came up with a small yellow envelope.

"Excellent! Anything else?"

"Uh...," I stretched my fingers to the utmost. "I don't think so."

"Oh, well, we'll hope this is a good one. There's no stamp or post-mark, which means it was hand delivered. That's promising. Tell me Smitty, how many more interviews do you feel up to?"

I bit my lip and stared at the ceiling.

"Me too. What time's dinner?"

"I'm supposed to call. Not before six, anyway."

"And what time is it now—?" He consulted his wrist as though there were a watch on it. "Hmm. The big hand is pointing to the bar, and the little hand is pointing to the bottle opener."

"Wow," I said. "Where can I get a watch like that?"

"You can't—the secret of its making was lost during prohibition. Let's go."

When we got back to the car I gasped.

"Chief!" I said, "someone broke the windshield!" It had a sizable nimbus of cracks in the center, as if someone had struck it with a brick.

"Don't worry about it," he said. "Get in."

Not 'til long after, on one of those occasions when the beer is flowing and one might tell anything to a friend, did he admit that he had sat in the passenger seat for several minutes, sick with anger, and finally punched the windshield with his fist.

"Okay. Let's take a look at things."

We were standing in Chief's study, and I was sipping my glass of pils and scratching Nietzsche behind what I guessed were his ears while Chief booted up his computer. This was an IBM PC clone, or rather two of them connected in some way, that he had assembled himself out of used components. We had an hour or so before dinner, and he wanted to put what information we had in some kind of order and look it over with me, mainly so we could develop a coherent plan for the coming week. Although he didn't say so, it was clear to me that he was anxious about having a significant body of evidence, if not the actual solution, by Friday, when Lieutenant Colonel Bragg was threatening to pull the plug on our informal investigation.

"Here come our suspects," he said as one of the printers started to make little zipping noises and spit out paper. "Behind that we'll have the material clues so far, and later tonight I'll come up with a draft time table. I'm printing them in 24-point print so we can pin them up on the chalkboard and see what we've got."

Shortly he tore off a long sheet and put it up on the board. It looked like this:

1. MERRICK, Andrew Jackson, Cpt
2. MERRICK, Kimberly, Mrs.
3. WORMS, Nancy, Mrs.
4. WORMS, John, Cpt
5. CRICK, Darrell, Col
6. CRICK, Rachel Gold, Mrs.
7. GRASON, Sabrina, Mrs.
8. BLICKWELL, Mercy, Mrs.
9. BRADLEY, Georgette, Mrs.
10. SUAREZ, Victor, Maj
11. Mystery German

"Now, you'll notice that I used the term 'suspect' pretty broadly; this is really just everyone, that we know of, who is connected with the investigation. The list won't become very interesting until we start connecting names with clues, and motives. Here's the clues. I must say, they make a fascinating list."

They looked like this:

1. CLUES OF THE BODY

  a) Dressed for Penthouse.
  b) Artificial tan.
  c) No apparent violence (bruise on cheek?).

   d) Body not moved (lividity).

   e) Rigor advanced. Time of death: midnight to 6 am.

   f) Scotch whiskey in esophagus.

   g) Nicotine stains on fingers of right hand.

   h) Needle marks between toes of both feet (approx. 20).

   i) Evidence of alcoholism.

   j) THC, cocaine use (by lab).

   k) No evidence of embolism or stroke (by lab).

   l) Multiple seminal fluids in vagina (by lab).

   m) Body temp 86.8, ambient 83.2; time of death 3 am.

   n) High blood alcohol level (by lab).

"I wondered why you took her temperature," I said.

"It's an excellent technique," he told me. "The body is mostly water, and the math for working out the rate of cooling is straightforward; under constant temperature conditions, it's usually accurate to within thirty minutes or so."

2. CLUES OF THE SCENE:

   a) Clean ashtrays.

   b) 2 ltr btl Vodka, 1/4 full, wiped clean except K's prints.

   c) Space heater turned all the way up.

   d) Footboard, mirror, space heater all wiped clean.

   e) Multiple prints on headboard.

   f) Apt. keys in coat.

   g) Missing purse.

   h) Bed not slept in since previous cleaning on Tuesday.

   i) Lingerie collection.

   j) Kitchen garbage old (w/only three cigarette butts).

   k) Paper towel with red grease stain.

   l) Liquor cabinet unused (except rum, also vodka bottle).

3. FROM WITNESS STATEMENTS:

   a) K. poor housekeeper. (M. Blickwell)

b) Neither K. nor Cpt M. home "lately." (M. Blickwell)

c) Dried mud on carpeting. (M. Blickwell)

d) Kitchen & Bathroom sinks used. Toilet paper gone. (M. Blickwell)

e) Front door bolted (probably). (M. Blickwell)

f) K's father wealthy? (Cathy)

g) Cpt M. not living in apartment since April. (Mrs. H., Cpt M.)

h) K. went out in evenings and stayed late or for several days. (Mrs. H.)

i) K. often picked up by silver haired man in blue Mercedes—other times by taxis. (Mrs. H.)

j) K. & Cpt M. used to fight loudly, but not recently. (Cpt W.)

k) K. & some LT's wife friends—Grason? (Cpt W.)

l) K. woman of easy virtue; had affairs (Hooker?). (M. Blickwell, N. Worms, Cathy, Cpt W., Mrs. Baker)

m) K. resembled cadavers of London street people. (Ginger)

"Well," he said after tacking everything in place, "what do you think?"

"It seems awfully sketchy, Chief."

"It is, and we need to get dozens of questions answered in the next few days. But that doesn't mean that the things we have got don't bear some close scrutiny; it's amazing what you can come up with sometimes from the scantest information." He pulled his stool up to the board and took out a large felt tip pen. "In fact, it reminds me of a riddle. D'you like riddles?"

"Eat 'em for dinner."

"Good, I'll save it 'til then. Pull up that other stool and let's study what we've got. Okay. Suspects."

"Too many," I said.

"Or not enough—depends on whether our murderer is on the list yet. I think we can cross off the Cricks." He did so.

"And Mercy?"

"I'm inclined to think so. Now, where does that leave us?"

"What about the victim herself? Shouldn't you cross her out?"

"Are we sure it wasn't suicide? Well, okay, I know *we're* sure it wasn't—but I think we better leave her there. Of the remaining possibilities, the husband is statistically most likely, and our first order of business will be to settle his alibi once and for all, and take it from there. Then we have the Worms's. What did you think of Nancy Worms?"

"I couldn't make that out, Chief."

"Me neither, but there are clearly some strong feelings there, and we need to find out what they're about. I'm guessing there's more between Nancy Worms and Kimberly Merrick than a little moral indignation."

I nodded.

"Then we've got Sabrina Grason. What did you make of her?"

"She's easy to look at—"

"Smitty! I'm ashamed of you. The woman is dangerous—that cuteness act is like a red flag to me. Besides, she lied through her teeth, if you want an expert opinion. Remember what the poet said about the female of the species."

" 'Deadlier than the male,' " I said, but added, "Kipling was a little sexist, Chief."

Chief laughed. "More than a little, actually. Okay, you got me." He sighed, then fixed me with a shrewd glance. "Still, I wonder if his point doesn't apply in this instance, even if it is a hundred years out of date."

"I'd probably let her lie to me...."

"I thought so. All right then—if she's the pretty friend Captain Williamson spoke of, we need to find out what she's hiding. That's next on our agenda." He scribbled a note next to her name. "Now, what about the man who was our main suspect?"

"Was?"

"Well, would you keep a rendezvous with a woman you knew was dead?"

"Oh. The mystery German."

"Right. I gave a friend of mine at the *Landsraat* that fragment of numbers you got off the license plate, and a description. We'll go down there tomorrow and see if he came up with anything. Unless he does, I think we're in a bad way; pretty hard to find one German male in a country of sixty million Germans, silver hair and blue Mercedes notwithstanding."

I drained my glass, and Chief asked me to bring two more bottles from the fridge.

"So," I asked while he poured, "where do we start in the morning?"

"I've been thinking about that. The really big hole in this case is, how did she die? I think we better start with her medical records, and find out who her doctor was at the clinic. She could have been diabetic, for instance, or had some other condition that will provide a clue. And then maybe Inspector Kriegmann will have something for us on that license plate."

"He's your buddy at the—what's it called?"

"*Landsraat*, the main police station here in Nürnberg. We worked together once on a drug ring that was selling to GI's. You'll like him."

"By the way, what are we going to do with that letter?"

"Letter? Jesus, I forgot all about it! Where is it?"

"In your pocket."

"Right. Quick, the kitchen!"

Chief's kitchen was scary. There exist people who only clean whatever part of the kitchen they happen to want to use at the moment and avoid looking at the rest, and my new boss was an exemplar of this class. The sink, full of dishes, was an obvious health hazard. There were overlapping stains and spills more or less everywhere, and stacks of cartons, boxes, and bags. In one corner was a tower of newspapers—nearly as tall as I am—leaning heavily against a stack of plastic crates filled with German beer bottles. In the center of the room was a heavy wooden table, its raw surface burned and pitted and scored with knife marks. Interestingly, it was half covered with chemical apparatus, including a bunsen burner and oddly shaped glassware of the mad scientist variety, and on the other end was a cereal bowl, a coffee mug, and a box of milk. I kept my distance from that box.

"You need a maid, Chief," I said bluntly.

He had lit the stove and was bringing water to a rattling boil in an old kettle. Wistfully he said, "They never stay...." When the steam was going strong he held the seal of the yellow envelope over it for a few seconds and then levered it up with a butter knife.

"Well," he said, "let's see what we've got here. It's in English, and in an American hand."

I got behind him to look over his shoulder, and read the following:

Dearest Kim,

I know you think it's over, but you're wrong—I still love you. I don't know what it is you've done to me,

but I can't think any more. I can't work. Meet me, for
God's sake. Thursday, our usual table, midnight. If
you don't come, I'll do something crazy. Please.

Love you,

Chet.

Chief threw the letter down on the table and went and stared
into the hallway. Then he took off his glasses and began to wipe
them with his shirt. At last he turned to me and said, "Okay, who
the hell is 'Chet?' "

7 Records... Anyone, Anyone?

Smitty's Apt., Nürnberg, West Germany,
Sunday, 29 June 198-, 1900 hrs.

"Chief," I said, "what about that riddle you promised?"

We had reached the coffee and cigarettes stage, having consumed the better part of a Beef Wellington baked to perfection with a Madeira sauce. It was a Maggie specialty for which she was properly famous at home; a dish furthermore known to induce a mellow satisfaction with life in even the most hardened, harried, and modern of human souls.

"All right. Sobranie?" he asked, extending a packet of those rich, expensive cigarettes. I declined, but Maggie, to my surprise, said she wanted to try one.

"Now then," he continued, "you recall our discussing that even the sketchiest clues can afford a useful conclusion?"

I nodded.

"Are you religious, by the way?"

I shrugged.

"I was raised a Baptist," Maggie said, not answering the question.

"That'll do fine; all we need for this riddle is an ordinary familiarity with the first chapter of Genesis."

We nodded.

"Okay, here goes: A team of archaeologists, on a dig in the Mideast, come across a very ancient burial site. Carefully excavating, they discover two bodies, a male and a female, in a state of almost perfect preservation. The bodies are naked, and there are no other artifacts at the site. After studying them for only a few minutes, the team conclude that they have discovered the remains—" He took a deep puff. "—are you ready?"

Maggie and I glanced at one another. "Are we supposed to guess?" she asked.

"No, no! I'll tell you. They are convinced they have found the original Adam and Eve. The question you have to answer is, how did they know?"

"Easy," Maggie said at once. "Adam was missing a rib."

"Well," Chief said, smiling, "the average human has twenty four ribs, but it's not uncommon to find an individual who's missing one or two, or has an extra. Like toes, you know. It's a good try, but I'm afraid we can't consider the ribs conclusive."

"Then I give up," she said.

"Aren't you going to say he had an apple in his mouth?" Chief asked.

"That would be dumb—they didn't die after eating the fruit! They were driven out of Eden, and had Cain and Abel." Maggie's tone was reproachful. "Besides, you said there wasn't anything else."

"You're perfectly right, of course, and that isn't the answer. It's just the one most people try after the 'rib' thing. Smitty?"

"I suppose fig leaves have nothing to do with it?" I said after a pause.

Maggie rolled her eyes.

" 'Fraid not," Chief said, amused.

"But what would be different about just their bodies? I'm drawing a blank, Chief."

"There's only one possible answer," he said, "and it makes perfect sense—as you'll agree when you discover it. It's a good exercise."

"You mean you're not going to tell us?"

"Of course not! Where would be the fun in that?"

Maggie stamped out her cigarette. "Men," she said.

Monday morning I took keen pleasure in driving past my unit as I was coming in through the gate to the *kaserne* and they were coming out, for I was warm in my car and on my way to an early breakfast, whereas they were chilled and sweaty in their t-shirts and running shoes, holding a tight column formation and singing a double-time cadence.

C-130 rollin' down the strip:
Airborne soldier gonna take a little trip...

I received not a few stares from my fellows, and an especially fine glare from the first sergeant, but I kept my face carefully blank as I stopped and rolled my window down to show the guard my ID.

Stand up, hook up, shuffle to the door,
Jump outside and count to four...

When the last of them had trotted past, however, I'm sure I smiled broadly. I know that there are many people who run for the sheer pleasure of it, but I think they must be a different species. (The sort of people, for instance, who would go airborne.) In any event, a legitimate excuse for missing a PT (Physical Training) formation is to me a cause for celebration, and I muttered "Thank you again, Chief," as I pulled into the lot next to the dining hall.

Specifically, my excuse was that I was to return to the evidence room and learn to fill out Department of the Army form 4137, Evidence/Property Custody Document. The clerk in charge that morning was irritable, and left me to figure it out for the most part on my own, with the result that I was barely able to finish recording the diverse list of artifacts we had collected at the Merrick's the Friday before, before dashing out to morning formation.

After muster I signed out the scarab and met up with Chief. He was feeling sleepy (I suspected him of having just gotten up), and we spoke little on the drive to Erlangen. I had looked forward to seeing how he filled out a uniform, but he disappointed me by wearing civvies—wool slacks with suspenders, a light cotton shirt, and a dull tie that hung loosely around his thick neck.

Our first stop was the brigade clinic, where the waiting room was filled with half a dozen soldiers on sick-call and at least a dozen wives with as many small children. The soldiers wore that expression of resigned boredom that every recruit learns in boot camp, while the children cried, whined, or otherwise misbehaved. The young Pfc who was running the reception desk and answering the constantly ringing phone looked a little ragged. When Chief finally got her attention, told her what he wanted, and showed her his identification, she stared at him with her mouth open.

"I ain't allowed to give out medical records to no one," she said at last.

"I see," Chief said. "Well, who is?"

"Just a minute."

It was many minutes before she could tear herself away from the phone and summon a sergeant.

"I can't give out no records without authorization," said the sergeant.

Several minutes later we were talking to a lieutenant.

"I'm sorry Warrant Officer Tobias, but medical records are controlled. Frankly, I don't think there's any way possible...."

At last we were talking to the clinic administrator, a civilian.

"I understand that Mrs. Merrick is deceased," said the administrator, "however, medical records are still highly confidential. May I ask why you wish to see them?"

"No," said Chief, "you mayn't."

"I see." The administrator frosted visibly. "Well, I think you'd better talk to the brigade surgeon, Major Suarez."

"Okay." There was a pause. "Well, bring on the good doctor, then."

"I'm afraid Major Suarez isn't here."

"Naturally. May I ask, where is he?"

If the administrator had said, "No, you mayn't," things might have gotten out of hand, but after a brief struggle with the temptation he said, "He's teaching a class this morning, at the education center."

"A class? No kidding!" Chief became jocular. "Something to do with medicine, I suppose?"

"Yes."

"And to soldiers?"

"Yes."

"Medics?"

"No."

"Oh...."

"It's a combat life-saving class."

"That's ridiculous. Combat is no way to save lives."

The education center was in a small building just a few hundred meters away and across a parade field, and we chose to walk, taking in the morning sun. Once inside we began peering into classrooms. There was a class in conversational German taught by a nervous young woman with thick glasses, a class in basic reading skills attended by somnolent soldiers hoping to pass the high school equivalency exam (necessary to become an NCO), and a class apparently devoted to the telling of amusing anecdotes, taught by a preening sergeant major with a keen sense of his own importance. At last we found the class being taught by Major Suarez, and stuck our heads in at the door at the back of the room.

"My God, Smitty," Chief whispered, "they're bleeding each other."

It certainly looked like it. There were a half dozen large tables in the room, and at each table a team of two or three soldiers with their shirts off. On the tables were bottles of rubbing alcohol, piles of gauze, saline bags with long tangles of rubber tubing attached to them, and large hypodermic needles which the participants were taking turns jabbing into the veins on one another's forearms. Once a vein was found, an event heralded by the sudden emergence of dark blood flowing from the back end of the needle, the needle itself was removed, leaving behind a slender plastic tube to which the longer tubing would be attached, and then the saline bag would be elevated, forcing fluid into the victim.

Major Suarez was going from table to table, helping to locate veins and offering helpful hints.

"Don't rush it!" he was saying. "Remember that in an actual combat situation your buddy's life might depend on getting fluid, and that can't happen if you don't take the time to find a blood vessel. If you can't find one on the arm, you can use the veins on the wrists and ankles, or at the back of the knee. Put that needle in the used box when you're done with it, Johnson! You don't want Tagget giving you AIDS or something, do you?"

"No sir."

Another soldier said, "You a faggot, Tagget?"

Tagget gripped a wad of gauze to his arm and looked resentful.

"All of you remember," Major Suarez continued, "that these needles must remain in their sterile packages—unopened!—until you have to use them."

" 'Morning, Major!" Chief said.

Major Suarez turned and gaped at us. "Oh, uh, good morning Mister Tobias."

"This looks like great fun," Chief said, "can we try it?"

"This isn't the place for humor, Mister Tobias."

"I'm as serious as a train wreck," Chief insisted.

"I think you've gotten me into enough trouble, don't you?"

"No trouble at all!" Chief said generously. "Here, Tagget, you been briefed on how to work this device? Yes? Excellent! Show me how it's done. Smitty, sit down and roll up your sleeve."

"It is rolled up, Chief. This is July."

"Then sit down."

"*Chief* Tobias—" Major Suarez began, but a sudden bark of pain and dismay from one of the other tables summoned him. "Just a minute," he mumbled, and then, "My God, Sergeant Grant, what have you done? Look, you've gone clear through the vein to the other side. Pull it out. Hold still, McManus! Now, gently.... "

"All right, Tagget, show us how this works."

"Well, sir, first he's gotta have this rubber thing 'round his arm, and start makin' a fist."

"Gotcha. Smitty, get your arm up here."

With grave obedience, I permitted the other soldier to tie a rubber strap around my biceps.

"Okay," Tagget said. "Now you gotta keep makin' a fist so's I can find your vein."

As I clenched and unclenched, Private Tagget, a gangly youth with an endearing twang in his voice and an Ohioan's simplicity of manner, tapped his fingers on the crease of my elbow several times, and then he and Chief leaned close and stared at where the veins should be.

"Smitty," Chief said, "you haven't got any blood vessels."

"Oh well," I said, "I guess that's that."

"Nope, I think I see one," Tagget said. He rubbed my skin viciously with an alcohol-soaked pad and unwrapped his hypo, holding it unsteadily over my arm like a dart.

"Uh, look, Chief—ouch!" I said.

"Dang," Tagget said, working the needle back and forth under the skin.

"Say, you know, this hurts, kind of."

"Looks like it would," Chief agreed.

"Well, I gotta try again," Tagget said, pulling the needle out.

"No, that's okay," I said.

"Smitty! Give the fellow a chance! Look Tagget, it looks kind of blue right about there, don't you think?"

"Ouch!"

"Dang," said Tagget.

By this time Major Suarez was back and staring down at us. And, just my luck, he was getting into the spirit of the thing.

"Having trouble, Tagget?

"Yes sir."

"Let me look. Hmm. A thick skinned one." He tapped my arm several times. "Here we go. Right there."

"Ouch."

"Nope, pull it out. Better disinfect it again, too." He felt in his pockets. "Somebody got a ballpoint?"

I handed him mine, and he drew a short line across the crease of my elbow.

"All right, Tagget. There's a vein there. Now, straight in, and keep going until you feel the needle enter the vein."

"Ouch! Oh great, there goes my shirt," I said, as blood flowed freely across my arm and onto my fatigues.

"Damn, Smitty, he got you!" Chief said, impressed.

"All right, Tagget, now push in with the tube while pulling out on the needle—nice and steady—that's it—now hook up the bag. That's right. Good job son."

"So, what's the point Major?" Chief asked. "I mean, these aren't medics, right?"

"No. It's Seventh Corps' idea. Most combat deaths occur because the soldier doesn't get to an aid station before he bleeds to death—"

"Hypovolemic shock," Chief interjected.

"Yes, that's right. Uh, well, anyway, they determined that if one member of every squad or tank crew had an I.V. kit, and could use it properly—"

"Right. It's a great idea." Chief thrust his hands in his pockets and stared at the apparatus. Suddenly he grinned. "Let's do Smitty's other arm!"

"Chief—" I began.

"Mister Tobias, what do you want?"

"Eh?"

"What did you come for?"

"Oh. Well Major, I'd like to see some medical records."

"You mean.. . ."

"Yeah. Seems they're classified, or something, and the clinic said we had to get your benediction."

"Come into the hall."

I followed Chief and the major with my eyes until they were out of the room, and then looked down to find Tagget raising the saline bag up and down, up and down, watching fascinatedly as my blood coursed into the tubing and then, when he lifted the bag, back into my arm again.

"Disconnect me, please."

"Can't. I haven't finished taping the works to you."

"Let's take it as read."

"Huh?"

I leaned close to Tagget, gritting my teeth. "Take it off."

By the time I got out to the hallway, the discussion had become somewhat heated.

"—precisely what I don't want," Chief was saying.

"There's no other way. You've admitted your investigation is unofficial, and without formal authority I can only give you the records with Captain Merrick's permission."

"How about just letting me study them for a few minutes."

Major Suarez sighed. "It would be improper."

"Look, the woman is dead. It won't harm her, and it might help in determining once and for all the cause of death. If she was diabetic, for instance—"

"She wasn't."

"—or subject to seizures, or had high blood pressure—"

"She didn't," the major said shortly.

Chief stopped suddenly, and gave the major a long look. "You were her physician, weren't you sir?"

Major Suarez hesitated.

"You were. And there is something ... something about her you don't wish me to know."

Major Suarez was becoming quite tense, and wouldn't meet Chief's eyes. Chief studied the doctor for a few moments, and then took off his glasses and began to wipe them on his shirt-sleeve.

"Major Suarez," he said, "whom are you protecting?"

"My patient, of course."

"Your patient is dead, doctor."

"She has a family."

"In fact, I believe your patient was murdered."

At this, finally, the major looked up, and his dark hispanic eyes studied Chief carefully. Chief put his glasses back on.

"What time will this class be over?"

"We're about done."

"I'd like to meet you at your office. Thirty minutes?"

Major Suarez started to go back into the class without answering, but turned at the door, glanced at us, and nodded. Chief stood staring at the closed door for a few seconds, making thoughtful little clucking sounds. Then he turned absent mindedly and put his hand on my shoulder before heading down the hallway to the outer door.

"How do you do that, Chief?" I asked when we were back outside. The sun had climbed high into the sky and the air was hot. Across the parade field, a small group of soldiers was at work, trimming the grass and sweeping the cobblestones with immense street brooms.

"How do I do what, Smitty?"

"Make people do what you want."

"What on earth makes you think I can do that?"

"Like just now, Chief! Major Suarez didn't want to talk to you, but he agreed to anyway, even though he probably could just refuse—I thought he was *going* to refuse. You always make him angry...."

Chief stopped by the curb and looked at me. "That embarrasses you, doesn't it?"

"No," I lied, "I just don't know why it works."

We paused to watch a short column of armored personnel carriers pass by, the whine of their diesel engines and the clatter of their metal track making the ground rumble.

"Let's get a cup of coffee," he suggested.

We detoured to the PX.

"Okay," he said when we were settled at a table. "First of all, there is only one way, that I know of, to get someone to do something they truly don't want to do, and that is to trick them. Even then it's difficult to do, and almost impossible to do to the same person twice."

"Well," I objected, "you could force them."

"How?"

"You could threaten them. They got me to do all kinds of things in basic training, for instance."

"I see your point," he said after a few seconds consideration, "but consider: didn't you want to finish basic training?"

"Of course. But that doesn't mean I wanted to do three hours of PT everyday."

"No, but you were willing to if that's what it took to get what you wanted. In that sense it's no different than my surrendering fifty cents to get this cup of coffee. It'd be nice to get the coffee for free, but that's not how it works."

I felt he was oversimplifying, and said so. "After all," I insisted, "you have to agree that people do manipulate other people."

"Ah!" he said. "And that's what you're accusing me of?"

"Oh no, Chief. I just meant... I don't know." Chief's tone was good-natured and certainly not contentious, but I felt backed into a corner and I was afraid of an argument with this man.

"What I'm trying to say, Smitty, is that nobody gets manipulated to do something they absolutely do not want to do."

"I just don't follow you, Chief."

"I can't manipulate you, and no one can manipulate anyone else, unless the person being manipulated is a willing participant in the manipulation."

"Hmm." I sipped my coffee. "Okay, how did you get Major Suarez to agree to talk to you, when he didn't want to."

"He *did* want to. That's just the point."

"Oh. It seemed like he didn't."

"That's because he is afraid."

This kept me busy for awhile, and it wasn't until we were mounting the steps to the clinic that I thought to say, "I wonder what Major Suarez is afraid of?"

Chief laughed. "Colonel Crick, probably. Let's find out!"

Major Suarez instructed the nurse who showed us into his office to bring him Mrs. Merrick's records, then invited us to take a seat. I sat and took out my notebook, as usual, while Chief remained standing, insolently inspecting the major's diplomas.

"University of Arizona!" he said. "That a nice place?"

"Chief Tobias," the major said, in a tone, for the first time since I'd met him, completely without annoyance, "you don't need to do that anymore. I understand the tactic, and I am quite prepared to be frank with you."

"Eh?"

"She was a prostitute."

Chief pulled up his chair slowly and sat, facing the major expressionlessly, but said nothing.

"She was a prostitute," the major repeated.

"That a diagnosis?"

The major turned as red as a tomato.

After a pause, Chief said roughly, "Look, sir, you think of me as a policeman, and I'd like you to stop. I'm not an MP, not a 'cop.' I'm a scientist, frankly, and you need to accept, doctor, that your patient is now my patient. The symptom is death by homicide, and it is my task to uncover the disease." Chief leaned forward intently. "You may not like my looks, or my bedside manner, but if you can set aside all your previous notions of what a policeman is or does and look upon me as a professional, in the *sciences*, and as one who is in great need of *facts*—well, you might find me a little less intolerable."

Major Suarez took a heavy breath, then slapped his intercom and asked for the nurse. He switched it off slowly then, and put his hand to his forehead in a gesture of fatigue.

"You're right," he said finally. "It's not you I don't like, it's the situation. There's going to be a bad season over this death."

The nurse knocked and entered, and Major Suarez asked her if she had found Mrs. Merrick's records.

"I'm sorry doctor," she said, "but there seems to be a problem."

"Delicious," Chief murmured.

"What problem?" the major asked.

"No one can find them."

"Have they been signed out by anyone?"

"No, they just aren't on the shelf."

"Keep looking," Major Suarez said severely, and when she had gone he said to Chief, "Let me tell you what I can from memory."

"Thank you sir. Have you been treating her since her arrival on base?"

"I first examined her about six months ago. She was pregnant. She was quite upset about it, and emphatic that it be kept secret."

"What happened?" Chief asked, glancing at me to ensure that I was writing things down.

"She terminated the pregnancy at a German hospital in Frankfurt."

"Did she give any explanation as to why?"

"No." Major Suarez leaned back in his chair. "I suspected though, even then, that she wasn't sure whose the baby was."

"What made you feel that way?"

"Nothing, exactly. Her attitude was odd, that's all. I might be embellishing the memory, though."

"In light of what came after, I presume."

"Yes. I saw her again several months later. Like her first visit, she wouldn't discuss her problem with any of the medics or nurses, or even the physician's assistant, but demanded to see me." Here the major paused and lowered his voice. "She had chlamydia."

"Chief?" I said.

"It's a venereal disease—" he began. "Oh, uh, c-h-l-a-m-y-d-i-a—is that right doctor?"

Major Suarez nodded. "You're a walking dictionary," he said to Chief.

"It's a curse," Chief said, shrugging his shoulders. "So, was that when you concluded she had turned professional?"

"No. I tried to get her to talk, naturally, but she was obstinate, even defiant. Then about four weeks ago she shows up with a galloping case of the clap."

"And would she discuss anything with you then?" Chief asked.

"She didn't want to, but by this time I had begun to hear some pretty ugly rumors about her. I confronted her, telling her that she was risking her own health and might very likely ruin her husband's career."

"What did she say?"

"She became enraged. Told me I was a 'quack,' and demanded to know why the Army couldn't hire real doctors. Really, she was nearly out of control. I wanted to give her a referral for counseling, but she was absolutely unapproachable. She repeated several times that if I violated her confidence she would see to it that I was ruined. All in all, it was as bad a confrontation as I've ever had with a patient."

"Fascinating. What did you make of that?"

"Obviously, she was in a poor state of mental health. What her precise condition was we'll never know now. Certainly she was borderline, maybe schizophrenic."

"Did you see her again before last Friday?"

The major shook his head. "I was still wondering what to do for her, or about her, when she died. I guess, now, that I should have come to you."

"To me?"

"Well, to the police I mean. She *was* breaking the law."

"Actually," Chief said, "she probably wasn't. U.S. jurisdiction ends at the gate for non-military personnel."

"Well, the German police then."

"Who would have done precisely nothing, for the simple reason that selling sex is perfectly legal in this country."

This was news to me, and from the look on his face I suspected it was news to Major Suarez as well.

"I'm sure you did as much as anyone could do, major," Chief continued. "Anyway, that's behind you now. I'm really grateful for this information—although I'd still like to see those records."

"I've told you all that's in them."

"All that you know of, sir. There would be a medical history there, and it may contain things of importance."

"Maybe," Major Suarez said, "but I read through all the documents there were and I don't recall anything unusual."

"Well," Chief said, "I also find the fact that the records are missing a very interesting, er, fact."

"They're probably just misplaced. The sergeant in charge of records will be coming back from leave by the end of the week. We'll find them."

"Who could have them?"

"No one, outside this building. Only the patient or a medical authority can sign them out, and then the sign-out card is used as a place-holder for them on the file shelf."

"What about Captain Merrick?" Chief asked.

"Nope. Medical records are confidential, even from spouses."

"Sometimes especially from spouses," Chief said. He was unsatisfied, but he could think of no further questions.

"Smitty."

"Chief."

"Lunch."

"Right," I said, nodding at the guard as we left Matson *kaserne* and swung the scarab out into a hail of bicycles.

"They're like locusts!" Chief said.

"Whoops," I said, throwing on the brakes.

"Not bad looking locusts, some of them," Chief amended. We both smiled at the student, a fresh-faced German girl in braids and cut-offs, who was smiling her apology at us for trying to get under my wheels.

"*Entschuldigen!*" she called, riding away.

"*Macht nichts!*" I said.

"Steady lad. How does giros sound? I'm going to share one of my best secrets with you, if you don't mind the detour."

At his direction I headed for the old countryside road that parallels the *autobahn* between Erlangen and Nürnberg. The immigrant population in Germany includes Turkish, Greek, and many Balkan people, and a happy consequence is that one can find a tremendous variety of cuisines. Chief directed me to an *imbiss* in a working-class suburb of Nürnberg and treated me to the best giros sandwich I've ever eaten—seasoned, roast mutton served on a pita bread with *suzaki*, a creamy cucumber sauce. We stood outdoors at an elbow-high table to eat, Chief with a *Pils* and me with a coke.

"Your fault for being in uniform," he said.

When we had taken the edge off our hunger he returned to our earlier conversation.

"So, Smitty, what do you think now: did the major want to talk to me, or no?"

"Yeah, but you had to piss him off again," I said with a grin.

"I did, didn't I," he chuckled.

"I thought he was going to throw us out. Then, like magic, he goes all friendly. I still don't know how you do it."

"Major Suarez' mental state is not all that difficult to understand," he explained. "In his world, he's in charge. Like many people who are not trained to leadership, he equates being in charge with being in control—and that's a fatal mistake, because of course one *can't* be in control. Successful leaders manage events—and people—in pursuit of common goals, but they don't expect to direct them because it can't be done. Consequently, someone like the major is saddled with a chronic anxiety, because he believes he must be in control and yet knows that he is not."

"Is that what you meant when you said he was afraid? I thought you meant he was hiding something."

"And so he was," Chief said. "You just had the cart before the horse."

"How do you mean?"

"He wasn't afraid because he was hiding something; he was holding back because he is afraid, just generally. He dressed it up in his own mind, of course—something about professional discretion or what not—but that was all a smokescreen for his own internal benefit, not for my sake."

Chief's analysis fascinated me. Although I had been along for every part of this investigation, he had not shared many insights with me and I hoped this new trend was going to continue.

"It's worth taking the time to really understand this mechanism," he continued, "because it's at the root of a great many behaviors. If you are saddled with a false concept regarding your relationships to other people, such as the major's about his role as a leader, then you will experience anxiety about those relationships. This anxiety will be very diffuse and non-specific—fear without an object. The tendency is to ignore the anxiety, to suppress it, so its source is hidden in the mind. However, if something happens to inflame that anxiety, the disturbed fear quickly precipitates into anger. Typically, the only way to get someone in this state of mind out of it again is to precipitate the anger deliberately. Then their mind will begin functioning, and you can communicate with them."

"And that's what you did to Major Suarez?"

"Oh," he said, "I just pushed a little bit—guessing that once he got some emotion expressed he would want to participate in the unraveling of this mystery. He's got a good mind."

"Just a little mental illness," I said.

"No, no! That would be far too strong a characterization. Like calling a hangnail a disease. His condition is common to all of us at one time or another. Don't make too much of it. I only brought it up again because you seemed interested, and because you were concerned by my behavior towards him."

"Yeah," I said, "I guess I was, a little."

"In fact, it was making you anxious," he said, smiling.

"Ye-es," I said hesitantly.

"And now? Do you still feel anxiety?"

I resisted answering. Chief had often made me feel self-conscious, but this was an explicit challenge to reveal my emotions. I looked at him and then glanced away—he was watching me closely. I suddenly felt the request was momentous; that perhaps the nature of our relationship hung on how I chose to respond. I took a deep breath and closed my eyes for a few seconds, repeating his question to myself mentally.

"No," I said then. "I don't feel anxious. Just curious."

"About what?"

"I'm not sure. I feel good, actually."

"Me too." he said, and slapped me on the shoulder. "Let's go meet inspector Kriegmann."

8 Minds over Mystery

The Police Station, Nürnberg, West Germany,
Monday, 30 June 198-, 1400 hrs.

Inner and outer Nürnberg, the *altstadt* and *neustadt* as they
are called, are like the inside and outside of a secret garden.
One passes from a barren wilderness of rude, industrial buildings
and grimy, four-lane thoroughfares through an immense medieval
wall—and suddenly into a wonderland of cobblestone streets and
cut-stone buildings. Here the Pegnitz river, as it meanders to its
confluence with the Rednitz, is spanned by graceful arches of
carved granite and sandstone; rock that is not solemn but wears
cheerful faces, weathered by centuries of wind and rain and bird-
droppings though they be, that poke out from nests of baroque tracery and smile in the bright sun. The ancient market squares that
overflow with stalls of food vendors and craftspeople are presided
over by two magnificent gothic cathedrals whose bells call out the
hours; the first is Saint Lawrence's, and the second, named for the
eighth-century patron saint of Nürnberg, is the cathredral of Saint
Sebald. The narrow, tightly twisting streets are hostile to traffic; it
is a place of pedestrians, of shoppers and tourists and passers-by.

We entered the medieval city through a gate on the north side,
skirting the towers of the old feudal castle, and worked our way
south through a maze of queer little streets to the *Jakob Platz,*

where we parked in the shadow of the wall on the south side of the *altstadt*, at a point where it overlooks what was once a formidable moat but is now a green and tree-lined park sunk strangely into the earth.

Chief led me to a brown building with a copper roof and the words *Polizeipräsidium Mittelfranken* displayed in large aluminum letters over the glass doors. He conversed briefly with a watchman behind a thick glass window who then buzzed us through the second set of doors. Inspector Kriegmann worked in a small office on the third floor.

"*Herr Chief Tobias!*" he said warmly after answering our knock. He was a short, red-faced man with short, graying hair, but he had an athletic build and seemed very energetic. He was dressed casually (for Germany), but wore a pistol in a shoulder holster.

"*Wer ist dieser gutaussehende junge Mann?*" he said.

"*Herr Kriegmann, dauf ich meiner neuen Assistenten vorstellen, Gefreiter Smith,*" Chief answered, placing his hand on my shoulder and beaming. "Smitty," he said, "Herr Kriegman."

"*Willkommen, Gefreiter Smith,*" he said, taking my hand in what felt like a vice grips.

"*Guten Tag, Herr Kriegmann,*" I answered. "*Danke schön.*"

"*Er ist ein sehr nette, junge mann!*" he said to Chief, "*Er spricht gut Deutsch!*"

"*Nur ein wenig,*" I cautioned him with a hesitant smile, hoping I was saying "only a little bit" correctly.

"*Das macht nichts,*" he said, "I can speak English for you. You have not been in Germany long?"

"Only a few months," I said, "but I like it very much. Nürnberg is a beautiful city."

"*Wunderbar.* I am glad you are liking it. Please come to me if I can ever be helping you."

"Thank you very much sir. I will."

"Now, Chief Tobias," he said, motioning us to chairs once the formalities were done, "you want I should tell you about this blue Mercedes, yes? Well, I cannot."

"I'm sorry to hear that. Not enough information, I guess."

"*Ja.* But, I can narrow it down for you. What was the model year and the number?"

Chief and I exchanged glances, and I shook my head.

"A recent model," Chief said. "A large sedan."

"Do you know what kind of blue it is in the color?"

"Quite dark, wasn't it Smitty?"

I nodded.

"Dark blue, good. Moment." He turned to a computer terminal and punched some keys. "That makes only eight, now. Before, it was over forty. You are sure the letters are N and U? Good. *Ach du lieber, sehr interessant!*"

"What is it?" Chief said.

"I will print it."

He did so, and we all bent over the list. There were two women's names and six men's. Inspector Kriegman pointed to one of them.

"This man I am knowing," he said. "A pornographer, who deals in cocaine."

"No kidding," Chief said, studying the name. " 'Gunther Buttenheimer.' Is he a tall man, with silver hair?"

"*Ja, ja.* Very big, very proud. You know of him?"

"Smitty and I saw him, if it's the right man, in Erlangen."

"I think maybe you should be telling me why you are interested in this man."

Chief explained about the death of Mrs. Merrick, and about her apparent link with prostitution and her reputed liason with one or more German men.

"We saw *Herr* Buttenheimer, if it is *Herr* Buttenheimer, waiting outside Mrs. Merrick's apartment Saturday evening. When he saw us watching him from her window he got in his car very quickly and drove away. I was unable to follow him."

"And you think he is involved in some way with this woman's death?"

"We don't know," Chief said. "She appears at this point to have died from alcohol poisoning, but we will have to wait on the autopsy to be sure. Also, there are indications that someone was with her at the time of death and is attempting to hide the fact. However, I doubt this man knew she was dead, else why would he return to her apartment, where she died?"

"That is reasonable," inspector Kriegmann assented.

"Nevertheless," Chief continued, "I would like very much to find out what his connection to the victim was."

"Naturally. I can ask him to come in for questions, of course."

"Yes," Chief said, but looked pensive. "Can you tell me more about him?"

Inspector Kriegmann was happy to oblige. He characterized Mr. Buttenheimer as a small-time underworld type, the owner of a photography business that specialized in pornographic layouts for magazines, and who was also known to be a conduit for the distribution of small amounts of cocaine. Although twice arrested, he had never been convicted of any crime.

"Is he under surveillance currently?" Chief asked.

"I will have to ask inspector Müller. That is his territory now."

"What about prostitution? Any link?"

"It is certainly possible," inspector Kriegmann said. "You are thinking of what you call, uh, 'primping?' "

"Pimping," Chief said, smiling.

"*Ja, ja.* Well, I do not think it so very likely. It is not legal, and any girls who participated in such a scheme would be in danger to have the license taken away."

"Ah, but Mrs. Merrick was an American. She would not have had a license."

"You are sure?" inspector Kriegmann asked. "I believe such women are here in Nürnberg."

"Hunh?" Chief grunted. "I hadn't thought of that. Could you check?"

"*Moment.*" Inspector Kriegmann tapped at the computer. "How you spell it?"

I spelled it for him.

"*Nein. Keine* Merrick."

"Does that list include Erlangen?"

"*Ja, ja. Und Frankfurt, und München.*"

"Min-chen?" I echoed, not knowing where that was.

"Munich," Chief said.

"Oh."

"Well," he sighed then, "you know, I think I'd like to hold off on official questioning for *Herr* B., at least for the moment. At least until you find out if he is under investigation currently. Also, I'd like to get another look at him surreptitiously. Can you give me the name and address of his business?"

"Of course. But please remember, my friend, that any questioning must be coordinated. You will not embarrass me, eh?"

Chief assured him, and got the information. Since inspector Müller wasn't in, inspector Kriegmann promised to check with him and call Chief if there was any other information, and then we left.

Outside, the afternoon sun cast widening shadows across the narrow streets, and a breeze had kicked up. Overhead, small clouds hurried across a brilliant sky. Chief stood on the sidewalk and lit a rare cigarette. Standing there in his cuffed slacks and suspenders, with his tie flapping in the wind as he sheltered the match in his hands and stooped over the flame, he looked like a character in an old movie. All he lacked was the fedora.

"Well, Smitty," he said, putting his hand on my shoulder, "how about a walk?"

"A walk, Chief?"

"Yeah—the peripatetic school of detection. You can be Aristotle." He grinned as he took the paper from his pocket on which was written Buttenheimer's business address. "This is only a few blocks, and in a neighborhood you should see if you haven't. Come on."

We walked east, keeping the wall on our right as we navigated the narrow ways.

"How do you like inspector Kriegmann, by the way?"

"He seems very nice," I said. "Very formal."

"It's the culture," Chief said. "How long did you say you'd been here?"

"Well, I got here in January, and Maggie and the kids came along in March after I'd gotten the apartment."

We stopped in front of an antique store and Chief studied the window display.

"You'll find," he said, "that people here, especially professional people, rely heavily on social conventions. It pays to respect the formalities. You did very well with the inspector, by the way. Quite well."

We continued on down the street.

"They warned us about that in the orientation classes," I said.

"Yes, but most soldiers, unfortunately, quickly forget it. Did you speak any German when you got here? No? Well, you should pick up all you can. Ah, here we go. I suppose a Dudley Do-right such as yourself has never been on this street before, hmm?"

"No," I admitted. It was a long, curving avenue cut through a deep canyon of four and five-story buildings with plain fronts and dark windows. At the ground level, however, were many glaring neon lights and garishly painted signs depicting the female form in greater or lesser degrees of unclothed detail. The nearest to the corner, on the other side of the street from us, had the words "Sexy Shop" flashing in orange and blue above a broad entrance from which the thumping bass of heavy rock 'n roll emanated into the street.

"When you hear soldiers speak of 'the wall,' " Chief explained, "this is where they mean. Although the oldest profession can be practiced legally anywhere, actual solicitation is restricted by law to small districts like this one in the largest cities. Pity you're in uniform, or you could get a more thorough education—" He stopped suddenly and put his hand on my arm. "Well, I'll be damned! Quick Smitty, let's check out this window!"

"What is it?" I whispered, turning with him and staring at a stack of magazines.

"Don't look," he said, throwing a brief glance over his shoulder. "All right, she's going the other way."

"Who?"

He chuckled. "I should make you guess."

"Chief—"

"Okay, okay! I won't tell you her name, but her initials are 'Sabrina Grason.'"

"You're kidding."

"All right, I'm kidding. C'mon."

We started to follow. When I saw her, I realized there was no mistaking that tight, peppy figure with its short curtain of bouncing brown curls and hip-hugging skirt. Chief proceeded slowly, but began to close with her as she neared the next corner. There was no need for concern, however, for she turned at a small doorway in the last building and disappeared into it. Chief smiled and dug in his pocket as we sauntered past on the far side of the street, reproducing his note with the address.

"Yep," he said, "Luitpold Strasse 19—site of *Herr* Buttenheimer's snapshot emporium. Smitty, this case might be coming into focus."

We continued to the end of the street and entered yet another tobacco and magazine shop. Chief gave me a few *Deutsche Marks* and asked me to buy him some Sobranies while he stood near the door and watched out the window.

"Smitty!" he called before I had gotten my change. I hurried over. "Nope, it doesn't matter—she's gotten a cab. Oh, well."

Back on the street, Chief stood and rocked up and back on the balls of his feet, his eyes shining.

"Well, Smitty, what's the obvious thing to do at this point?"

"Check out that place," I said, nodding to Buttenheimer's building. "Or else, get ahold of Mrs. Grason and make her tell you what's going on."

"Yes," he agreed, "those are the obvious things to do. So let's not."

"Chief?"

"Both of those will keep, at least for now."

He turned and walked on, not back to the car but towards the central market, and I followed.

"One important aspect of directing an investigation," he continued, "is *not* letting it direct *you*. There's an awful lot going on, just now, in one way, but in another way we're in something of an intermission. It'll be tomorrow before the lab can tell us anything about most of the evidence we collected, for instance."

We crossed the street, entering a pedestrian zone. Musicians and other performers dotted the walkways, playing tunes, singing, or even dancing for those whose goodwill was expressed by tossing coins into hats and guitar cases. Children with ice cream cones tugged at their mothers' skirts or chased one another through the crowd, while the spires of St. Lawrence cathedral rose up before us like the masts of some fantastic ship plying the cobblestone sea.

"We may learn something from those fingerprints, or we may find there was something on her clothes that will narrow our leads. Also, the memorial service is tomorrow, and we will have an opportunity to speak to her family, and re-interview several witnesses. There are stories to track down, alibis to confirm, and much evidence to be sifted through—perhaps new evidence to be collected. Potentially, at least, there's a mountain of work ahead of us."

We stopped under the enormous doors of the cathedral, and sat at the base of the steps.

"You can see, can't you, that an investigation is something of a labyrinth, and that it's possible to wander in it endlessly without getting anywhere in particular?"

"Yes," I said, and we sat quietly for a minute or two watching the crowd.

"What's needed at this point," Chief said, "is some organizing principle. A hypothesis, or a system of hypotheses, to begin to narrow things down. Then we can break our work up into a logical sequence of tasks."

"How do we do that?" I asked.

"We need to step right outside of it, and give our higher functions a chance to help us put things into perspective. In fact, Smitty, we need to meditate."

After another minute he got up and stretched, then settled his gaze on the rose window of the cathedral front. "Beautiful," he said; "just the thing." He signaled me to follow, and we walked around to the side entrance, a heavy medieval door with wrought iron fittings, and went in.

If I had a gift for poetry I would write about cathedrals, but I am stuck with prose—a meager instrument for conveying the effect upon the mind and emotions that a genuine Gothic cathedral can have, particularly upon a person entering one for the first time. St. Lawrence's is not even one of the great cathedrals (it would disappear into the shadow of Rheims or Notre Dame, for instance) and it had to be almost completely reconstructed after World War II—yet it has the magic. How can I describe it? The stone, to begin with, is dark and rough and shows plainly the erosion of countless generations of careless human habitation. Also, each block is obviously hand-cut, with subtle irregularities that are strange to we who flourish in the environs of a machined and mass-produced age. Yet, it is this very quality that works upon the senses an unaccustomed wonder. We apprehend that each small part of the place is precious in itself, each stone a distillation of human aspirations.

One can almost still detect the mingled odors of faith and perspiration. It is this—the rude comfort of stone flags underfoot and the gritty surface of the walls and pillars near at hand—which strikes the tonic chord in our emotional response, a response that builds like the slow swell of an orchestra as our attention progresses from the parts to the whole, our gaze wandering up chorus after chorus of upright stone, until the crescendo of a vaulted ceiling towers above us like the vault of heaven, lit with a fire of crimson and gold from the filtered light of the stained glass windows on every side. If the builders meant to make a place where faith might find a home, and where the natural tendency of men and women to be struck by the mystery of existence might be given full expression, let it be said that they succeeded.

I followed Chief to a set of pews near the front and we sat facing the choir. Over our heads, perched on a wooden arch that spanned the width of the nave, was a life-size crucifix painted in a very realistic style. The figure itself looked emaciated, and the face was contorted in a kind of sobbing grimace. The blood, painted in glistening streaks from the wounds on the hands, feet, ribs, and scalp, looked so real that I was struck by a sudden fancy that it might drip onto our heads. I shivered and looked away, wishing Chief had chosen somewhere else to sit.

Chief's head was tilted up, but his eyes were closed. I wondered if he was praying, and then I wondered if he was religious. Like most people I'm pretty much an agnostic if pressed, but I generally don't like to think about it and I am sometimes made uncomfortable by people who are openly faithful. Here, however, in such a crucible of faith as this ancient cathedral, such reactions seemed petty. Nevertheless, the thought that Chief, with all his humor and zest and practical sense, might be devout, gave me a real shock. It was one thing to admire religious expression (like the cathedral) objectively, but it was something else again to confront it personally. I felt apprehensive—my admiration for Chief was threatened.

"What are you worrying about?" he said suddenly, still with his eyes closed.

I hesitated. "Are you religious, Chief?" I asked.

He laughed a loud, short, bark of a laugh. "You're supposed to be thinking about this case!" he said.

"Right. Sorry." I took a deep breath and tried to focus my mind on the investigation, but before long I was thinking about Chief again. I was thinking that I had no real experience of truly religious people, and that I wouldn't know how to handle it if Chief turned out to be one.

But then I realized that I did have experience, of a sort: my favorite author when I was a teenager was J.R.R. Tolkein, and I not only read *The Lord of the Rings* several times but everything else by or about him I could get my hands on, including his biography. He was a devout Catholic, and I would have sold my soul to spend one afternoon with him.

I began to relax. If Chief was religious, I would be okay. At least, if he was a Catholic, or something solid and ancient and rich like that, which he probably was if he was in fact praying, because this was a Catholic church, about as Catholic as Catholic gets.

But he wasn't praying, he was thinking about the investigation—he had just as much as said so—and here I was, sitting there like an idiot having a neurotic episode.

"Well, Smitty, any thoughts?" he asked quietly.

"Uh, not really Chief."

"Hmm. You're not very focused, I think. You can't meditate

if you're not focused."

"I don't really know what meditation is, Chief," I admitted.

"Well, we'll have to fix that. The basic idea is simple: one's mind is a chatter-box, and to meditate it is required simply to turn the chatter-box off, but remain alert. Make sense? Okay, now: there's no mystery about it. You just focus your mind on one thing, and ignore any and all other thoughts that enter your mind."

"That sounds easy. What's the point?"

Chief laughed. "I assure you, you will not think it easy after the first time you try it for five minutes. As to the purpose—" He looked around. "Let's try a demonstration. Come over here."

He led me to one of the pillars. Attached to it about eight feet from the floor was a large sculpture, of a scene from the book of Genesis.

"All right. You trust me? Good. I want you to stand here and stare at this sculpture. Don't think about it, just stare at it, and at nothing else until I come back."

"How long?" I asked.

"Long enough. I promise I won't let you die standing here."

With that he walked away. After a few moments I turned to see where he had gone, but he was standing just a few feet away obviously waiting for me to do exactly this, and gestured at me to do as I had been told. Chagrined, I turned back to the sculpture and stared, trying not to think about anything. Shortly, I realized my thoughts had strayed to home. I was thinking about Maggie, inspired I think by the graven images of the first couple. I forced myself to stop. I stared. The sculpture was of the temptation scene, with the serpent entwined about a tree and Adam and Eve standing to either side, Eve with the fruit in her hand. That got me to thinking about Mrs. Merrick and the investigation, and I rationalized that it was okay to think about that because that was what I was supposed to be thinking about earlier—but my conscience stung me as I thought of Chief, probably still watching me, and his instructions to think about nothing and to just stare. I stared. My feet hurt, and I had to go to the bathroom. I wondered if he'd be angry if I quit to go to the bathroom. Really, I suddenly had to go very badly. Oh hell, I was doing it again. With a supreme effort, I stared. I don't know how long I stared, but I did finally succeed in doing nothing but paying attention to the statues, without chattering to myself about them, for some time.

And then it hit me. Chief must have seen me giggling, because he came and put his hand on my shoulder.

"Belly buttons!" I said, turning to him in a kind of ecstasy. "They don't have any belly buttons!"

"The intelligence is a wonderful thing," he said, smiling. "But it works in the quiet spaces, between our conscious thoughts. Let's go sit down."

"Wait 'til I tell Maggie!" I said, following him back to the pews.

"I'll bet you five dollars she's already guessed it," he said.

"I doubt that!"

"Then it's a bet?"

I didn't hesitate to shake on it.

"Now," he said, "let's see if we can get similar results concerning the untimely demise of Merrick, K."

"Right!" I said, still enthused, but then I sobered. "Actually Chief, I've been thinking about it a lot, but I feel frustrated. I feel as though I should be able to deduce things from the evidence, like Sherlock Holmes, but nothing comes to me."

"Ah. Well, I shouldn't feel bad about that if I were you. You are asking something of yourself that doesn't make any sense."

"Hunh?"

"Well, you know that Sherlock Holmes is fictional, don't you?"

"Of course."

"All right then. So were his methods."

"Oh." I said. "Could you explain that?"

"Don't get me wrong," Chief said, settling himself comfortably and stretching his legs; "they are wonderful stories, and even instructive. But when Conan Doyle made Holmes 'deduce' solutions with his so-called 'deductive methods,' he actually led generations of readers down the primrose path to idiocy. Holmes practically never 'deduced' anything—he inferred."

"There's a difference?"

"Yes, and a very important one. Let's take the case of Adam and Eve. You know as a general principle that anyone who was born from the womb has a belly button, and you know, intuitively at least, that the contrapositive of an implication is always true—in this case, that anyone who has no belly button cannot have been born. Thus, when you admit for sake of argument the literal truth of the Genesis myths, you may safely deduce that the bodies without navels are those of Adam and Eve, the only people who ever lived who were made, not born."

"That makes sense."

"Good. The proper term for a deduction of that sort is *modus ponens*. The classic example is, 'All Cretans are liars; I am a Cretan; therefore I am a liar.' You have a general principle, and argue to a particular case. It's not that I might be a liar, or that I'm probably a liar, but that I *must* be given the premises. Now, in contrast take an example from our investigation. We have as evidence that

Mrs. Merrick, a heavy smoker, smoked no cigarettes as she sup-
posedly sat in her room drinking herself to death. However, there
is no general premise to the effect that she would *have* to smoke
under those conditions, only the fact that she ordinarily would,
leading to the inference that there was something unusual in the
circumstances. There are many possible explanations. She may
have quit, felt sick, or even flushed the butts down the toilet and
cleaned the ashtray before passing out. We can conclude nothing
for certain, but we may note the oddity of the circumstance and
seek possible explanations. See the difference?"

"I think so. It's what is meant by circumstantial evidence."

"Exactly! Of course, as Thoreau said, some circumstantial
evidence is very strong—as when you find a trout in the milk."

"That would convince me."

"It would certainly be suggestive. Indeed, it might lead to an
inference."

"Got it," I said.

"Our first goal, really, is to be able to make enough inferences
to form a credible theory—or theories—of what happened. Then
we may test our conjectures and try to find compelling evidence,
the kind that leads to reasonable certainty or, in other words, a
conviction. If we are very lucky, we might even be able to prove
our result."

"How?"

"Oh," he said, "by finding missing belly buttons, say."

"And if we can't?"

"We don't have to. In court, as in life, a reasonable certainty
is sufficient."

"So we just have to find the trout in the milk," I said, leaning
back in my chair and trying to look thoughtful.

"Oh, well," Chief said, dropping his hands out in front of him like Jack Benny, "we've got that. What we need is the fella with the fishing gear who's been hanging around the milking house—preferrably one with a grudge against dairy products."

We sat in silence for a few moments.

"Actually," he said with sudden animation, sitting up and turning to me with an intent look, "our problem is more subtle—damnably so. We didn't find a trout in the milk at all, we just noticed the funny taste. Our hardest job may be convincing others that something is—"

"Fishy," I offered.

Chief made a sour face. "All right, I think we've about bled that analogy dry. Let's be serious, and see if we can't structure our thoughts about this. Assume it was homicide. The fundamental issues to be confronted are means, motive, and opportunity. Let's start with means."

"Already we've got a problem," I said, "because we haven't discovered the cause of death."

"Right. Nevertheless, we should remind ourselves of what we do know, even if it's all negative information. We know the death wasn't violent, wasn't caused by narcotics overdose or any other common chemical agent, and wasn't asphyxiation. On the other hand, we do know that she had enough alcohol in her to do her in. So... suppose that was the means."

"Okay, but Ginger said she could have had an aneurysm—"

"Yes, and we'll consider that later, but we're assuming for the moment that it was homicide, remember? You'll see why in a minute."

"All right."

"Now, if she died of alcohol poisoning, it could still be homicide, even premeditated."

"How?"

"That's easy. Once someone is really drunk, it is not hard to keep them drinking until they begin to pass out. Then just pour it down their throat."

"Hmm. I suppose you could."

"All right. The reason I like this theory is two-fold. First of all, her physical appearance makes it pretty clear she was a heavy drinker, and heavy drinkers know how to nurse a drunk. Also, their bodies are used to metabolizing the alcohol, so their system is not so easily shocked into a coma. Second, the booze she'd been drinking was scotch whiskey, yet the body'd been staged with the vodka bottle and there was no open scotch bottle in the house. That all but forces the inference that someone else provided the scotch and then cleared out after she was pretty much gone, wiping their prints and taking the bottle along with them."

"That works," I said, getting the idea. "This person probably also washed whatever glasses they'd been using, cleaned the ash-trays, and, and...,"

"And vamoosed. Now, there are two other things I'd like you to consider, one that reinforces this theory and one that threatens to dash it to pieces. The first is the mirror. Remember? The one with no prints?"

"Yes."

"What would you use a mirror for, if you were a murderer?"

"Well," I said, my mind blank. "Am I vain?"

"Try again."

"Oh! To see if the person was still breathing."

"Excellent. You get a gold star. Now the bad news: Why didn't we smell any scotch on her coat or the bed? If it was forced down her throat at some point, it would almost certainly have spilled here and there."

"Well, would we still be able to smell it after it had dried? There were other odors," I reminded him. "Strong ones."

"So there were. We'll conduct an experiment later with some whiskey and a sweater or something." He looked pensive.

I sat back reflectively and, while my eye traced the shape of some ornate carving or other, thoughts began to take shape in my mind. At last I was focused. Then I became aware that Chief was watching me, closely.

"Out with it," he said, after a pause.

"Hunh?"

"You were thinking," he said.

"Well—" I began. It was oddly difficult to form the words I needed. "If she was forced to drink scotch... I mean, if she got drunk there, why a vodka bottle? Why not just leave the scotch bottle, I mean, if someone forced her to drink that, you know? Or did she get carried home after she was already passed out? Or dead? And where did the vodka go if she didn't drink it?" I was afraid I was being incoherent. "You know?" I ended lamely.

"What are you really trying to say?" Chief coaxed.

"Um ... I'm not sure."

"Give yourself a chance. Take a deep breath. Okay, now, wait a minute, and think it over again. Then tell me."

"I think," I said, slowly, "that it doesn't make... any sense. Unless—wait a minute. Okay. Unless she was killed somewhere else, but in the way that you said, and then the person brought her home and left her on the bed—all right, I've got it! It's simple! It had to look like she'd done it herself—"

"There you go," he said.

"—and so whoever it was poured out half the vodka bottle and left it there so whoever found her would think she died there, and not somewhere else."

"So, why was she dressed like that?"

"Okay. Because she was, well, 'entertaining,' at whatever place she was when it happened, and the murderer didn't bring her clothes back when he brought her. Or the scotch. He didn't think of that part, maybe, until after he got her home. In fact...," I was getting excited, and feeling rather impressed with myself. "In fact," I repeated; "in fact, he—it must be a 'he'—didn't know she was dead! Not at first, anyway—that's why he didn't bring her clothes back, or dress her or anything, and... and when he realized it he used the mirror to make sure! Then he got the vodka out of the liquor cabinet, emptied part of it out, set her up with it, wiped off his prints—it's perfect!"

"So it wasn't murder, then," Chief said.

"Oh." Odd how this felt like a setback. "Well, no, I guess not. But still, it explains everything. The clean ashtrays, the scotch—"

"The heater?"

"The heater? Oh. The heater. Damn. Oh! Because at first he didn't know she was dead! He turned the heat up because she was practically naked, and he didn't want her to get cold. Simple."

"Not bad, Smitty, not bad. Now, who was he?"

"Buttenheimer. Had to be."

"Why?"

"Because that's who was always picking her up and dropping her off. At least, assuming he's the one Mrs. Hernandez saw. You know, the blue Mercedes?"

"Yes," Chief assented, "and I agree that Buttenheimer is far the most likely. And if it was him, and if it happened like you say, then the death was indeed accidental—although Buttenheimer would still have some hard questions to answer."

"Wow," I said. "I feel like we've solved it."

"Whoa, hold the phone! You've got a *theory*."

"But it works! It explains practically everything."

I was convinced.

"Define 'practically,' " Chief said.

"Hunh?"

"Look at it like this," he continued. "You've made up your mind the death was accidental, and I admit your theory is pretty good as far as it goes. But suppose you'd concluded it was murder. Would you be willing to put Buttenheimer in the chair and throw the switch? I mean, would you do it now?"

This didn't seem to me like a fair question, and I said so. "I don't think there's a death penalty here, anyway," I added.

"Suppose there was."

"Okay. Yes, I think it's a pretty strong case."

"But that's not what I asked," Chief insisted gently. "Here's Buttenheimer, strapped into the chair. Here's the box with the switch that turns it on. I'm handing it to you. Will you throw the switch? Will you do it?"

"I suppose I wouldn't. I don't know." Whatever Chief was driving at, it didn't make sense to me.

"But," he pressed, "you just said you were certain."

"I said I was certain it wasn't murder."

"I know," he said, "and I was saying, 'suppose your line of reasoning had led the other way—what then?' My point is, when you come to a conclusion you need to realize the gravity of what you are doing. This isn't a game show. We're talking about someone's untimely death. There are many possible outcomes to a homicide investigation. The first is, we find out who did it. The second is, we don't find out who did it. See if you can tell me some others."

I could think of one easily: "We convict the wrong person."

"Yes, or...?"

I shrugged.

"We might conclude, as you just did, that it wasn't homicide—"

"Oh, yeah."

"—and we might be right. Or...?"

"I see. Or we might conclude it wasn't homicide, and we might be wrong."

"Precisely."

"So, you're saying I'm wrong." I was only a little put out.

"Not at all! I'm saying you could be. And, I'm saying it matters to be as sure as possible."

I was feeling obstinate. "But I am sure—you just said so."

He laughed. "All right, Sherlock. You're sure there are no holes in your theory?"

"Yup."

"Covers everything?"

"Yup."

"Would you be terribly upset if I mentioned about six things that rip your admittedly lovely theory to shreds?"

It was my turn to laugh. "Yup," I said.

"Then I'll only tell you one of them, and leave the rest for you to think of on your own, while you're at home practicing meditating. Ready? Okay. According to you, Mr. Buttenheimer brings Mrs. Merrick home, discovers she is dead, and goes to elaborate efforts to hide the fact that he has ever been there. That is on Thursday night. Then on Saturday night—"

"Uh-oh," I said.

"On Saturday night," Chief continued, "the incorrigible Mr. Buttenheimer drives back to Erlangen and loiters in front of her apartment, as though he expected a woman he already knows, on your account, to be stone-cold dead to come down from her apartment and go galavanting about with him. Would you mind telling me why?"

"Fine," I said, and we rose to go. Outside I said, "It was so we'd see him, and think it couldn't be him, for otherwise why would he come back? He was establishing an alibi. That's what it was."

Chief laughed. "Somehow, Smitty, I don't think so. But I admire your tenacity."

"Don't think he's as smart as me, eh?"

" 'As smart as I', and no, I don't think so. At least, I hope not."

We walked up the street in silence. The shadows had deepened, and the sidewalks were less crowded. As we approached the wall, Chief slowed down and became watchful.

"Do we scan Buttenheimer's again?" he mused aloud, and looked at me. I nodded.

The street, however, was deserted, and Buttenheimer's door didn't open as we went by.

At the car Chief stopped and lit a cigarette.

"Plans for tonight, Smitty?"

"Not really, Chief. You?"

"Yes, I think so." After a pause he said, "I think maybe you do too. Why don't you take the car and go back to battalion. After it's put away go home, eat something, then change into something you'd go out on the town in, and wait to hear from me. If you don't hear from me . . . well, never mind—you will."

I opened the door to the car. "Chief," I said, "what are the other five things?"

"Hunh?"

"You said there were six, altogether. The things that make my theory no good."

"Oh! Well, think about it. I'll give you a hint: think about Mercy's testimony, about the condition of the body, and about the things we found in the apartment. It'll come to you."

He set off down the street with a wave and a grin.

On the way home I bought some whiskey.

9   Gunther Speaks

Smitty's place, Nürnberg, West Germany,
Monday, 30 June 198-, 1630 hrs.

"Honey, what are you doing?"

Maggie stood in the doorway, her arms laden with grocery bags, and looked at me with some concern—for my sanity, presumably. This was because I was sitting at the dining table pouring whiskey into a large mixing bowl and kneading it through an old sweater.

"You know my methods, Watson," I said.

"That's what worries me," she retorted. "I suppose this has to do with your investigation?"

"Yep. If you're a good girl I'll let you help," I said playfully.

She put the bags in the kitchen and returned, snaking her arms around my neck and putting her lips to my ear.

"What if I'm better than good?" she said softly.

"Mmm!" I responded, but then the kids came in from the hallway, Mikey valiantly struggling with his own grocery bag while his sister walked behind him, watching him carefully. When he saw me he dropped the bag with a crash and ran over to me, nearly jumping into my lap like a small dog.

"Daddy!"

"Hey tiger. What'd you drop?"

147

"Uh-oh," he said, looking back.

"Mikey," Maggie said, picking up the bag and checking its contents, "you get to eat this banana."

"Who's cooking?" I asked, following Maggie into the kitchen.

"I am."

"Then I'll use Susan. Susan!" My eldest stuck her head around the corner with the air of someone indulging a nuisance. "Do you know how to use the dryer in the basement?" I asked.

"Yes," Maggie answered for her, "but not alone—especially not at night."

"Ah," I said. "Well, I guess I'll do it."

"Do what?" Susan asked, inquisitive now that she was shielded from the call to duty.

"Actually, you can still help," I said. I got the bowl with the sweater and handed it to her. "Take this into the bathroom and wring it out in the sink. Don't rinse it, just wring it and hang it up on the shower rod."

"What—" she began, sniffing the bowl closely, and then, "Ugh! What is it?"

"Demon liquor," I said. "Let that be a lesson to you!"

When she had gone I grabbed Maggie to say hello again. She said hello back.

"I got the answer," I said in a sing-song.

"The answer? To what?"

"Chief's riddle."

"Oh, that," she said blankly. "Belly-buttons. I thought of it after you went to bed."

"Damn! And you didn't tell me?"

"You were asleep."

"You could have told me this morning!"

"I forgot," she said disinterestedly.

Glumly, I went to practice meditating while sitting on top of a dryer in the basement.

We were eating dinner when Chief buzzed from the ground floor. He was in a hurry, and declined an invitation to come up and join us in our meal. Instead, I grabbed the sweater and met him downstairs.

"I've asked them to bring in Buttenheimer," he said as we got into the Toyota and sped away.

"You think he did it?" I asked excitedly.

"I hope we'll find out. What's that?"

"Smell it," I said, handing him the sweater. He sniffed it, shook his head. "An hour ago," I said, "it was soaked with whiskey."

"Hmm. Good work. What does it tell us?"

I shrugged.

"Yeah. Well, the 'death by the liberal application of scotch' theory is intact, I suppose."

"I thought of something else," I said. "I was practicing meditating—"

"Good man!"

"—and I remembered a couple of things. First, there was the paper towel with the grease on it."

"Yes?"

"Well, nothing. I just remembered it."

"Well, it's worth remembering. What else?"

"Didn't Mercy say there was mud on the carpet?"

Chief didn't say anything. We were stopped at a light, and when it turned green he failed to notice until the driver behind us honked.

"Chief?"

"Dried mud. She said it was dried mud."

"Right," I said.

He said nothing else. After a while I asked him if he had gotten ahold of Sabrina Grason, and he said he had tried, but that she was not at home. At least, she wasn't answering her phone.

At the *Landsraat* we met inspector Kriegmann, and he introduced us to inspector Müller. The latter didn't speak much English, and Chief conversed with them in German. The conversation was brief, and we then walked down a long corridor to a large interrogation room. Inside, Gunther Buttenheimer was sitting, looking disheveled and angry, on one side of a big table, with a uniformed policeman standing behind him. His face was red and puffy, and he started nervously when we came in. He stood, protesting loudly in German. It was obvious he felt ill-used. No one responded to him, however, and when we had all taken seats he sat down slowly and stared at us with bilious blue eyes.

"*Herr Buttenheimer*," inspector Müller said to him, "*da ist Herr Inspector Tobias, von der americanishen Armee.*"

Buttenheimer said nothing, but stared at Chief coldly.

"*Sprechen Sie Englisch, Herr Buttenheimer?*" the latter asked.

"*Nein. Kein Englisch.*"

"A pity," Chief said in English, "We will be somewhat delayed, then. I had hoped to get you back home tonight."

"What do you want?" Buttenheimer said, also in English. "I am not American. You have no business to question me."

"*Ah. Sie sprechen gut Englisch, Herr Buttenheimer!* I thought so. Somehow, I didn't imagine Kimberly spoke much German."

At Kimberly's name, Buttenheimer lost a little more of his

composure.

"What do you want?" he repeated.

Chief had brought two cases from his kit, and instead of answering he opened one of these and took out a tape recorder. Putting it on the table with a glance at inspector Kriegmann, who nodded, he turned it on and cleared his throat.

"You have a little hobby, I believe. Uh, photography?"

"That is my business. I am a photographer."

"Oh? I thought cocaine was your business."

Buttenheimer half rose out of his chair with an angry exclamation, but the officer behind him put a hand on his shoulder and pushed him back into his seat.

Chief shrugged "Perhaps I was misinformed," he said. "This photography business—it involves models, I believe."

"What of it?"

"Some American models, even."

Buttenheimer said nothing.

"How long was Kimberly Merrick working for you?"

Buttenheimer hesitated. "I do not know this person."

"Come now, Gunther," Chief said, rudely using the given name, "this is well known. Kimberly was your star. She was practically living with you."

"I have said I do not know this person."

"You own a Mercedes, license number NU1828. With this car you picked up Kimberly Merrick at her home in Erlangen and took her to your home, to your place of business, and to parties—where she performed a variety of services."

Buttenheimer was breathing heavily.

"On Friday last," Chief continued, "you used the same car to drop her off at her apartment. Only this time, she wasn't in a very good state of health. In fact, this time she didn't even make it into bed. This time she was found dead—"

"I did not know this woman!" Buttenheimer yelled. "I am telling you, I did not—"

Chief stood up and grabbed one of his cases, opened it, and took out a glossy magazine, which he slammed down on the table in front of Buttenheimer. It was a girlie magazine, with a photo of Kimberly Merrick on the cover. All of her.

"And I am telling you," Chief roared, "you *did*."

"*Mein Gott. Ach, mein Gott....*"

"You took that picture, did you not? *Herr* Buttenheimer, did you not?"

"*Ja.*"

"She was your *Hure*, was she not?"

"*Mein Gott.*"

"And you took her home on Friday, did you not sir?"

"*Ja. Ja. Meine Kim, meine Geliebte, sie war so schön....*"

"Why did you kill her?"

"*Was? Nein....*"

"You killed her. I know this. Why did you do it?"

"*Nein! Ich hätte ihr nicht weh tun können! Das müssen Sie mir glauben!*" Buttenheimer was almost shrieking. It was not clear, at least to me, whether he was consumed by guilt and fear, or simply in an agony of grief.

"You did," Chief insisted. "You killed her, took her home, carried her upstairs—"

"No! *Nein!* I could not do this." He began to cry.

"Is smoking permitted?" Chief asked the inspectors. Inspector Kriegmann nodded, and Chief gave Buttenheimer a Sobranie. He lit one himself, picked up the magazine, and leafed through the pages.

"A beautiful woman," he said. "How long did you know her?"

"Ten ... er ... *Monate*," Buttenheimer said.

"Ten months. You were in love with her."

"*Ja.*"

"And yet, you pimped her around, to your friends."

"I am not understanding."

"You sold her—used her for sexual favors—for what? Cocaine?"

"You do not understand," Buttenheimer said. "It was her way. She was ... she was a lover. A great lover."

"It made you jealous."

"No. It was her way. You do not understand."

"I guess not." Chief examined the ash on his cigarette silently, took a drag. "How often were you in her apartment?"

"I was not!" Buttenheimer looked surprised.

"Not ever?"

"Yes. I was not ever in her apartment."

"Except," Chief insisted, "last Friday night."

"No. I was not ever in her apartment."

"Tell me about last Friday. Where was the party, your house?"

Buttenheimer hesitated. "No."

"Well, where?"

"Please do not ask me this."

"All right," Chief said. "We'll come back to it. You took her home. What time?"

"Uh ... *um ein uhr. Es war sehr früh. Verstehen Sie?*"

"About one. Why did you take her home then?"

"She said for me to do this."

"Why?"

"She would not say. She insisted. I could not understand, but I would not say no to her."

"She was very drunk, yes?"

Buttenheimer nodded.

"You took her upstairs."

"No."

"You did not take her upstairs?"

"No."

"She walked upstairs?"

"Yes. I was staying in the car."

"What had she been drinking?"

"Uh," he hesitated, "it is called Johnny Walker, yes?"

Chief sat down and drummed his fingers.

"I have the name correctly, yes?" Buttenheimer continued. "She liked this drink very much. Too much."

The interrogation went on for another hour at least, Chief asking the same questions a second, a third, even a fourth time. He stopped pressing Buttenheimer for a confession, and Buttenheimer became less overwrought. He stuck to his story, insisting he had not entered Mrs. Merrick's apartment, insisting she had gone up from the car herself, and refusing to say where they had been for their "party." He confirmed her outfit, saying she had gone home in her lingerie and fur coat. She had been wearing a pair of red, high-heeled shoes, and carrying a small red handbag.

At the end of it there was another conference among the detectives (which I could not understand, naturally, it being carried out in German), and it was agreed that Buttenheimer would be sent back home. Before letting him go, Chief repeated one more question.

"Why did you come to the apartment on Saturday?" he asked.

"I have told you this. We were to go out together."

"Right." Chief went around to Buttenheimer's side of the table and leaned close to him. "Buttenheimer, go home. But just do one thing for me, will you? Tell Sabrina it will be much easier for her if she comes to me."

Buttenheimer was startled. *"Entshuldigen?"*

"Just tell her."

"The hell of it is, Smitty," Chief said to me outside.

"Yes?" The night was warm and clear, and the air fragrant with summer.

"I believe him."

"Yeah," I said.

"Which, you'll not have failed to notice, sends your 'accidental death' theory to its grave."

"I suppose it does," I admitted.

In the car he said, "I'm not sure where this leaves us. We could be wrong, and he could be lying, but if he's not... well, who was there when she died?"

I did my best to look thoughtful.

"There are three categories of possibility," he continued. "First, Buttenheimer could be lying. He could be our man. If he is, which I doubt, then proving it is probably impossible. Müller says he thinks he knows where the party might have been, and will do some checking on it for us; find out who else was there, when Kimberly and Buttenheimer left, and so on."

"Maybe someone else was with them when he took her home," I offered.

"Yes, I had thought of that, and I hope Müller will be able

to nail that down. That also brings up the second category of possibility: It might have been someone else connected with Buttenheimer—someone he is protecting, probably out of fear. It is even possible that someone from that party followed them to the Merrick's, and went up after Buttenheimer dropped her off."

"I like that idea," I said.

"I don't. It doesn't fit in with the information we have, and leaves us back where we started at the beginning—hankering after motive, as well as means and opportunity, and saddles us once again with a mystery man about whom we know absolutely nothing."

"What about a mystery woman," I said, thinking about how Kimberly Merrick must have aroused a good deal of jealousy, not to mention envy, almost everywhere she went.

"Right," Chief said, becoming more animated. "That is our third category of possibility. There are plenty of people who may have had the motivation—people we already know something about, and about whom we can probably learn a great deal more—and any one of them is far more likely to have gotten themselves into her apartment that night after Buttenheimer dropped her off." He looked at me with a good-natured frown. "Let's see if you can guess who I'm presently most interested in—?"

"Sabrina Grason."

"Holed it in one. Tomorrow's the funeral—let's see if she shows." He started the car.

"Chief," I said, "are you saying you think it *was* Sabrina?"

"Not at all," he said. "I just think she's got a lot to tell us." After a minute he admitted, "Well, I think she certainly could be. She's a hard, sharp little girl. Scares me, a little. But," he said, holding up his hand and counting off his fingers, "we've got a goodly list of suspects still. There's the husband, for one. His alibi *must* be settled. Second, there's the Worms woman. I doubt she'd have said what she did the other day if she were the one, but you never know. People are odd creatures, at best. Thirdly, there's Chet, whoever he is."

"Oh yes," I said, "the heartsick lover."

"Right. And finally, there're a whole *kaserne* full of jealous wives and God knows what scandals involving their husbands."

"Man!" I said, impressed by the range of possibilities.

"We have another stop, by the way," Chief said. "Ginger's on night shift tonight, or so he said. What do you say to having another look at the deceased? We should be able to get copies of the medical lab reports, too, instead of waiting 'til tomorrow."

"Sounds good," I said, stifling a yawn.

"He may not be glad to see us," Chief said. "I gather the powers-that-be were none too happy about his doing all those invasive tests I asked for."

We found Ginger in the lab, hunched over a table with a scalpel in one hand and a needle-like probe in the other. He wore some kind of headband contraption on his head that had several lenses sprouting all around it and a pair of bright little lamps on flexible stalks. He looked up, at our step, through a magnifying lens that seemed to turn half of his face into one huge blue eyeball.

"No!" he said when he saw Chief. He jumped up and backed away, twirled this way and that, and then leapt to a back doorway. "No!" he repeated, and almost flung himself into the hallway outside.

"Ginger—! Oh the idiot," Chief said. We went after him.

"Ginger!" Chief called. We just caught the sight of his black Nikes disappearing around a corner. "Ginger, you know full well— Ginger! What about your karma—!" When we got to the corner and looked around, however, he was gone. "Hell," Chief said.

"This is bizarre, Chief. What do we do now?" I asked.

"Go back to the lab and wait for him. He usually comes back."

"You mean he's acted like this before?"

"He's really a good guy," Chief said apologetically. "You get used to it."

When we got back to the lab, to my astonishment, Ginger was waiting for us. He must have run a circuit and come back in the front way.

"Chief Tobias, Pfc Smith," he said in formal, clipped tones, "so good of you to come by." He extended a gloved and blood-smeared hand. It was as if we had just that moment walked in on him for the first time.

"I'm really sorry, Ginger," Chief said, pretending not to see the outstretched hand.

Ginger held his hand up and looked at it, apparently surprised at its condition. "No need to apologize," he said, "it's only my job you nearly cost me; my job, my reputation, the roof from over my family's head, and the food from my children's mouths. Really, think nothing of it."

"I'm *sorry*, Ginger. What can I do to make it up to you?"

"Donate your body to science," Ginger said after a moment's reflection, "and mention my name."

I sniggered, and he gave me a sharp look.

"And what plans have *you* made for the afterlife? It's not too soon to make arrangements. Now *I* should like to be eaten." He removed his gloves and went to the sink to wash up.

"You'd be stringy," Chief said.

"I've thought of that. I think I'd like to be made into some sort of processed food spread—the sort you squeeze from a plastic tube, you know—and used on rye toast, with cheese."

"That would work," Chief admitted. "Tell you what: I know some people in the food business—I'll put in a good word for you."

"You are too kind."

"It's no problem at all! Now, I was wondering if you could possibly—"

"*God!*" Ginger howled. "What a piece of work is a policeman! how base in reason! how infinite in guile! in form and movement how—"

"All right, Ginger," Chief interrupted him. "I delight not you. I'm aware of it."

"— how acute in observation."

"And your Hamlet is marvelous. But calm down, old fellow! I'm not after anything but lab reports. Well, and we'd like to see the body again."

"The lab report is there, on the table, and the body's in the basement. I give them to you. There, you are a king of infinite space. May you have bad dreams!"

Chief picked up the report and scanned it. He whistled. "Ginger, you didn't tell me the alcohol was this high."

"I told you it was enough to kill two seasoned topers."

"You weren't kidding. Point-five-five! Is that possible?"

"Certainly. People are picked up behind the wheel all the time with a point-four percent BAT or higher—still conscious and still functioning. Well, so to speak."

"I know that, but Ginger—" He flipped up the top page and flipped it back again, scanning. "— this was just her blood, wasn't it? Did you do a vitreous sample?"

"What would be the point? Isn't a five-five good enough for you? I don't like sucking the juice out of a cadaver's eyeballs. It makes them look icky. I prefer to let the autopsy johnnies do that if they want to—"

"Think man!" Chief said, breaking in on this gruesome reflection. "She'd been dead at least twelve hours before she got here! When did you take the samples?"

"It's on the report."

"Uh—five-thirty! Ginger, if your report is accurate—"

"I beg your pardon!"

"If it is, she must have had nearly a point-seven blood alcohol, or even higher, when she died!"

"Ridiculous," Ginger said. "That's not possible. She'd have to have drunk pure ethanol—which would have come straight back up and her stomach with it. I can't possibly imagine why she didn't puke as it is."

"Then you explain it."

Ginger was silent.

"Sounds to me like you'd better get that vitreous sample. C'mon, Smitty and I will go with you."

Ginger got his equipment grudgingly, and we trooped downstairs. I had never been in a morgue before, but it turned out to be just like in the movies: a big fridge with lots of steel doors, and behind each one a body. The devil's filing cabinet.

"You all right, Smitty?"

I nodded.

Ginger slid her out and unzipped the bag. My jaw dropped and Chief muttered, "What the hell?" There was a large blotchy patch on her right cheek.

"I told you there was a bruise," Ginger said.

"I know you said so, and that's why I wanted to see her again. But dammit, that wasn't there before. Now what in the hell—?"

Chief and I found something else to look at while Ginger took his sample, and then Chief examined the bruise carefully.

"I'm gonna need a picture of that," He said.

"I'm not a photographer," Ginger said irritably.

"We'll do it! Not tonight, though—she'll keep. Ginger, what causes a bruise like that?"

"Contusion. The capillaries are damaged by trauma, and blood leaks into the surrounding tissues. Is this a test? You already knew that, Chief Tobias."

"But Ginger, *it wasn't there*. Now, what causes a bruise post-mortem?"

"Same thing, except that there is no blood pressure, so the contusion has to be low on the body or otherwise the blood won't—"

"That's it!" Chief said, snapping his fingers. "Ginger, did you lay her on her stomach at any time?"

"Ah!" Ginger said. "Do you know, she came in that way! I had quite a talk with the ambulance drivers about it—the lazy bastards just rolled her into the bag instead of lifting her, and zippered her up backwards."

"And the blood in her skull settled in the face. It's as clear as day." Chief was getting that thousand-yard stare that signalled a withdrawal into his own thoughts.

Ginger looked concerned. "I thought you said she died in bed."

"She apparently did."

"Well, what did she do, *fall* into bed, smacking her face on the headboard?"

"Somehow," Chief said distantly, "I don't think so."

We said goodnight to Ginger, and left. We drove in silence for several minutes.

"Chief," I said, after a while, "what do those numbers mean, about the alcohol?"

"Just simple percentage," he said. "Actually, if you want the textbook answer, it's 'grams per 100 milliliters.' But that works out to about the same thing. If you have a point-one BAT—legally drunk—then your blood is about one tenth of one percent alcohol. That is, about one part in a thousand. In a normal person, a level of point-three-five or a little higher is lethal. An alcoholic develops a tolerance, however. Their blood chemistry changes, and they can still function with a point-four or even close to a point-five."

"Why do you have to take the fluid out of her eye?" I thought that was really gross.

"Because the body's cells continue to metabolize the alcohol even after death occurs. The blood alcohol level can drop quite a bit. The only way to know exactly what the alcohol level was at the time of death is to check the vitreous fluid."

"Hmm."

"I guess a career in forensic medicine isn't in your future?"

"No."

He chuckled. "Me neither."

When we reached my apartment building, I voiced a concern that had been growing on me since earlier in the day.

"Chief," I said, "do you sometimes have ones that can't be solved? I mean, that you never find the truth about?"

He sighed. "Yes, Smitty. Sometimes."

We sat for a bit, and he lit a cigarette. I noticed he was smoking more than he had been.

"A lot of times," he said then, and wagged his finger at me, "but Smitty, this isn't one of those times."

"Yes Chief."

"The funeral's at ten. You got a black suit?"

I shook my head.

"Well, you'd better wear your Class A's, then. You can ditch the jacket afterward. Grab the scarab and pick me up at home, about eight, okay?"

"Willco," I said.

"Roger. Out!"

I was putting my key in the front door when he called me back. He was going through my notebooks, of which there were now several.

"Smitty," he said fretfully, "about that purse. We never found any but the empty ones in the closet, right?"

"Right," I said.

"Were any of them red?"

"Uh," I said, thinking back, "two, I think—both large, with straps and side pockets and things."

"Yes, here they are," he said, "and both empty. Damn, damn, damn...."

He drove away.

10   The Mourners, Part I

Matson Barracks, Erlangen, West Germany,
Tuesday, 1 July 198-, 0930 hrs.

Tuesday morning was gorgeous. The sun's rays shot through an atmosphere crystal clear and blue, like the glory at the heart of a star sapphire. The countryside was verdant, and when we came into Erlangen the brilliantly colored bunting on the stone buildings seemed to praise by imitation the gaily colored flowers at every window box and along every walkway. Students swarmed and shoppers bustled, save those who luxuriated on the grass or on benches in the deep green shade of the trees.

It was a strange day for a funeral.

Well, not a funeral, I guess, since Mrs. Merrick herself wouldn't be attending, but a service, anyway. Chief, who had chosen to drive, parked near the parade grounds, about a hundred meters from the brigade chapel and directly across the field from the brigade headquarters building. He had no sooner done so than the sound of helicopters approaching filled the air, and soon we were treated to that raucous thumping they make when passing directly overhead at low altitude. There were two of them, a Huey and a Cobra gun-ship, and they landed in front of us on the parade field. The rank of the chief occupant was prominently displayed on the door of the Huey.

"Hmm, two stars," Chief said. "Must be the division comman-der."

"With his own side arm," I added.

The choppers disgorged, there was a flurry of salutes, and a tight group of middle-aged soldiers walked into the headquarters building, their subordinates dangling at their heels.

"I suppose he's come for the service. Nice of him. Well, Smitty, we've got a few minutes before the show begins—let's look at those fingerprint reports."

We had gone to battalion before coming to Erlangen, both for breakfast and to pick up the lab reports. The fingerprint report was mainly a photocopy of the prints Chief and I had taken the morning the body was discovered, with a written inventory identifying the prints as belonging to "A," "B," and so on for each sample. I dug them out of their Manila envelope and handed them to Chief.

"Okay, what have we got?" he said. "Let's see, 'A' is Kimberly Merrick, 'B' is Mercy Blickwell, 'C' is Captain Merrick, 'D,' 'E,' and 'F' are unknown."

"How did you get Captain Merrick's prints?"

"Didn't you get fingerprinted when you enlisted?" he asked.

"Sure."

"All right then. Captain Merrick belongs body and soul to the United States Army, just as you do—and if there's one thing the Army does well, it's keep a careful inventory of its possessions. I could have your prints by this afternoon if I wanted. I have friends in low places."

"That's a little scary, Chief," I said soberly.

"Mmm. Looks like that palm print on the wall was Captain Merrick's, and the headboard prints are only what they should be: the Captain's, Mercy's, and the deceased's. The doorknob is too cluttered to be worth much, and the prints we took in the rest of the apartment are almost all Mercy's. I'll bet 'D,' 'E,' and 'F' are accounted for by the doctor and the other wives who were there."

Chief took off his glasses and was, I'm sure, going to wipe them on his shirt, but he was dressed for the funeral and his shirt was tucked in. He put his glasses on again and sighed.

"I'm going to stop looking for clues, Smitty," he said with resignation.

"Chief?"

"It doesn't pay. Whoops, here we go!"

A large group had emerged from the headquarters building, and was cutting across a corner of the parade field to the chapel. I recognized Colonel and Mrs. Crick, Captain Merrick, and Major Suarez.

There were others I didn't recognize. A very fat man in a black suit walked next to Colonel Crick. Walking beside them, hanging on Captain Merrick's arm, was a frail looking woman in a gray dress and black scarf. Behind them came Mrs. Crick and another woman, in the company of Major Suarez and a short man in uniform I guessed to be the division commander.

"Still ten minutes," Chief said, looking at his watch. "We'll wait."

No one else appeared to arrive, however, and eventually we got out and walked over to the chapel, straight on ten o'clock.

We entered quietly. The only other person attending, outside the party who had come across the parade field together, was a tall woman who must have arrived very early. She wore a black tweed outfit complete with a pill-box hat and a veil. Chief and I sat in the back, and although her black hair was pulled up into a bun I couldn't see her face. Sabrina Grason was certainly not there.

The chaplain was the only one who spoke. He was brief, general, and carefully nondenominational; it was barely twenty minutes before everyone rose to go. Chief and I stayed in our seats as they filed out, permitting us to see that the veiled woman was Nancy Worms. She avoided our glance as she walked by, and exited quickly before the others.

When they had gone, Chief grunted. "Well," he said, "ready?"

We walked out to find that the group, save for Mrs. Worms, who had disappeared, were gathered in a loose clump next to the street. We had barely cleared the door when the frail spinster who had been with Captain Merrick detached herself and approached Chief.

"What do you want?" she demanded.

"I'm afraid I haven't had the pleasure—" Chief began.

"You've no business to be here," she cut in shrilly, "accusing people and making trouble!"

Captain Merrick approached. "Mother, it's all right," he said, taking her by the arm.

"It is not! You leave my son alone, d'you here? I won't have it!"

"Mother! You've said your piece. Come along now."

She let herself be led away, not without throwing several venomous glances over her shoulder. Chief was speechless. He recovered himself when the group moved to cross the street, however, and called out to Colonel Crick. The party stopped on the far curb, and Colonel Crick spoke to Major Suarez, who came back while the others continued on.

"The colonel instructs me to tell you that any information you have for him should be forwarded through channels," Major Suarez said in formal tones.

"Damn his eyes!" Chief said, with a quiet explosion.

The doctor looked shocked and began to turn away, but stopped and regarded Chief. "What have you found?" he asked quietly.

"I guess you'll find out through 'channels,'" Chief said with considerable resentment.

"Tsk, tsk, Chief," Major Suarez said with uncharacteristic humor, "you've lost your temper."

"Damn it, Doc," Chief said, softening, "that's my game. Careful, or we'll find ourselves becoming friends. Did you find her records?"

"No."

"When's that clerk getting back?"

"Well, I've seen her around post, actually, but she's not back on duty 'til Friday."

"Too late," Chief said. "Look, Doc, how about a favor? Can you track her down for me? I want those records, badly."

"I'll see what I can do. Now will you answer my question?"

"What? Oh. What have we found out? Let's see. What shall we call it—Smitty? Well... how about 'squat.'" He took out a Sobranie. "The fact is Major, I don't know for certain what I've found, but I'll tell you this: it seems to want to stay unfound, in the worst possible way."

Major Suarez looked thoughtful. "Well," he said, "good luck. I'll find those records for you."

As we walked to the car Mrs. Worms emerged from a nearby sedan and approached. She greeted Chief demurely, in contrast to her manner the previous Friday.

"I owe you an apology, Chief Tobias," she said.

"You were upset—" he began.

"Yes. You see ... well, I just wanted to apologize, and to tell you that I did not intend to mislead you; that is, there was nothing between Mrs. Merrick and me."

"I see," Chief said.

"I hardly knew her, in fact."

"Ah."

After an awkward pause she said, "Well, thank you again," and walked away.

"For what?" Chief said when she was out of earshot. He did not have long to muse, however, for next we found ourselves hailed by the large man in the black suit who had been with the mourning party.

"Chief Tobias!" he called, and, waving, hurried as best he could across the parade field. Approaching, he held out his hand and repeated, breathlessly, "Chief Tobias."

"Sir?" Chief said politely.

"I'm Mr. McKenna, Kimberly's father."

"I thought you might be," Chief said, shaking hands. "I'm glad for the opportunity to meet you, and tell you how sorry I am at your loss."

"This is my hotel," Mr. McKenna said abruptly, handing Chief a card. "Can you meet me later? In the bar."

"Of course," Chief said, somewhat taken aback. "Er, this is my assistant, Pfc Smith."

"One o'clock?" Mr. McKenna pressed, ignoring the introduction.

"Sure, uh, that'll be fine," Chief said.

And then the man was gone, puffing his way across the parade field again. Chief sat on the hood of the scarab and stared at the man's retreating back.

"Smitty," he said, "how weird do you suppose this day is going to get?"

"It's off to a great start," I said.

"That's for damn sure. Let's take a little walk."

"The peripatetic school again?"

"I want to visit Captain Merrick's battalion."

The 1st Battalion of the 28th Armored Regiment, the "Iron Tigers," were billeted on the east side of the *kaserne*, and our walk took us past both the PX and a vast motor pool which was mostly empty, but parts of which still sheltered battle tanks and a hodgepodge of trucks, humvees, and other vehicles under immense corrugated metal shelters. Here and there tanks had been pulled forward from their shelters, and soldiers in brown t-shirts and fatigues were working on the tracks with tools like automotive tools but much bigger, or cleaning and carefully arranging equipment on tarps on the ground (for inspection, I didn't doubt), and some were ramming enormous rods with wire bristles on the ends up and back in the gun tubes, a procedure which took three or four of them heaving together on the rods.

"It sounds like an airport, Chief," I said. "How come they sound like that?"

"I don't know," he admitted. "Hey!" he called, waving his arms. Several soldiers looked up, and one detached himself and walked over to the fence. "Say," Chief yelled above the noise, "what unit is this?"

"One-Two-Eight," the man said, coming up to the fence.

"First Battalion, Twenty-eighth Armor?"

"That's right."

"Just back from the field? I mean, gunnery?"

"Who are you?" the man asked, after a suspicious pause.

"Oh, sorry," Chief said. "I guess curiosity's against regulations, isn't it? And rightly so. Here sergeant," he said, digging out his wallet. "I'm a soldier with 501st Intel. Here's my ID. My friend and I were just wondering, er—these must be M1's?"

"M1A1's," the man corrected.

"Oh, right. Why d'they sound like that? Just wondering."

"It's the engines," he said slowly.

"Right," Chief said. "What kind, if it's okay to ask?"

"Oh, I get what you're after," he said. "It's a turbine engine. No pistons."

"You mean, like a jet?" Chief asked incredulously.

"That's right."

"Hunh! What d'you need all that power for?"

"Well sir," the man said, warming to his subject, "that baby weighs 60 tons, give or take, but it'll do 60 kph on a flat."

"No!"

"Yessir. I'll tell you what; you talk to the first sergeant, and maybe we'll give you a ride sometime."

"That'd be great. Thanks sergeant." Chief returned his salute, and we wandered on. "Well, Smitty, now I know something I didn't before. Specifically, I have a much better idea of why those damned things cost more than a million dollars a piece to make—"

"You're kidding."

"—and why their fuel consumption is rated in gallons-per-mile."

"I can believe that."

Captain Merrick's battalion occupied a quad of World War I era buildings that ringed their own little parade ground. The headquarters building was marked by a large wooden sign with the battalion's crest painted on it: a green shield with the silhouette of a great cat crouched to spring, with "Iron Tiger" written across the top and the motto *Valor Vincet Omnia* emblazoned beneath. The ground floor appeared to be a mess hall, and the stairs to the first floor were decorated with photographs, drawings, and maps delineating the unit's history.

I had noticed this feature of combat units before. While more technical units, such as my own, saw themselves in terms of their modern role in the military establishment, combat units had a very strong sense of history and of their own past achievements. The 28th Armored Regiment (I learned while climbing the stairs) was evidently a cavalry unit in World War I, was reestablished at Ft. Knox, Kentucky in 1942, served in France and Germany in the period 1943-46, fought in Korea and Vietnam, and was reposted to the 1st Armored Division in Germany in 1972. The regimental flag behind the charge of quarters desk at the top of the stairs was thick with battle streamers.

Chief showed the sergeant on duty his badge and asked him if the entire unit was in the field.

"Yes, sir," the sergeant said, "Charlie left on Friday morning, and they was the last to go."

"I need to see a battalion roster."

"You'd have to see the duty officer about that, sir," the sergeant said dubiously.

"And where would I find him?"

"Lieutenant Michelson, sir. He's the S-1."

"I didn't say 'who,' sergeant, I said 'where.'"

"Yes sir. Just down the hall on your left. Uh, I can't leave the desk. Sorry sir. But you won't have trouble finding it."

"S-1?" I whispered as we went in search of Lieutenant Michelson.

"Staff officer for personnel," Chief said. "Here we are."

The S-1 office was large, containing a half dozen desks, a phalanx of filing cabinets, and several desk-top computers. It was empty of people, but as we stood in the doorway a young soldier came up behind me, tapped on my shoulder, and squeezed past while precariously balancing a coffee cup and a doughnut on a tall stack of computer print-out paper.

"Can I help you?" he said, putting his load on a desk.

"Frankie Bottoms, or I'm damned!"

The soldier wheeled about as if he had been struck. "Chief? Chief! Chief Tobias!"

"How you doin', Frankie? Still wearing knee-pads, I see."

"Chief, what are you doing here? When did you leave Ft. Lewis?"

"Shame on you, Frankie. I was never there."

"Oh, 'course not," the young man said with a grin.

"Smitty, meet Frankie—the finest cheese-eater in the enlisted force."

In the manner of young black soldiers, instead of shaking hands he tilted his head up with a sharp nod and said, " 'T's up?"

" 'T's up?" I echoed.

"When did you get transferred out of CONUS, Frankie?"

"Right after you left—uh, I mean... well, hell, Chief, you know what I mean! Happened damned fast, too."

"That was your guardian angel at work. This where you're pushing paper now?"

Frankie nodded.

"And you a highly trained grunt. It's a damned shame. Listen, I need some info. Wanna help?"

"You got it! And hey, I ain't a grunt no more. I got retrained soon as I got here," he said righteously.

"Okay, okay, so your a *licensed* pencil pusher."

"Uh, that'd be key-pusher now, Chief," I interjected. "This is the modern Army."

"That's right," Frankie said. "What d'you need?"

"A roster," Chief and I said in unison, and stared at each other.

"You got it," Frankie repeated. He plopped into an office chair, pushed off with his legs, and rolled and swivelled gracefully until he was facing one of the computers. "Whole unit? Enlisted? Officers? Everybody?—or what?"

"Let's start with command and staff, down to company level," Chief said.

Frankie whistled and grinned. "You got it." His fingers flew, and in a few seconds one of the printers began to sputter. "This is my own system," he said impressively. "The Army's got one they paid a stack o'money for, but it don't work. Now see, here I can get you any personnel stats you want, any way you want it, and I don't got to memorize fifteen different dumb-ass commands." He ripped off the print-out and handed it to Chief. "Not bad, huh? I can also do casualty reporting, personnel replacement, reassignment—"

"Frankie, what ever made you think you wanted to be an infantryman?" Chief asked.

"Oh, well," Frankie said wistfully, "I thought it'd be cool, y'know? Like the movies and shit."

"I been there," I said sympathetically.

"When does the unit come back from the field?" Chief was looking at the roster, and his eyes were shining.

"Different times," Frankie said. "Uh, Alpha'll be back first, probably Friday. Then Delta, Bravo, and Charlie, each about four days apart."

"What about staff sections?"

"Hell, Chief, staff just comes and goes. But the light bird don't usually come back 'til the last company's home."

"Colonel Serway?"

"Yeah. He'll send back the XO, Major Bell, about a week early to run battalion here in garrison. The colonel likes to watch his tanks shoot."

"Hmm," Chief mused. "Then what about the S-3 section? They'll be back with the XO?"

"Naw, Ops has gotta run the range."

"So their lieutenant stays in Grafenwöhr?"

"Yeah, that's right. Hey, Chief, what's up anyway?" Frankie's curiosity was finally catching up with him.

"Now, Frankie, you don't really want to know that, do you? But hey, can you run me some addresses on these people?"

"Sure. You even want the commander's?"

"No, you can leave him off," Chief said with a smile.

"What about the XO? Or the company commanders? Do you want—"

"Frankie, just do it, okay?"

A lieutenant was coming up the hallway as we were leaving—the S-1, I was sure—but we passed him by without a word, leaving him to stare at our retreating backs. I wondered what Frankie would tell him.

As we walked back across post, Chief showed me the roster.

"Lieutenant Grason is in the S-3," I noticed.

"Look at Charlie company," he said.

"Captain Worms. What about it, Chief?"

"I gotta hunch. Let's see if we get lucky."

He led us to a small, obscure building behind the PX. It's tiny sign read, "Brigade Legal Office." Inside there was a small waiting room, like a dentist's or doctor's office, complete with magazines and a receptionist's window. Chief rapped loudly on the window.

"Sergeant Bellows!" he hollered.

The soldier who came to the window said, "Damn, Chief, what if the JAG was here?"

"He isn't. Lemme in."

The soldier disappeared, and momentarily a door opened and Chief stomped through, me behind him.

"Damn, Chief," the man who let us in repeated, "Sergeant Bellows ain't here neither—how come you didn't know that then, if you know so much?"

" 'Cause he's not tied by an umbilical cord to a shiny red BMW, unlike your precious JAG officer."

"Precious! Not to me. I don't think Captain Dinkerson is precious to nobody."

"That's a nasty thing to say, Dupree. So Sarge isn't here?"

"Hey, you said it, man, not me. No, Sarge went to lunch."

"That's all right," Chief said, "you can do it. I want to see the Article 15's from One-Two-Eight for the last six months."

"Sure you do," Specialist Dupree said with a grin. "And of course you've got a DA Form 3824b, authorizing me to show 'em to you."

"Son, your momma ever whup you when you were a boy?"

"What about it?"

"You're gonna wish I was her if I don't see those Article 15's in 10 seconds."

"Shee-it," Dupree exhaled, opening a filing cabinet. "I'd like to see you and my old lady go at it. She'd snap you like a broken rubber band. She damned sure would!"

Chief laughed. "I'm sure she would," he said. "But it wouldn't do any good. It obviously didn't work on you."

"That's a fact," Dupree laughed in his turn, and handed Chief a bulging Manila folder.

"Say, these have been some naughty boys! How many years' worth is this?" Chief asked.

"You said six months. Those are back to January one."

Chief whistled.

"It's more than half Alpha Company. Their CO, Captain Merrick—" Dupree paused. "Hey, Chief, I can tell you this, right? I mean, you wouldn't—"

"Dupree, I am your father confessor. Unburden yourself, son."

"That man is a super-prize, A-number-one dick-head."

Chief chuckled. "Let's take a look Smitty. Dupree, are these by company, or what?"

"Naw, man, by type, then date. Department of the Army regulation 29-5, paragraph 3, subparagraph 'd.' "

"You made that up," Chief said, sitting at an empty desk. "Oh well, we'll browse."

Devised by Congress, the "Article 15"—so called after the section in the Uniform Code of Military Justice (UCMJ) that specifies its use—is the means by which commanders exercise discipline over their troops without being hobbled by the Constitution. Military members are citizens, after all, and as such are protected by the "due process" clause of the Bill of Rights. However, discipline would be non-existent if commanders had to say, "do what I tell you or I'll take you to court" every time they gave an unpopular order. Hence, "non-judicial punishment" was created. If a soldier commits a misdemeanor, his commander can invoke Article 15, under which, following a hearing in which the commander responsible is both judge and jury, punishments ranging from a mere reprimand and extra duty to reduction in rank, loss of pay, and confinement for up to 30 days can be imposed. Prior to an Article 15 proceeding a soldier can demand a court martial, even for a minor offense, and then the commander must either drop the charge or hand the matter over for a full jury trial—with all the constitutional trimmings. This happens rarely, however; a court martial is a federal court of law, and a conviction usually means going to jail, with subsequent ejection from the military under other than honorable conditions. This gives the company commander a considerable amount of power, and each commander handles this power in his own way. Some wield it like despots. Most use it as sparingly as possible, and ninety percent of Article 15's are glorified hand-slapping.

Captain Merrick was into hand-slapping with a vengeance. Chief wasn't taking much interest in Alpha Company's, however, but was flipping through the whole stack rapidly.

"Here we go," he said, and then, with a little jump, "Hot damn! Dupree, make me a copy of this!"

"Sure, Chief," Dupree said, glancing sidelong at Chief as though he'd gone crazy, "anything you say."

As soon as Dupree handed him the photocopy Chief grabbed my arm and headed for the door. "Dupree," he said over his shoulder, "Next time you commit a felony I'll look the other way."

"Wha'd'you mean, *next* time?"

Outside, he thrust the document into my hands as we headed up the street. I read it carefully. It was from Company C, and

signed by Captain Worms. Apparently a soldier had been keeping
hard liquor in his footlocker, and had been sentenced to twenty
days extra duty and forfeiture of a week's pay (a hundred and
twenty-nine dollars and five cents—depressing). When I was done
reading it, I handed it back to Chief.

"Well?" he said.

I shrugged my shoulders.

"Oh, Smitty, Smitty, Smitty," he cried, stopping and grabbing
my arm again. "Look at it! I wanted summary Article 15's precisely because I knew that they are always hand-written. Do me
proud, Smitty—look at it again."

I looked. "Oh my God," I said suddenly. "That letter we
found...."

"Now look at the signature."

It had been signed, "John Chester Worms."

"Hot damn!" I said, mimicking unconsciously. "So Chief,
does this mean he did it?"

"Oh for Christ's sake, Smitty! No, it doesn't mean he did it. It
means we've got a lead. Finally."

"Right, Chief. Sorry."

"It's all right—I did act pretty excited, I guess."

"How did you know?"

"I didn't know, I guessed. The fact that the letter was hand-
delivered was the first thing—what simpler than for someone who
lives in the building to drop a letter in her box? Then I wondered
what in the hell Nancy Worms was up to this morning... but the
biggie was finding out C Company hadn't left town 'til Friday.
That was like flashing lights and sirens saying, 'this way to the
lead!' "

"Sounds simple when you explain it."

"Everything sounds simple when you explain it," he said matter-of-factly.

"Oh, I don't know about that. I had to drop out of calculus."

"You took calculus? I'm impressed."

"Did you?" I asked.

"Oh ... I guess you might say that," he said cryptically. "Well, where are we?"

"At the car."

"Right. What time is it?"

It was really odd that Chief didn't wear a watch. "Twelve-thirty."

"Hmm. Hungry? Me too. Well, let's hope her father feeds us." He took out the card Mr. McKenna had given him and studied it, and we both got in.

11   The Mourners, Part II

Röter Adler *gasthaus*, Erlangen, West Germany,
Tuesday, 1 July 198-, 1300 hrs.

Since downtown Erlangen was only five minutes drive from
post, we had plenty of time, and after we parked we mean-
dered among the shops and *imbisses* before heading to the *Röter
Adler*, Mr. McKenna's hotel. Germany does have shopping malls
and department stores, of course, but the real centers of retail activity are still the *pedestrianzönen* in the hearts of the towns, dense
with boutiques, specialty stores, and cafés, many of which extend
their displays right out onto the sidewalk. Chief bought a copy
of the International Herald Tribune at a newsstand (kind of a con-
glomeration of the New York Times and the Washington Post pub-
lished for Americans abroad), and we enjoyed ourselves looking
at the goods for sale and (to be candid) at the equally interesting
shoppers.

The hotel turned out to have an outdoor café, separated from
the sidewalk by a low stone wall, and as we approached we saw
that our host was watching and waiting for us at a table. He rose
and shook hands with Chief, and with me this time. I wondered if
his natural instinct for courtesy had been restored or if, like so
many men of his age and (probably) standing, he looked upon
good manners purely pragmatically, as a social tool to be used

181

when it served a purpose. He had changed since the service, and I quickly concluded that Maggie's customer's rumor—concerning his wealth—was not idle; the suit was well tailored to his bulk, and his gem-studded ring and Rolex watch were conspicuous.

"Have a beer, will you? *Garçon!*" he called, signaling to the waiter.

"You mean '*herr kellner*,' sir," Chief offered.

"Whatever. They're all Europeans. He knows what I mean."

The waiter, who turned out to be a *fraulein* in any event, came up to the table and said, in a neutral tone, "*Bitte?*"

"Yeah, look honey," Mr. McKenna said, "we want some beer."

"*Drei biere?*"

"*Mineral wasser, bitte*," I said, in the politest tones I could.

"*Pils für mich, danke schön*," Chief said.

"Uh," Mr. McKenna hesitated. "Hell, I just want a beer.... "

"*Meiner freund hat ein hell gern*," Chief offered.

The waitress's eyes sparkled with humor. "*Pils, wasser—und helles bier!*" She twirled away with a smile.

"What the—?" Mr. McKenna began.

"It's all right, sir," Chief said. "You tell a German girl you want a little hell, she knows just what to do. Sobranie?"

Mr. McKenna waved the cigarettes away. "No, thanks. Uh, Chief Tobias, I need to talk to you about Kimberly."

"I'm sure you must be very concerned," Chief said. "I'll be happy to offer you any information or help that I can."

"Good. I was hoping you'd say that."

"Perhaps, too, you may be able to tell me something—"

"The fact is," Mr. McKenna went on gruffly, "I've had a talk with the general, and he and I don't see any reason why Kim's body can't be released immediately."

"Oh." Chief was taken off guard by this. "Well, sir.…"

"From what Colonel Crick and that doctor of his said, it seems you're the only one holding things up. What about it?"

"Well, that's not entirely true. The fact is, Army reg's are pretty firm on this point. When a dependent dies overseas, there are procedures that must be followed."

"I was told that's what you'd say, so I called a friend of mine. From what he tells me, there's no reason for delay since the death was natural. Now, I want her back home—"

"Natural?" Chief interjected.

"An alcohol coma's natural, as far as I'm concerned," Mr. McKenna asserted. "Accidental death. Natural as you want."

Just then our drinks arrived, and Chief used the interruption to gather his thoughts. After sipping his pils and staring at it for a few moments, he wiped the foam from his mustache and said, "Well, Mr. McKenna, I understand your feelings. It will take some wrangling with my people, but maybe I can get them to see it your way."

"Now you're talking," the other man said.

"It will help me a great deal, though," Chief continued, "if you can tell me a few things."

"Like what?"

"Well, uh, let's start with a little history. How long were she and Captain Merrick married?"

"Not quite two years."

"Do you think they were happy?"

"What's that got to do with anything?"

"If I can just establish a few facts, Mr. McKenna, it will make it much easier to get your daughter home to you."

"All right. Sure, they were happy. Andy's a solid kid."

"To your knowledge," Chief said, picking his words carefully, "there wasn't any trouble between them?"

"To my knowledge, no. We done?"

"Had Kimberly ever mentioned to you about unhappiness in her marriage?" Chief persisted.

"Look, Chief Tobias, I'll be frank with you. My daughter and I weren't on the best of terms. She didn't tell me much."

Chief tried a different tack. "Was Kimberly ever diagnosed with any conditions—physical problems, say—for which she might have been taking medication?"

"No," Mr. McKenna said. But there was the slightest hesitation.

"What about emotional or mental problems?"

"Oh hell! I don't know what this has to do with anything."

"Was she under treatment?" Chief asked quietly.

"Kim had a lot of problems. She was a mixed up kid, but I think after she married Andy she was all right. I don't really know. It doesn't matter anymore—it's over now, all right?" The man was getting flushed.

"Mr. McKenna," Chief said, "I'm afraid... that is, I think there may be more going on here than an accidental suicide—"

"Oh, go to hell." He got up awkwardly, upsetting his beer mug. "I just want her home, you got that? Just get my daughter home!" He threw his napkin down on the table and stormed away.

Chief said nothing at first, and shortly our waitress was back with a towel, asking our pardon and wiping up the spilled beer. At last he said, "What the hell, I'm still hungry. And Smitty, you need a beer. Don't worry about your uniform; the morals squad doesn't hang around joints like this. *Entshuldigen Sie, bitte*," he said to the waitress, "*Wir wollen speisekarten*—wait, schnitzel okay

Smitty?—*zwei schnitzel, bitte, und nach ein pils—nein, dunkel—*
für beide uns."

"Two schnitzels, and two dark beers, yes sir," she said, and
strode away.

"Damn it, they always do that," Chief snapped, "especially
the pretty ones: wait until you've massacred their language before
letting on that they speak English." He lit a cigarette and puffed at
it angrily.

"Was that grief, Chief?" I asked after a minute.

"Dunno. Maybe."

"Seemed more like fear and anger," I said.

"Yeah. Well, at least it's consistent. Everybody connected
with this case acts like they've sat on a hot poker as soon as you
start asking questions."

"Do you think he's trying to cover up something?"

"No—yes," Chief said, "but I think it's probably personal, not
connected with her death *per se.*" He shrugged in a thoughtful
way. "Certainly, if she'd been my daughter, I'd have a lot on my
conscience."

Our lunch arrived and Chief browsed through his paper as we
ate, though I noticed he seemed to spend less time staring at it
as past it, into empty space. As we walked back to the car he
discussed his plans for the afternoon. His purpose in getting addresses from Frankie was to find out where the Grasons lived, and
he wanted to stop there first. Then, he felt, it was time to confront
Mrs. Worms.

The Grasons lived in a high-rise on the edge of town, across
the *autobahn* that led south to Nürnberg and north to Bamberg.
Like all German buildings, the only way in—absent a key—was to
be buzzed in from the foyer by an occupant after ringing them up

from the intercom. Accordingly, Chief found the Grason's name and buzzed; waited, and buzzed again. After a couple of minutes he found the manager's buzzer and pressed it. Immediately an immense *hausfrau* came to the inner doors and demanded, through the glass, to know who we were and what we wanted.

"*Gruss Gott*," Chief began, then continued with other forms of greeting I didn't understand and held up his ID and badge.

The woman seemed much perturbed, but eventually came into the foyer. After some discussion, she tried the Grasons' buzzer herself. When there was no answer, more discussion ensued. At last she let us in, and escorted us up two flights of stairs to the Grasons' apartment.

Here Chief rang the bell and rapped on the door, but still there was no answer. Talking a mile a minute, the landlady led us back down the stairs to the front door. Her tone had changed considerably, and as we stood by the door I became aware that Chief was doing his polite best to get us out of an invitation for coffee and cake. Before we left, he took my notebook and scribbled a note to Sabrina. He tore it off, folded it tightly, and left it sticking in the jamb of her mailbox.

"That woman's coffee is no doubt excellent and her cakes sublime," he said as we got back into the scarab, "But, lord—!" He gathered himself. "She hasn't seen Sabrina for at least two days," he said. "Which may mean nothing at all," he added as we pulled into traffic.

"Are you worried she may be escaping?" I asked. "Fleeing the country?"

"Smitty," Chief said, "you mentioned that you write stories, didn't you?"

"Yes."

He pulled into a parking lot next to a phone booth. Turning to me he said, "So, are they all cheap thrillers?" He yanked viciously up on the parking brake, got out of the car, and stepped into the phone booth.

This was the first time Chief had ever shown irritation with me, and I was a little shaken. I wallowed in hurt feelings for a few minutes. Then suddenly it occurred to me that Chief might be worried about Sabrina... and I felt a little ashamed. I pulled myself together.

"Sorry, Chief, that was stupid. Something might have happened to her," I said when he got back into the car.

He stared at me. "I hope you'll always keep surprising me, Smitty."

Back on the road he said, "That was inspector Müller."

"And?" I prompted. Chief's attention was somewhere else.

"Uh, well," he said, "it sounds like Buttenheimer's story stands up: Müller had a pigeon at the party, who reports that Buttenheimer left with Kimberly about one in the morning. Then Buttenheimer returned alone, before two o'clock. That makes the times about right, since the party was just outside Nürnberg."

"Wow," I said. "Anything else?"

"Yeah. Sabrina was there."

I whistled. "Does he know where she is now?"

"No."

I tried to think out the implications of this. Sabrina was still a suspect, no question. Now more than ever. But was she also a possible victim? If so, whose? It sounded like Buttenheimer was cleared, so why would he hurt Sabrina if he was innocent? Or was Buttenheimer shielding someone, as Chief had suggested (hadn't he?), and was that someone also apt to kill Sabrina? By the time we reached the Matson *kaserne* housing area, I had a shallow headache going.

Chief didn't park in front of Mrs. Worms building, but behind the next one down, and after shutting off the engine he just sat with his shirt tail pulled out, wiping his glasses.

"Chief?" I prompted.

"Oh, it's all right, Smitty," he said. But he still didn't move. At last he said, "It's one thing to know your husband is in love with another woman. It's something else again to know that others know it too." He looked at me. "Smitty, we're about to go in and stab this woman through the torso with a burning spear . . . and we've got to, because it's the only way to get at her husband's alibi."

"You think she knows?"

"You were there on Friday—what do you think?"

"Maybe we could talk to *him* first," I said, starting to realize how uncomfortable this was going to make me feel.

He didn't answer, but got out of the car. "Well," he said, as we strolled up the sidewalk, "let's just see how it plays."

When Mrs. Worms opened the door, she stared at us expressionlessly. She was pale and tired-looking, and wore a long, flowered robe.

"I'm sorry to disturb you, Mrs. Worms," Chief said. "When you spoke to me this afternoon, I—"

"Come in," she said, opening the door wide. She seemed composed, much more so than the previous Friday, but it was a grim kind of composure, like that of someone condemned. Again I was struck by the strength of her build and features. Altogether, her height, the prominence of her face, the rich shock of black, wavy hair that today draped across her shoulders, and her upright carriage suggested to me that she had never been a candidate for the role of "vulnerable, delicate little woman." I wondered if it ever occurred to anyone that she would sometime need to be protected, and comforted.

Once we were seated on the couch, Chief asked plainly, "Why did you come to see me today?"

Mrs. Worms curled into a large chair, drawing her bare feet up under her robe. "I didn't expect to," she said. "I went for the service."

"Given what you told me on Friday—"

"Naturally," she interrupted. She seemed to be weighing something in her mind. "Chief Tobias, did someone murder Kimberly Merrick?"

Chief paused. "Do you think so?"

"I do now. I thought she was just dead, and I was glad. But then I saw you at the chapel, and I realized...."

"What did you realize, ma'am?" Chief prodded.

"That there must be more to it. And of course, now...,"

Chief waited while Mrs. Worms drew herself together.

"... now I suppose you must suspect me. Isn't that right?" she concluded, her voice slightly elevated.

"Actually, ma'am, no. Not you." Chief cleared his throat, leaned forward slightly, and held Mrs. Worms's gaze for long seconds.

She broke. "Oh, Jesus...." she said, her throat suddenly very tight and her Adam's apple leaping up. She looked away, and tears squeezed from the corners of her eyes.

"All I need, Mrs. Worms," Chief said gently, "are the plain facts. That will make it easier."

She nodded mutely.

"John was home Friday evening." Chief paused, but there was no response. "But he left, didn't he?"

She nodded.

"What time?"

"About eight-thirty. He said he had to make sure his company was ready to move out in the morning."

"What time did he return?"

"Twelve forty-two."

"And you know what time it was because—?"

She looked at Chief. "Because I was watching—closely."

"You are absolutely sure that was the time?" Chief persisted.

"Yes."

"What time did he go out again?"

She looked surprised. "He didn't, not 'til morning. He didn't get any sleep, either," she added, in a tone that made her meaning plain: she had confronted him.

"What time would that have been?"

"About five. They were rail-loading at seven."

"Ma'am?"

"Rail-loading. The tanks."

Chief sat back and stared at his knees for a few moments. "Mrs. Worms, how does it stand between you and your husband, now?"

"I thought all you wanted were facts," she objected.

"You're right," Chief admitted, "and you don't have to answer that if you don't want to."

She hesitated. "I think...," she began, but then she seemed to have too many considerations and qualifications in mind to give voice to them.

"Are you afraid your husband might've killed Kimberly Merrick?"

"Oh no, it isn't that! I don't know that he wouldn't have, for certain," she said after some reflection, "but I know that he couldn't have."

"I see. I'm sorry, I interrupted you."

"When he left, Friday morning, I felt like maybe we were going to be okay. I think he was really sorry. But.... " She started to crumble again, but regained control. "You see, I'm pregnant."

"You haven't told him," Chief said.

"No."

"But you haven't packed your bags, either."

"No."

Chief got up. "Mrs. Worms, I am sorry. I wish you the best and, somehow, I think you're probably going to be okay. Smitty and I will be going now."

"Chief Tobias," she called, when we had reached the door.

We turned back.

"Thanks."

"What do you want to do now, Chief?" I asked when we got to the car.

"What do I want to do? I want to find John Chester a.k.a. Chet and give him a swift kick in the butt."

"Okay. Then what?"

"Kick him again, 'til he squeals."

We drove onto post, and stopped at the brigade headquarters. Inside, Chief asked to see the commander.

"Not here," the CQ said. "Gone to Graf."

"What about Captain Merrick?"

The sergeant shrugged his shoulders.

Disgruntled, Chief decided next to look in on Major Suarez, but he wasn't in his office, either. The head nurse admitted that Mrs. Merrick's records had still not been found.

It was getting on for four o'clock, and Chief, frustrated and concerned, asked me to drive him home. He talked little on the ride, but stared out of the window, occasionally muttering to himself.

He invited me up when we got to his building, but once I was settled with a bottle of pils he ignored me and worked at his desk. I took the opportunity to examine Chief's enormous collection of books. Many of them were old, especially the multi-volume collections of literature and essays, and there were few paperbacks. He would tell me on another occasion that although he bought and read paperbacks he couldn't keep them—there was no room. A great many of the books were reference works, covering topics from history to science to mythology, and he must have had a dozen dictionaries. A dozen English dictionaries, that is; there were as many more in other languages, including Latin, Greek, and Russian.

I paused briefly to scratch Nietzsche on the head and to wonder what lizards thought about, before continuing down the stacks. There was a philosophy section, and next to that there were several shelves of books on mathematics. This struck me, and I remembered Chief's odd response when I had asked him if he had taken calculus. I took one titled *Non-Euclidean Geometries* off the shelf and flipped through it. Geometry had been the only mathematics class I really liked in school, partly perhaps because I enjoyed making designs with ruler and compass, and partly because the teacher had been very good, but this book made absolutely no sense to me at all. I put it back and tried another one called *Modern Algebra*, and was shocked to find that it contained nothing that resembled algebra in the least. There weren't even any numbers, and the equations—if you could call them that—contained all sorts of arcane symbols. It might as well have been a book on sorcery, for all I knew. Or cared to know, I told myself. I snapped it shut and replaced it on the shelf with a shake of the head.

"Better stick to the four branches of arithmetic," Chief chuckled behind me, " 'ambition, distraction, uglification, and derision.' "

"Oh," I said, "um, damn...."

"Lewis Carroll."

"I knew that."

"Have you got a copy of *Alice* at home? No? Here," he said, rummaging down the shelves on the other side of the room, "take this one. I've got two."

"Oh, thanks."

"Start by rereading 'The Mock Turtle's Story.' C'mere, I've got something to show you." He picked up a large sketch pad and propped it against a computer screen. "Here's the time table for last Thursday night, with our cast of characters' supposed whereabouts."

Chief had drawn a kind of grid, with times running across the top and names down the side. Some of the names were in red ink, and I asked him about that.

"Those are the people whose whereabouts want checking up on, or at least verification."

"Hmm. Sabrina, Captain Worms, Mrs. Worms, and Captain Merrick. Oh, and Major Suarez! I didn't know he was a suspect."

"He wasn't, really," Chief said, "and I'm not sure I consider him one now, but since he turns out to have a history with her—even if only a professional one—I thought maybe we'd better start taking that possibility more seriously. For one thing, the disappearance of those medical records...."

"Yeah," I said. Then, "Yeah! I didn't think of that! If nobody outside the clinic could take them, then it had to be somebody inside."

"Maybe so. Still, as far as I'm concerned, Suarez's name is on here as a formality. I'm not inclined to think he could have done it."

That reminded me of something. "Chief," I said, "let me in on some magic."

"Hunh?"

"You already knew Mrs. Worms was pregnant, when nobody else did. How did you know? Is there, like, some subtle mark or something?"

He laughed. "Yes. It's called 'a distinct uterine bulge on a woman who is otherwise lean as can be.' On a build like Mrs. Worms's, it's hard to mistake, even at just six or eight weeks on."

"I didn't notice it," I said.

"You weren't looking for it."

"So," I asked after a pause, "Captain Worms isn't cleared by her testimony?"

"Nope."

"You don't believe her, then?"

"Well, just between you and me, Smitty, yes I do. But, just between me and you, I can't afford to."

"So what now?"

"I see a trip in our future."

"Someplace nice, I hope."

"Oh yes! Beautiful countryside, rolling hills, lush forest—"

"Grafenwöhr. When do we leave?"

"In the morning. Tonight, we have other business. We've got to find Sabrina Grason."

"How do we do that?"

"The old-fashioned way—we look."

"Where?"

Chief gave me a very disquieting grin.

12 The Wall

"Now, you sure you feel up to this, Smitty?"

I nodded. The thumping rock 'n roll washed over us in an unending flood of sound, making speech difficult. The bizarre colors of the flashing neon sign—one moment depicting a woman with the feathered veil of a stripper hiding her torso, the next moment depicting the same woman with the feathers flung away—gave Chief's face a frightening otherworldliness, especially as the changing sign was so perfectly reflected in his glasses, hiding his eyes.

"Good. You're just after information. Try to look harmless, and see if you can get some girl or other to talk to you. Oh, here's some money." He dug in his wallet and handed me a wad of 20-*Mark* bills. "Try not to spend it, but use it if you have to. You'll need some just to get in."

I tucked it away.

"I'll start in that one," he said, pointing up the street. "If we miss each other, we'll meet at that hamburger joint, up around the corner. Let's say, not more than an hour, hour and a half, max."

I entered the building. The contrast with the dingy street outside was stark: every surface seemed to be either a mirror or a

196

flashing light, and the noise was deafening. The first room was filled with banks of what looked like video games. On closer inspection they turned out to be video machines indeed, but a one-*Mark* coin bought you, not a game, but a few minutes of hard-core action on the screen. The room was ringed with small booths, each of which had a red and a green light over the door to indicate whether it was occupied. There were few people in this room however, and the main action, as well as the source of the music, seemed to be on the other side of a cage-like door at the far end. I noticed that every patron had a military haircut, and I hoped I wouldn't run into anyone I knew.

At the cage-door a bored looking attendant took six *Marks*, and I went in. This room was truly amazing. On three walls were immense glass cases, and in two of these naked women were adopting utterly candid poses on slowly rotating, carpeted platforms. On the fourth wall was a bar. There were maybe thirty-five young men in this room, leaning against the bar or standing at chest-high tables and watching the show. I went to the bar and asked for a beer, and was startled when the bartender slammed a can down in front of me. I hadn't seen beer cans in Germany before—everything was half-liter bottles. Not only did he give me beer in a can, but he wanted five *Marks* for it. My money wouldn't have lasted long if I had been there on pleasure instead of business.

At the moment, however, there was something more pressing on my mind: everyone in the room was an American. There were no girls. Somehow, I doubted I could get what I was after by yelling my questions through the protective glass of the rotating stages.

The music stopped momentarily, and one of the models slipped through a door in the back of her fish bowl, then another arrived to take her place as a new "song" began. In the brief intermission of silence, I was spotted.

"Hey, Smith!"

Uh-oh. I wheeled around and said hello to one of the fellows from my old platoon, a Private Turner, whom I didn't like. Vulgarity I can handle, and I don't especially mind someone being stupid. But stupid *and* vulgar gets old in a hurry.

"Escaping from the old lady, eh?"

"Uh, yeah," I said.

"Damn, look at the tits on that one!" he said, and went on to share with me what he might do with them if he had the chance.

"She's pretty," I allowed.

"You doughboy!" he taunted. "You been here before?"

I admitted I hadn't.

"There's this redhead comes on you gotta see. The face ain't much—but damn!" He looked me over with an alcoholic stare. "Hey, tell me something," he said, and I knew exactly what was coming: "What's all this shit about you getting transferred to the MP company?"

"Uh, somebody needed a driver." Think fast.

"Not what I heard. They say you're workin' for some spook—"

"Hey, Turner," I interrupted him. "How come there ain't any . . . uh, you know, any girls here? I thought the wall—"

"You're in the wrong place, man. You wanna get laid?"

"Um. . . ."

"C'mon. Buy me a beer and I'll initiate you."

Suddenly I was glad of Turner's distinguishing traits. He led me outside and up towards the end of the street, to a hole in the wall right next to Buttenheimer's. It had only a small sign, and appeared to be just a run-down *gasthaus*. Inside, however, was the same gut-wrenching music (although not so loud), a bar, a dance floor, and several tables. The place was tight with GI's. And girls. Turner immediately hailed a crowd at one of the tables and pulled me over.

"Hey, this here's my buddy Smith! He says he'll buy the beer if he gets laid."

Jesus. This wasn't going to work. I needed anonymity, or at least privacy. I let myself be pushed into a chair, however, and handed Turner a twenty as one of his "friends," a slinky little creature in green hot pants and a pink blouse that ended above her navel, climbed into my lap.

"What's your name, GI?" she purred.

"Uh, what's yours?" I tried, removing her hand from my hair.

"Heidi."

Of course it was.

"You're handsome!"

I was learning quickly that sitting in a lap could be done, well, intimately. My body, like any man's, had no concept of obedience given that kind of encouragement, and I shifted, trying to move her off at least far enough that I could save myself from inadvertently encouraging her.

"Hey! Don't you like me?"

"Oh, sure, sure. It's just that I, uh, I need to go to the bathroom."

She smiled and kissed me on the cheek. "You come back?"

"Of course."

"Okay," she said, moving off, but she grabbed my hand as she did so and held it to her. "Remember, you're coming back," she said.

I staggered up and stumbled towards the back of the room, my pulse pounding in my ears and the weight and shape of her breast still tingling on my left palm.

Once in the bathroom I entered a stall, shut the door, and sat down. This was so far out of my experience that I wasn't sure I could continue. Besides, how could I ask for the information I wanted unless I got the chance to talk to some of these girls away from the other fellows? Well, maybe it wasn't that big a problem. If I stood at the bar the girls could come to me, and if they didn't know anything I could tell them I wasn't interested.

I went out. There was an open stool at the end of the bar, near the restrooms and almost out of sight of Turner's table. I quickly stepped up and claimed it, noticing as I did so that Heidi was sharing one of Turner's buddies with another girl. Competition, I supposed. Or was it collaboration? Maybe she was just keeping her motor running.

I ordered a beer. Looking around, I caught the eye of a tall, dark-haired girl in a one-piece, black leather outfit, sort of like a teddy, but not quite as bed-roomish. She smiled at me demurely, and I sort of half nodded, half smiled back. I turned nervously to take a sip of my beer, and when I looked up, she was at my elbow and staring into my eyes. It amazed me how easily intimacy can be aped.

I said hello.

"Buy me a drink?" she asked, in a voice nearly free of accent.

Naturally. I dug in my wallet while she signalled the bartender, who seemed to know what to mix for her without having to ask. It would be mostly water, I supposed.

"What's your name?" she asked.

"Rocky," I said without thinking, and then nearly laughed out loud at myself.

"Hi, Rocky. I'm Ilsa."

"Hi." Now what? I felt like someone who hadn't learned the script. "You're very beautiful, Ilsa," I tried. She was, too. Huge dark eyes, a shapely mouth, pleasant skin—and a becoming manner; she took my compliment by dipping her head shyly, and then giving me a look of such sincere admiration that I had to remind myself to breathe. "Um," I said, thinking of a useful way to follow this up, "do you ever do any modeling?"

"That is very sweet for you to say," she said, clearly pleased.

"No, really, do you?"

My tone caught her attention, and she hesitated, not sure if the compliment was quite the point. "Maybe," she said. "Sometimes."

"Oh," I said, wondering what to say next. "Um, because I'm really interested in that."

She smiled and leaned into me, running her hand along the back of my neck. "You want me to, for you?"

"Do you know Buttenheimer?" I said quickly. Too quickly.

She froze. "What—?"

"I'm trying to find someone. Her name is Sabrina."

Ilsa turned abruptly and picked up her drink, putting her elbows on the bar. "What do you want, GI?" The warmth had gone from her voice.

"I'm sorry, I just need to find her. She's a friend of Buttenheimer's, and her name is Sabrina—wait!"

But she was gone. She walked out quickly—out the back way—and I wondered if I should follow her. I decided against it: my plan was still intact. I pushed her drink to the back of the bar, and thought about the encounter. Somehow, I had to keep their interest long enough to introduce my questions, but do so in a way that didn't make them run off. I wondered how Chief was managing, and if this was the way he was going about it. Somehow, I was sure, Chief would just say the things that worked, and get what he wanted if it was there to be gotten. I wished he'd let me go with him to see how he did it, but then this wasn't the sort of job you could do with a partner—as he had pointed out when he was talking me into it. But how he thought I was ever going to get anywhere on my own....

I paused to flirt with resentment.

But that was stupid. Really, he was showing a tremendous amount of confidence in me just by letting me participate in this part of the investigation. Perhaps, if I made it clear right off, even though I didn't want to buy their services, that I was willing to pay for the information, I'd start to get somewhere. If I'd done that with Ilsa when she asked what I wanted, she might not have left in such a hurry.

I felt confidence return. Ask, then show the money. It'd work.

I picked up my beer and took a healthy swig. Suddenly I coughed, getting beer up my nose and nearly spewing foam across the bar; arms had encircled my waist and a hand was groping down under my belt buckle.

"Hi, hi!" said a bright soprano under my right ear.

It was Heidi.

"You are naughty!" she said, "You promised."

"I'm sorry," I said. "Uh, drink?" I signalled the bartender, who looked at me oddly, then shrugged, removed Ilsa's glass, and went to mix another one.

"You want to be my friend, yes?" she said.

She sidled along my flank, one hand on my thigh and the other running up my arm, and I wondered what kind of commitment would be entailed if I answered in the affirmative. I chose to smile at her instead, hoping it kept me on neutral ground. She returned it with that same cow-eyed look of submissive admiration Ilsa had shown, but without the same potency; this one's quality was several notches lower. Still, there was a girlishness about her that had its own peculiar effect.

When her drink came she picked it up and tugged at me with her other arm.

"Come, sit," she said.

"Uh, not over there."

She looked around, and led me to a small booth in a dark corner. I tried to let her in first, but she succeeded in maneuvering me onto the bench and pushing me against the wall, then climbed in against me.

"I am forgetting your name," she said.

"Rocky."

"This is a *strong* name," she whispered. She crossed one leg over both our knees, and put her hand in my lap again. I straightened, wondering what to do, and decided it wouldn't seem too much like a brush-off if I put my hand under her thigh and gently uncrossed her legs. She countered by curling one leg under her buttocks and sitting on it, which brought our faces to a level. She leaned very close.

"Uh, Heidi, what I really want is—"

"Yes?" She put her hand on the back of my neck.

"Uh, look—" I was getting panicky. I yanked my wallet out and hurriedly fumbled for bills, grabbing the remaining twenties.

She smiled as big as Texas, and suddenly pulled me forward and put her mouth on mine in a wet kiss. I was too stunned to stop her when she grabbed the bills from my hand and stood up, waggled her hips at me, and took off with a giggle.

"Hey!" I said. I banged my knee viciously on the table leg getting up, and hobbled after her.

She was by the back door, waiting for me to appear, and then darted out. She was waiting, too, on the other side, and grabbed me and kissed me again, dragging me down a hallway as she did so. Again she let go and scampered on with a giggle, running lightly up a staircase.

"Heidi, wait!" I called. "That's not what I—"

"Come, come, GI!" she called from above. "I am having sugar for you!"

"At least she's an honest whore," I muttered as I climbed the stairs. "She could have just taken the money and run. There's hope yet."

At the top of the stairs was a long empty hallway with many doors. This looked like defeat, but then I heard her again.

"Gee—aye, aye!" she called in a sing-song, and I realized that one of the doors was open. I went to it and looked in, but didn't see her. I stepped in a little further, and the door shut behind me. She'd been hiding behind it.

"Ta-daa!" she said. Her blouse sailed off over her head as if tugged by hidden strings, and she threw her arms around my neck, kissing me and pushing me back onto the bed. I tripped backwards onto it and she straddled me, tugging at my belt.

"Wait! No!" I cried, grabbing her hands, "I just want to talk!"

"What?" she said, as if hearing me for the first time.

"I just want to talk," I gasped.

"GI, why you are making stupid talk?"

I looked at her—and my head spun. Her shorts had disappeared, somehow, so she was naked but for her panties, and her pale white belly undulated as she rocked her hips gently back and forth. Her hair was let loose, and the blond tresses curled and teased about her nipples. Her eyes were big and blue, the lips wet and pouty.…

"I just… I just need to talk to you," I managed weakly.

"Talk *mit diesen*," she said, and putting my hands over her breasts she leaned down and stuck her tongue in my mouth.

I don't know how I did it—forever in my imagination there will be another version where I didn't—but somehow I tore myself away, dumping her awkwardly on the mattress and jerking myself upright.

"I'm sorry," I panted. "I can't. I just—*Jesus*—I just want to talk to you. I'm looking for someone—a woman—she's—"

"You don't want me?"

"No, I—yes, but no. I just want to know if you can tell me—"

"Get out."

"I—what?"

"Get out," Heidi repeated. She got up and grabbed her clothes.

"Look, I'm sorry. You can keep the money if you can tell me where I can find Sabrina—the woman—if you know where.…"

"I don't know any woman," she said. "Now get out of here."

Suddenly I was angry. "Look, I'm sorry and everything, but if you can't help me then give me the money back."

She didn't answer, but turned and started to walk away, towards another door that led God-knows-where.

"Hey!" I said, and stepping up behind her I grabbed her by the arm.

With a speed and viciousness I would never have expected, she spun around and punched me in the eye. It was a practiced punch, delivering all the strength and weight she had, and I went down with a yelp.

There I was on the floor, and there was a naked girl half my size screaming at the top of her lungs at me in German. I crawled backwards a little ways, got to my feet, and left with my hand over my face.

It really hurt.

I was aware of other doors opening in the hallway and of heads peeking out, but I didn't look. I stumbled down the stairs and along the hall toward the bar, but when I got there the thought of making my way through the crowd in my present state—and past Turner's table of friends—filled me with despair. I leaned against the wall, wondering what to do, and then sank down and sat on the floor.

I hadn't sat long when the door to the bar opened, and I was aware of someone standing over me. I opened my good eye. There was a pair of black shoes, from which sprouted stockinged legs. Tilting my head back, I traced them up to where they met a pleated skirt, then a blouse, and finally a head of springy brown curls framing a familiar face.

"You!" she said.

It was Sabrina Grason.

Chief was waiting for me, luckily, in the hamburger place, and I burst in with the news.

"Good work, Smitty! Where is she?"

"Waiting by the car. At least, she said she would."

Chief bounced up and headed for the door. "What did she say when you found her?"

"Well," I admitted, "she sort of found me."

"Then she doesn't know we were looking for her?"

"Oh, I think she does. I think Ilsa—er, one of the girls I talked to—must have told her, but I don't know. I didn't tell her anything, except that you wanted to talk to her."

We walked hurriedly back up that hellish canyon of buildings to the other end of the street. There, sure enough, Mrs. Grason was waiting by Chief's blue Toyota, smoking a cigarette.

"Mrs. Grason," Chief said. "I'm glad we've found you."

"But, Mr. Chief, I wasn't hiding!" Her tone was the same she had used during our first interview with her, and it was a tone I now recognized—to my regret. It was an up-town version of that which Ilsa and Heidi had each used, and if the medium was the message then the message was simple: "You are a man: you must be stupid."

"I'm relieved to hear you say that," Chief responded, and his tone now made sense to me too: "If it suits you to believe me stupid, then it suits me to let you."

"You must be thinking awful things about me, running into me down here! But you see, I know someone who lives above the bar where I found your friend."

"Yes," Chief said. "I think we've met him."

"Him?" She looked puzzled.

"Say," Chief said after a pause, "this street is no place to talk. Let Smitty and I buy you a cup of coffee." He took her by the arm and we all walked together into a *gasthaus*. After taking her coat for her and holding her chair in the old-fashioned manner as she sat down, Chief ordered coffee for each of us, and sat back to regard her in a parody—a quite intentional and offensive parody, I realized—of infatuation.

"So, what can I do for you?" she said finally.

"Oh, well," Chief said, keeping it up, "I just have to ask questions, you know. Er, this friend of yours, do you stay with—her—often?"

"Mr. Chief! I was just *visiting*." She was keeping it up too.

"Of course! Silly me. You know, it's funny that you should have a friend in that building, because I have a friend there too. A new friend—I always love to make new friends! Maybe you've met him? His name is Gunther."

It was fascinating to watch her face at that moment. She didn't bat an eyelash, and the shape of her mouth didn't change, but somehow I knew that something inside her had just shattered, like an icicle hitting the pavement.

"I'm sure you'd like him," Chief continued. "He's a photographer, you see."

"No," she said then with a little laugh. "I—"

"Yes, you see, I've been making a collection of his work. Some of it is very artistic! Uh, Mrs. Grason," he said, taking out a cigarette, "do you have a light?"

She seemed not to hear him at first, but then gave a little start and leaned down to dig in her purse, which she had set on the floor by her chair. Chief leaned slightly to watch as she did so, then straightened with a startled look and signaled me silently with his hands to start taking notes.

"Thank you so much!" he said, as she struck a match and lit his cigarette for him. "Now, I wonder if you'd let me look in your purse."

Their eyes locked. Mrs. Grason attempted a laugh, but broke it off. She glanced around self-consciously then, and finally said, "I think I'd like to leave."

"That's *not* a good idea," Chief said.

She calculated. "I'm not in the military," she attempted, "so you have no authority over me."

"That is true," Chief said, "and we are on foreign soil. Would you prefer it, then, if I called my friends down at the Nürnberg police station? Just say the word."

I'm not sure if Mrs. Grason was capable of saying anything at that moment.

Chief leaned down and picked up her purse. "Do I understand, then, that I have your permission?"

She was motionless, and growing pale. At last she nodded slowly.

"Yes or no, Mrs. Grason."

"Yes."

Chief opened the brown leather purse, a large, zippered one with a shoulder strap, and drew out a much smaller one, a hand bag, covered with red sequins. He sighed then, and looked at Mrs. Grason carefully.

"Sabrina, listen to me," he told her. "I have to ask you some questions. Before I can ask you these questions, I have to tell you that you have certain rights, do you understand that?"

"Yes." She was still as death.

"You have the right to refuse to answer these questions—to say nothing at all. You also have the right to have a legal counselor with you when I ask them, if you wish. Your answers, and anything else you say, will be recorded, and may be presented against you at any later time, including in a court of law. Do you understand?"

I was afraid she was going to pass out.

"Sabrina, do you understand?"

"Yes."

"Sabrina, why do you have Kimberly's purse?"

"May I have my cigarettes, please?"

Chief handed them to her, and she lit one.

"Now, what were you saying?"

"I asked you why you have Kimberly Merrick's purse."

"What do you mean?"

Chief tilted his head back and blew a large sigh at the ceiling. He took my notebook from me and wrote in it, saying, "Smitty, this is inspector Kriegmann's home number. Go and call him for me, would you? Ask him to meet us here."

"Wait."

I paused, half out of my chair.

"I took it," she said.

I sat back down, and Chief handed me back my pen.

"Why?" he asked.

"So no one would find out about—us."

"From her purse?" Chief asked, picking it up and opening it.

"There's an address book."

"So there is," Chief said. He flipped through it. "Now, when did you take it?"

"That morning, when she was found. It was on the dresser, and when Mrs. Crick wasn't looking I . . . I picked it up and dropped it into my bag."

"What were you doing there, anyway?"

"I'd come to meet Kim. I was just getting there when Mercy started screaming."

Chief thought about this. "Where were you Thursday night?"

She took a long time to answer, and I began to wonder if we were going to go through the "call inspector Kriegmann" routine again. Finally, however, she said, "I was at a party."

"Whose?"

Answering seemed to be painful, but she did. "It was one of Gunther's," she said.

"And what time did you leave?"

"I didn't. Not 'til the next morning. I took a taxi home about eight-thirty."

"A taxi? From Nürnberg?"

"I didn't have to pay for it."

"Sabrina," Chief said, "I have the means to check that. Now, I'm going to ask you again: what time did you leave that party?"

"It was eight-thirty, give or take ten minutes."

Chief was silent for a long time, and seemed to be weighing things in his mind very carefully. Then he said, "Sabrina, I'm fairly bound, by duty, to turn this whole thing over to the German authorities."

She took a deep breath.

"But I'm not going to. Not yet. Whether I do tomorrow, or the next day—or at any time—may depend on you."

"What do you want me to do?"

"I want you to let me take you home, and I want you to stay there. Can you do that?"

"Yes."

"I'm serious. I'll be checking to make sure you do." He handed her back her purse, picked up the small red one, and got up. Outside, he had Sabrina get in the back seat and told me to sit next to her.

"Sabrina," Chief said on the way to Erlangen, "just how long did you think you could keep your, uh, 'job' a secret?"

"That's not hard," she said. "They're always in the field."

"What did you plan to do when some bright lad decided to show his platoon leader a picture of his wife?"

"That wouldn't happen."

"Why not?"

"Because Gunther doesn't sell his pictures in Germany."

"What makes you think that?"

"Because," she said, "he told us ... Kimberly told me.... "

"Sabrina," Chief said—and I think he enjoyed it—"your pretty little butt is for sale on the corner newsstand. I know it is, because I bought a picture of it there myself just yesterday."

He turned to look at her in the back seat, but she had twisted around to look outside at the passing buildings, as though she expected to see herself on a poster in some magazine shop window. Which, I realized, she might sometime.

She was silent the rest of the ride.

"Remember now," Chief warned her as he pulled up to her building, "you are either here when I call, or I'll have you arrested. Got it?"

She nodded.

"All right. Good night."

We waited until she was inside the building, then drove away.

"She's in a lot of trouble, isn't she Chief?"

"It's a self-inflicted wound," he said brutally.

"She was crying."

Chief didn't seem very impressed.

"Chief, you wouldn't really have called inspector Kriegmann, would you?" I asked him.

"I may be getting myself in trouble for not doing so. If she hadn't told us herself about being at Gunther's party, I would have done."

"I don't understand."

"It's their jurisdiction, Smitty—she was absolutely right about that. If she's our murderer, she'll be tried under German law and in a German court, and on evidence provided by German police. The investigation will no longer be ours to conduct."

"So, you don't think she did it?"

"I really don't know," he said. "But there's no way, I think, she could have known that we knew she was at that party. Since we can probably verify when she left, I'd like to do that before having her held on suspicion. She's a perverse young fool, at best, but maybe—just maybe—no worse."

Chief pulled over by a phone booth and set the brake. "She's on a bad road, though," he added, and I was struck again by how the "Sabrina" aspect of the investigation got under his skin. He got out to call the *Landsraat* and leave a message for Müller.

Back in the car, he was silent until we got onto the *autobahn*.

"So," he said then, "when are you going to tell me about that eye of yours?"

"Never," I said after a minute.

He didn't push it, and neither of us said anything for a mile or two.

"I got hit by a hooker, Chief."

When he didn't answer, I looked over at him. He was looking the other way, out the window, but I thought his shoulders were shaking.

"Her name was Heidi—"

He started making funny snorting noises, and I looked at him closely. He was suppressing laughter, and when he looked back at me he lost control of it. Completely.

"You don't understand! She took me to her room, started taking her clothes off—"

He broke into loud guffaws.

"Chief, she practically raped me—it's not funny, Chief! She decked me! She kept all the money too—"

"Whoo!" he said, and was contorted with laughter.

The car drifted, and I almost had to grab the wheel to keep us from scraping a guardrail.

"I don't know what I'm going to tell Maggie," I said, trying to preserve an injured tone, but my mouth wouldn't cooperate: I was having to suppress my own grins.

"Oh, Smitty, Smitty, Smitty," Chief wailed between hiccups. He had to take his glasses off to wipe his eyes. "I wish I could have seen it!"

"I think I'm scarred for life, Chief."

"Poor Smitty," he said chuckling. "Do you really think Maggie'll be mad at you? If you want, I could, you know, maybe say something. Tell her it was—"

"—in the line of duty?" I finished for him. "Jesus!" I said, putting my hand over my eye. Laughing made it hurt.

"Seriously," he said when we were breathing normally again.

"I think I better handle it," I said, with far more assurance than I felt. "Are we still going to Graf. in the morning?"

"Let me call you. How's your field gear?"

"I can get it together."

"All right. It'll be early."

He pulled up in front of my building, and I opened the door, sighing heavily.

"Maybe she'll be asleep," he said.

"Yeah."

13 Grafenwöhr

Woods Barracks, Nürnberg, West Germany,
Wednesday, 2 July 198-, 0845 hrs.

B y the time Chief phoned I was dressed, breakfasted, and nearly two hours bored. I don't like getting up at 5 o'clock, but in the Army it becomes a habit.

"I was beginning to wonder, Chief," I said.

" 'Bout what?" He sounded a little groggy.

"I just thought you were planning to call early."

"Ye gods, man, it's hardly nine o'clock yet! Just a minute." It sounded like he dropped the phone, and then I heard him swearing. "I want one of those newfangled air phones," he said then, "the ones with no cord. So, you ready to go? How's about going down and getting the scarab, and picking me up here?"

When I got to his building at 9:30 and buzzed him, he told me to wait for him downstairs. After about 10 minutes he came huffing down, toting a duffle bag and a brief case, and wearing camoflage fatigues.

"Chief," I said, "you're wearing BDU's!"

"Don't you laugh, or I'll punch your other eye. Here, take this."

We stowed his gear in the back seat with mine and headed off.

"I talked to Müller," he said. "It's certain that Sabrina was still

215

there at Buttenheimer's party at four in the morning. We have no
way to tell when she might've left after that."

"Then she couldn't have done it," I said.

"I don't think so."

"Did she stay home? I mean, did you call her?"

"Yeah," he said. "She came to the phone when I called at four."

"Four in the morning?" I said.

He chuckled. "Yeah. Pull over here, and I'll make sure she
stayed put."

He got out and used a pay phone. She was still at home, evidently, and we headed to the highway. Chief got a map out of his
briefcase and studied it.

"Stay on the *autobahn* when you get to Lauf," he said, "and
we'll drop down through Auerbach and enter Grafenwöhr on the
west end."

"Okay. Did you ever get ahold of Major Suarez, by the way?"

"He was with patients."

Once we were out of the city I pressed my foot down until the
gas pedal was on the floor, but the scarab topped out at about 110
kph (65 mph) and I kept well over into the right-hand lane. It was
unnerving to drive on the open *autobahn*, because different vehicles drove it at such widely varying speeds. Often, the trucks (like
in the U.S.) could barely keep the legal minimum, and eventually
I felt like I just had to pass them. I'd watch my rearview mirror
for several minutes, until there was absolutely nobody behind us,
and pull out around them as fast as I could, but then suddenly I'd
see flashing lights in my mirrors and hear the urgent beeping of a
horn, and as soon as I pulled back into the right-hand lane some
red or blue or green streak would whiz past at twice my speed.
When there are accidents one doesn't see a wreck *per se*, but just

a quarter mile or so of parts strung out along the road. Or so I've been told.

Chief still seemed to be drowsy; he was slumped in his seat with his head down and his eyes closed. I thought he had fallen asleep. In fact I think he did, but after about twenty minutes he gave a jerk, the way people do when they're sleeping lightly, and then sat suddenly upright and put his hand on the dashboard, blinking and taking a deep breath. Then he sat back and grunted to himself.

"My problem, Smitty, is that I don't have any dependents."

I didn't know what to say to this.

A few minutes later he muttered, "Three ack-emma," and got out the map again.

I wondered what was going on. "What was that about dependents, Chief?"

"Hmm? Oh. Just a minute." He continued to study the map. Finally he put it down and said, "When you get transferred, what do you have to do before you go?"

"Um, outprocess. Is that what you mean, Chief?"

"Yeah. Tell me about outprocessing."

"Well, after you get your orders they give you an outprocessing form with all the places on post on it—you know, supply, finance, the clinic, even the library. The commander has to sign it, and then you take it and about a bajillion copies of your orders to all those places, where they stamp your form and everything, and you get all your finance records and personnel records and education records and... and finally you're done. Then you're cleared to leave."

"And when you get to your new duty station—?"

"Then you do it all over again, in reverse."

"Inprocessing."

"Yeah."

"And the English language," he said ironically, "is the richer for it."

"Don't you have to do that?" I asked.

"It's been a while, Smitty. I just wanted to know if the procedure had changed. Hungry?"

We stopped and picked up some sandwiches. We ate in the car, and Chief took a turn at the wheel while I enjoyed the scenery. We were off the *autobahn* now, and traveling through open countryside. Every three or four kilometers there was a village, always a neat cluster of buildings, uniformly white or cream-colored with red, tiled roofs, with names like Plech, Höfen, Hammerschrott, and Krottensee. Between the towns the green fields dressed the gentle hills like a tailored garment, bordered with copses of pine and bramble, seamed with meandering rivulets of water, and dotted by ponds. Once in a great while I could glimpse the ruins of stone battlements on some promontory, and quite often there were roadside shrines, with a statue of the virgin or a large crucifix, cowled in mortared stones and bedecked with dry flowers.

I had always lived in the western United States, where the land is devalued by its very abundance, and to see such densely inhabited farm-country kept like a garden, without heaps of decaying equipment, tumble-down sheds, and rusted barbed wire strung carelessly about, was an education.

It was pleasant to fantasize how it might have looked, say, five hundred years ago. I could imagine horses in colorfully decorated tack on the road in place of automobiles, the farm families working the fields with scythe and hoe instead of a tractor, and the battlements occupied by knights and nobles, their banners flying in the breeze.

Suddenly we were pulling down into a sizable town on a river, and here were the tell-tale signs of a nearby military community: a McDonald's restaurant, a used car dealership, and signs with advertisements written in English. Not far beyond was a dense wood, into which we drove until stopped by a broad gate with a brightly painted guard shack. The guard shouldered his M16 rifle and lingered over our identification.

My little historical daydream underwent a transformation. There was a sound like distant thunder in the clear sky, which I knew to be the thumping of cannon-fire, and now I thought of us transported in time only forty years back, into the heartland of the great war—its cradle as well as its last bloody field—with fear and battle everywhere at hand. Perhaps it is the influence of so many movies, but there is something about a military setting that reeks of drama. Its tableau is familiar: the open trucks and jeeps with their whining engines, the coordinated yet ever hectic activity of men in fatigues, who carry weapons the way students carry books or businessmen carry briefcases, as constant companions, and above all the acrid aroma arising from its hellish end—a close commerce with death. It is strange, even incredible, that the aura of violence shining above a battlefield should be so seductive, and I thought of the remark attributed to Robert E. Lee, that it is well that war is so terrible, lest we should grow too fond of it. The romance of war might be a dark and even a shameful thing, but its allure is real.

My daydreams evaporated quickly—not without leaving a trace of dramatic tension in my mind—when Chief began talking about our plans for the afternoon. He was eager to tackle Captain Merrick's alibi, and he hoped for an opportunity to question him again.

"What about Captain Worms?" I asked.

"Yeah," Chief said, as though he'd forgotten all about him, "I guess we'd better talk to him too."

We stopped at an operations center for a map, and to learn where the 1st Battalion, 28th Armor was located. One of the largest military reservations in West Germany, Grafenwöhr was where most of the NATO units stationed there went for their gunnery practices. Fifteen kilometers long and eight wide, most of its interior was "down range" to the tank and artillery units that took up positions near its perimeter, pointing their muzzles in at computer-operated targets that popped up on motorized levers in a carefully orchestrated attack simulation. It ran virtually twenty-four hours a day, year round.

It turned out that Alpha Company was billeted nearby. On the way there, Chief asked me if I had formed any new theories of the case.

"Yes," I said. "Chief, how come we haven't asked Major Suarez yet where he was Thursday night?"

"Ah!" he said. "Why do you ask?"

"Well, I'm thinking, maybe... since he's a doctor, wouldn't he be able to kill someone in some way that we couldn't detect?"

"No doubt he could. But we've detected it—she died of alcohol poisoning."

"Chief! I thought you thought that somebody killed her, and made it *look* like alcohol poisoning."

"So I did. Until this morning."

"Hunh?"

"Ginger phoned and got the lab report for me on the sample he took the other night. Sorry, I should have told you sooner. I was talking to him on the phone when you came to pick me up."

"Well?" I said.

"Her blood alcohol was point-seven-two."

"Ginger said that's impossible."

"So it is."

"I don't get it, Chief. What does Ginger say now?"

"Claims he's quitting medical science and taking up a career in the arts," Chief said grinning.

"So what does it mean?" I tried.

Chief shrugged.

"It was Doctor Suarez did it," I said after a minute. "He injected her with rubbing alcohol."

He laughed. "That's a damn fine try, Smitty. I only wish it were that easy. Unfortunately, rubbing alcohol is a completely different kind of stuff from the kind you can drink. It would be about the same as drinking anti-freeze—exactly the same, in fact. Besides, I already had Ginger check for it."

"I still vote for Suarez," I said, determined. "Why don't you think he did it?"

"No good reason, I guess," Chief said after a thoughtful pause.

"I bet he destroyed her records—"

"Why?"

"Well," I said, "because he was hiding something."

"Such as?"

"That's what we should try to find out!" I was feeling annoyed by Chief's unusually casual attitude towards the possibility.

"Tell you what, Smitty, we'll try calling him from here, and see if he can't tell us something interesting."

We pulled into a large gravel lot next to some low buildings. There were a couple of humvees and a truck "combat parked," that is, backed in so as to be driven away in a hurry if need be, and next to one of the humvees stood a knot of soldiers. I recognized

Captain Merrick among them.

Chief pulled alongside the group, rolling his window down. "Captain Merrick, I'm glad to see you again!"

"You—! What in the blue blazes are you doing here?"

"Just my duty. I need to check on a couple things, that's all."

"I'm busy, Mister Tobias," Captain Merrick said, and calling to his driver he got into his humvee.

"Say," Chief said, "I guess you're transferring soon, huh?"

"What? No, I . . . no."

"Oh. Sorry. My mistake."

"Top," Captain Merrick said to his first sergeant, "make sure this man has anything he needs. I'll be back, uh . . . I'll be back." He signalled to his driver, and was gone.

Chief rolled up his window and backed up to park.

"That was sudden," I said. "What—"

"Got the bastard!" Chief said. "Now, if only . . . ,"

"If only what, Chief?"

He didn't answer, but seemed to be thinking hard. Then he looked at me with the same bright gaze he'd had when the case first began, in the Merrick's apartment, when we were gathering clues and he had become convinced there was something to be investigated. He clucked his tongue and smiled. "C'mon!" he said.

My emotions were mixed. I was glad to see the end of the weary frustration he'd worn the last couple of days, but I was also a little hurt that he was forgetting—was it just forgetting?—to share things with me, like the lab report.

But mostly, I wished to hell I knew what he was so excited about.

Captain Merrick's first sergeant was a bulldog of a man, short, round, and pugnacious. His name-tag read simply, "Frigg."

"So, who the hell are you?" he bellowed in that stentorian voice which puts every enlistee in mind of boot camp and makes him jump. First sergeants are often ex-drill instructors, making them effective in their role as top NCO in a company. "Oh, and head-gear ain't exactly optional."

Chief, who had forgotten his cap, went back and got it out of the car. When he put it on, his warrant officer insignia glinted in the sunlight.

The first sergeant wasn't impressed. "Oh, I'm sorry, who the hell are you, *sir*."

Chief dug out his ID and handed it over.

"Oh... er, what can I do for you?"

The letters C-I-D are like magic, universally potent.

"How's about we get out of the sun?" Chief suggested.

The first sergeant led us to one of the long, low buildings. The inside was open from end to end, but it had been divided into sections by the use of camouflage netting as partition material. He barked irritably at the few soldiers who were there as we walked in, yelling that the grounds outside were a mess, and assigning a rash of details to fix the problem. Every visible soldier found a rake or a broom and evacuated the building. He led us to an area at the back that evidently served as an orderly room, and sat on the edge of a desk.

"All right, sir," he said, digging into his breast pocket for a Marlboro, "what's up?"

"You run a crack outfit," Chief said, looking around. "I sometimes think we could use a few combat NCO's to put things in order around the MI battalions."

"Whole damn army's goin' to hell," the first sergeant said, "but I keep my corner of it dress-right. I've got some damn fine soldiers."

"How about the officers?"

The first sergeant gave a disdainful shrug. "Officers—!"

"Your CO been with you long?"

"About six months."

"Like him?"

"Best CO I ever worked with."

Chief pulled up a chair and sat down, stretching his legs. "When did the unit come up to Grafenwöhr? Two, three weeks ago?"

The first sergeant moved behind his desk and consulted a calendar. "We rail-loaded the fourteenth. Look, uh, sir—"

" 'Chief' is fine.

"—can you tell me who you're investigating?"

"Captain Merrick hasn't mentioned anything to you?"

"*Hell* no," the first sergeant said, but his temper wasn't directed at us. He lit his cigarette and extended the box to Chief.

"Well," Chief said, "it isn't you—er, do your soldiers call you 'Top?' "

"Only if they want me to step on their heads."

"Good policy. I'm not after you or any of your men, First Sergeant. I'm not *after* anybody. He, uh, he did tell you his wife died?"

"Sure—hey, Johnson! What the hell are you doing?"

"Nothing, First Sergeant," said the hapless boy who had just walked in.

"That damned parking area's dicked up. I want it raked smooth. Grab whoever's still outside and get on it. So," he continued then, "is that what this is about?"

Chief answered by not answering. Instead he got up and walked over to a window. "Captain Merrick went down on Friday, when he heard about his wife. Had he been down any time before that, since the unit came to Graf.?"

"Couple of times, for command-and-staff meetings. Battalion didn't get itself up here 'til the twentieth."

"What were the dates?"

The first sergeant had to consult his calendar for some time. "Let's see, I think it was the eighteenth, and, uh, well, the twenty-fifth."

"I thought you said battalion came up on the twentieth."

"Yeah, I guess that's right."

"Why'd he go down on the twenty-fifth?"

The first sergeant didn't answer at first. "I don't believe he said."

"POV's aren't permitted up here, isn't that right?"

"Yeah, uh, Chief Tobias—"

Chief turned around.

"—if you're thinking the CO had something to do with his wife dying, you can forget it. He was here that night."

"And you know this because . . . you share quarters?"

"No. He has his own quarters. But we didn't get off the ranges 'til after midnight, and he was here when I woke the troops at five. He took his tank down range that morning. Look, Captain Merrick's a damned fine officer. He's a little heavy handed with the troops, maybe, but he cares about his unit. Hell, he oughta be on leave what with his wife dyin', but is he? Hell no! His troops are in the field, and that's where he's gotta be. Whatever you might think, he—"

"First Sergeant," Chief broke in, "is a humvee about as fast as any vehicle the company's got up here?"

"Fast? What d'you—? Yeah, I guess so."

"I need to borrow a humvee. Just an hour or two."

The first sergeant was at a loss for words.

"Captain Merrick's orders were pretty specific. That's what I need."

Reluctantly, the first sergeant took a dispatch folder out of his desk, and handed it and a pair of keys to Chief.

"Thanks. Tell Captain Merrick that I—"

"At ease!" somebody hollered outside, and another short, round figure came into the building, looking at first like a clone of First Sergeant Frigg. It wasn't, but it was pretty close: a sergeant major.

"I'm Command Sergeant Major Kline. Is there a Chief Warrant Officer Tobias in here?"

"Yo!" Chief said.

"Colonel Crick asked me to remind you that you do not have the run of this brigade—and that includes my battalion."

"We were just on our way to see the colonel—"

"Good! I'll take you there."

"You're very kind, Sergeant Major," Chief said.

The sergeant major turned a little pink. Or maybe he was always pink; he looked like someone who lived in a perpetual state of apoplexy. In any event, "kind" was evidently not a compliment to him.

"As it happens," Chief continued, "we have a vehicle already. Perhaps you'd like to follow us there." He left abruptly, me at his heels. He grabbed his maps out of the scarab and jumped into the first sergeant's open-top humvee, and I got in next to him.

The sergeant major had apparently decided to stay and talk to his subordinate. His mistake.

"Shit," Chief said, looking at the controls. "Smitty, I don't suppose you—?"

We climbed past each other.

"Hurry," he said.

I started the engine and popped it into gear. As we pulled out onto the road, the sergeant major came running out of the building and waved his arms at us to stop.

"Step on it," Chief said through his teeth, grinning and waving back. "That'll teach 'em to park these things backwards! Makes 'em too easy to steal."

"Chief," I said, "if you go down, do I go down with you?"

"Smitty! Where's your sense of adventure? Isn't this what you enlisted for?"

"That stuff's just for the TV commercials, Chief."

"Balderdash! Turn here." He consulted his map. "Okay, up ahead turn left."

In a few minutes, we were at a gate. The guard waved us past.

"There's a town up ahead," he said, "and past that a nice straight stretch of road. Let's stop and pick up a snack on the way through."

There was an *imbiss* in the town, and Chief bought us a couple of sausages and some fries, and two bottles of beer. He put them in the back seat and we headed for the open road.

"Okay," Chief said when we got to open country, "let's see what this baby can do. Put'cher pedal to the metal."

We accelerated.   The humvee (which is a phonetic of

HMMWV—High Mobility, Multi-purpose, Wheeled Vehicle) was the Army's replacement for the time-honored jeep. It was as big as a full-size pickup, but with an over-designed transmission and suspension intended to make it the premier cross-country vehicle. It definitely wasn't designed for racing, and the speedometer hovered just above 80 kilometers per hour (about 50 miles per hour) and refused to go any higher—and at that speed it vibrated like a clothes washer on the spin cycle.

"All right," Chief yelled over the wheel and engine noise, and I backed off the accelerator. "Find a place to pull over."

There was a roadside shrine under a clump of trees just ahead, and we stopped next to it, sharing its shade. Chief pried the caps off our beer bottles on the seam of his door, and handed me a sausage on a bun. Then he spread his highway map out on his knees, muttering and dripping mustard on it.

"What's up Chief?"

He didn't answer; he was tracing the *autobahn* with his finger and talking to himself. "Nine, twenty-two, forty-four kilometers to Pegnitz, then seventy-nine, eighty-seven—and forty-two makes one hundred and twenty-nine, plus say five for getting into town and maybe eight getting out of Grafenwöhr. Call it a hundred and forty. Now, if you go the other way—" Again he counted off numbers. "Hmm, only about a hundred and thirty, but less than half of it is *autobahn*."

"What's up Chief?" I repeated.

"How long would it take you to drive this humvee to Erlangen if you went as fast as possible?"

"Two hours, at least."

"Yeah." He stared at the map again, then flung it on the floor in frustration. "It won't work. It couldn't cover the miles there and back, and still leave time to murder her and rig the scene."

"So much for Captain Merrick," I said.

"Oh, you think so, do you?"

"Don't you?"

He sighed, and folded the map up.

On the way back, I asked what he would tell Colonel Crick.

"What do you mean?"

"Well," I said, "you did tell that sergeant major we were headed to see him."

"Quite so. I've been keeping a sharp eye out, too. Have you seen him?"

"Chief! I can't believe you'd disobey a direct order."

"Which order would that be?"

"Well, didn't he say . . . no, I guess he didn't actually say the colonel *said* for you to go and see him."

"A sharp eye for detail, Smitty—that's what it takes to stay ahead of the opposition. Still," he said, "I guess we'd better go pay a visit. I wouldn't know what to tell Maggie if you ended up in the stockade."

I did my best to laugh without sounding nervous.

The brigade was headquartered in another section of Grafenwöhr, and by the time we got there the afternoon was wearing on. Chief made me combat park ("Good practice, Smitty—you need to learn this war stuff!") with the result that I dented the first sergeant's rear bumper against a concrete pole.

"He'll never notice."

"Sure Chief. I'm gonna say you were driving."

Inside, Chief walked up to the nearest desk and asked to use a phone.

"Are you in this brigade, sir?" the sergeant at the desk asked.

"I'm in this division. Doesn't that count for the same thing, sergeant?"

"Uh, I guess so." Chief had a way of responding to officiousness that always made his victim feel flustered. The sergeant handed him the phone, but as Chief was reaching for the receiver he picked up a pen. "Social security number?"

"I beg your pardon?"

"I need it for the log, sir. It's field SOP."

"Sergeant, you ever hear of the Privacy Act?"

"Sir?"

"Never mind. Uh, one-five-nine, nine-five-one, oh-six-six-six."

"Uh, that's too many numbers, sir."

"You callin' me a liar, sergeant?"

"No sir, but—"

"I'm from Utah. Just write it down, son. Why doesn't this damned thing work?"

"You have to dial nine first."

"Got it. Hello? Is this the clinic? Major Suarez, please. Well where—? Oh. You the nurse? Oh, okay... maybe you can help. You got two ways of telling when records have been checked out, don't you? Medical records. I mean, one for temporary, and one for permanent, right? That's right, when a soldier is outprocessing... permanent change of station, right. Okay, now listen carefully. I want you to write down a message for the major. Ready? My name is Chief Tobias. Tell him to look there, and if he finds it to call me back with the date. The date, that's right. This is urgent now; tell him to leave a message for me at brigade headquarters in Grafenwöhr. You got that? Yeah, that's right. In Graf. If I'm not here tell him to leave it with, uh—" He looked at the sergeant's name tag. "—with Sergeant Greenberg. ASAP, you got that? Oh, and what's your name?"

While Chief was talking a group of officers walked past, one of them a tall, lanky, balding man with captain's bars on his collar and "Worms" on his name-tag. The group went out the way we had come in, apparently headed to the parking area.

"Chief!" I said when he hung up, and nodded towards the men who had gone outside. "Captain Worms."

"That's luck—" he began.

"Sir," Sergeant Greenberg said, "about this social security number—did you say three sixes, or—"

"Just leave one of the numbers out if there's too many," Chief snapped impatiently, and headed for the door.

"Chief Tobias!" boomed a familiar voice. It was the sergeant major. "The colonel has been waiting for you."

"Oh, hello Sergeant Major—"

"He understood that you were coming directly. What's kept you?"

"Wrong turn. Awfully sorry. Smitty here can't read a map to save his life. Uh, Sergeant Greenberg, make sure I get that message when it comes in, alright? Now, Sergeant Major, I sure don't want to keep the colonel waiting. Is that his office?"

"The colonel's not in. He's got better things to do than wait for you."

"Ah. Of course. Well, we'll be happy to come back. When do you suppose—"

"You can wait. Sergeant Greenberg, call Top Frigg and tell him to come get his vehicle." The sergeant major turned on his heel and disappeared the way he had come, slamming the door behind him.

Sergeant Greenberg picked up the phone and dialed, but at the last moment Chief walked over and put his finger on the disconnect.

"No need for that, Sergeant. We borrowed it, we'll return it." He headed for the door. "Don't forget about that message, now!"

We didn't quite run to the parking lot—more of a dignified trot.

"Good thing you combat parked, Smitty."

"Which way?" I said, spinning gravel onto the grass as we careened out the driveway.

"Hell, I don't know. Which way did Worms go?"

"I didn't notice."

"Smitty! Well, go that way, then."

"Chief," I said after a minute, "do sergeant majors really run the Army?"

" 'Sergeants major,' you mean—and you bet they do. Just ask one."

14 Gunnery

Grafenwöhr, West Germany,
Wednesday, 2 July 198-, 1600 hrs.

Chief was torn in three directions. He wanted to return First Sergeant Frigg's humvee before an armed posse was dispatched to run us down, but he also wanted to follow Captain Worms, and for some reason he wanted to go to the post clinic before it closed for the day.

In the end discretion won out, and we returned to Alpha's billets. The ride was uneventful aside from a wrong turn that took us onto a bad stretch of road, full of ponds and potholes that were difficult to miss among the shadows of the trees. Also, we seemed to be near a gunnery range, and the massive retorts of the cannons added to the unnerving effect of the bumpy ride.

"Try turning here," Chief said, holding his map first this way, then that.

We were dead-ended by a thick stand of trees.

"Maybe we should just turn back," I offered.

"Nope, I see the way. Here, turn right. No, wait a minute— that'll put us down-range. Straight ahead, and *then* right."

"Chief—"

"Trust me. We're almost back to the main road. Look out!"

Splash.

"I think we scraped bottom that time," he said when he had stopped bouncing. "I hope these things are as sturdy as they look. Top Frigg'll have something to say about all this mud, I'll bet."

"Is it all right if I just wait in the scarab when we get there?"

"It is *not.*"

When we found ourselves and got to Alpha Company, Captain Merrick's humvee was in the parking area, and a young soldier was wiping it down with a rag. I pulled in next to the scarab and looked nervously toward the billets, but no one seemed to be watching for us. When we got out Chief stopped and stared at the buildings also, but his look was more thoughtful than nervous.

"Hey, soldier!" he called to the man by the other humvee, and waved him over.

"Sir?"

"Is your first sergeant here?"

"Yes, sir."

"What about your commander?"

"Yes, sir."

"You his driver?"

"Yes, sir."

"Hmm. Your CO's been back to post a couple times, I'm told. Did you drive him down both times?"

"Yes, sir."

"And brought him back?"

It seemed to occur to the young man to wonder who this imperious stranger with all the questions was. Also, perhaps, he was stymied by the need to answer with more than two syllables.

"Are you that investigator, sir? Captain Merrick said if you asked me anything, I was to tell you—"

"I'm an officer with Criminal Investigation Division, son,"

Chief cut in, showing the soldier his badge, "and you'll answer my questions. That's an order. Did you bring Captain Merrick back from Erlangen both times you took him down?"

"No, the second time he sent me back early, and came up with the mail. Sir."

"With the mail...?"

"Yes sir, in S-1's humvee."

"Oh. How do you know that?"

"That's what he said he was gonna do."

"Of course. Sorry. Dumb question. I want you to do me a favor, son. Take this dispatch in to the first sergeant, and tell him thanks from me."

"Er, yes sir."

"Oh, and by the way, what did Captain Merrick say for you to tell me?"

"That you was to talk to him, sir."

"Well, rest easy son. I will."

We wasted no time getting back on the road. Charlie Company was nearby, and Chief decided to stop there next in hope of finding Captain Worms. When we got there, however, the billets were all but deserted, and the few soldiers who were there claimed not to have seen their CO since earlier in the day. It turned out that two of their three platoons were slated for night gunnery exercises, and we were assured that Captain Worms would be found on the range by dusk if not before.

We were leaving when the phone rang. It was for Chief.

"Hello? Yes, Sergeant. Yes, I'll wait." Chief looked at me and raised his brows in a gesture of resignation. Evidently, we'd been caught up with. "Yes, sir! I'm glad to have gotten ahold of *you*, sir. We were just headed—sir? Yes, sir." He hung the phone up delicately.

"I take it," I said when we were outside, "that you just received a direct order of some kind."

"Of a most emphatic kind," he said. "Shocking language for a field-grade officer. And no, you may not wait in the car when we get there."

"Chief," I said, as we approached brigade, "you seem to have a theory of the case."

He looked at me and smiled. "Theory number seventeen-dash-b. It's not time for champagne yet, Smitty."

"No, but still . . . I can tell that you're on to something."

"I think so. I think I understand quite a bit, now. But there are still some major problems, and I could be completely wrong. I'm not, of course, but I could be. I think, if you won't feel terribly put out, I'd like to keep my thoughts to myself a little longer. I want to see how this plays out, and check some things."

"Okay," I said, trying my hardest not to sound put out.

Getting out of the car he mumbled, "Besides, I'm nowhere if I haven't the vaguest idea *how*. There's the rub. Well, that and this confounded colonel. He's terrified his sweet vision of a brigadier's star is going to be irretrievably tarnished when I discover dirt under the rug." He stood staring at the field headquarters building with his hands on his hips. "I wish I was on the promotions board. I'd retire his battle-dress, dress-right butt for him. But then," he added, "he's probably gonna try to retire mine right here. You want to wait in the car, after all?"

I didn't answer, but strode to the door and held it open for him.

"That's the spirit! Onward—to fight! Our nostrils flare at the welcome stench of battle! Mayhem and blood—oh, hello sir."

Colonel Crick was waiting for us, the sergeant major at his side. "In my office, Chief Tobias. Your driver can wait here."

Bummer, I thought, watching their backs, but I was cheered by Chief's posture; he was almost insolently jaunty as he followed the other two men to the colonel's office. He stopped at Sergeant Greenberg's desk and, after scanning it, grabbed up a sheet of notepaper and whistled a short, triumphant melody.

"*Chief* Tobias!" the colonel called.

Chief winked at me, and was gone.

That half-hour was one of the longest on record. The sergeant major came out after five minutes and headed in my direction. I stood and came to parade rest, but he continued by me—not without leaving his enraged glare hot on my cheek—and went outside, slamming the door behind him.

"Hey, what'd you guys do?" one of the clerks laughed, "steal the T-rations?"

"I wish somebody would," another said.

For a few minutes I joined in the common recreation of condemning Army food. T-rations—standard field rations packaged in large baking tins and theoretically distributed hot to the troops—are pretty sadistic. Even MRE's (Meals, Ready to Eat), the combat rations, are preferable.

Before long, though, I was sitting, silently, studying the second hand on the wall clock. It wasn't very interesting.

Chief emerged at last. He looked happy, and gestured for me to follow him as he went outside.

"Well?" I said when we were in the car.

"We got two choices," he said, starting the engine, "we can beg a cot with one of the companies and share their delightful dinner—

and their even more delightful breakfast—or we can go in search of civilization among the surrounding towns."

"That's not what I meant, Chief—"

"Priorities, Smitty! Everything in life is priorities. If you like, we can swing by Alpha Company and I can drop you off...."

"No thanks! Uh, you buying?"

He grinned and headed for the gate.

"So, are we busted, or what?"

"He smelled my blood from afar, and hungered after it. I was the stag, and he the pack of slavering hounds!"

I sat back and waited patiently.

"Insubordination! Unauthorized snooping! Grand theft auto! That is, if such a thing could apply to a humvee—it's hardly very grand. He thought he was going to make a meal of me, Smitty. For about three minutes, it was almost entertaining."

"Chief, are you afraid of death?"

"One question at a time, please. I apologized most abjectly, of course, and declared that I would depart his garden at once, deposit the whole affair with 1st Armored Division headquarters in Ansbach, and let them deal with 2nd Brigade's little murder problem, together with its attendant scandals of prostitution, drug use, pornography, falsification of records—I had my hand on the doorknob at that point—"

"This is beautiful! What did he do?"

"He excused his sergeant major, somewhat hoarsely I thought, and invited me to sit down."

"Did you tell him everything?"

"Nope. For twenty minutes or so, I told him approximately nothing. Pissed him off."

"So, now what?"

"I had to promise to brief him fully on Friday, before I give my report to Lieutenant Colonel Bragg. That gives us one more full day. In return, he is going to put the word out that we are to be given every courtesy—no matter where we choose to poke our inquisitive noses."

"You'd make a good poker player, Chief."

"Well, with Colonel Crick I held all the cards. Nothing scares an ambitious officer like the prospect of being investigated by a higher command. That can quickly turn into a career-ender. Anyway, he'll be back in Erlangen Friday morning, and so will we."

"With the solution?"

He took a deep breath. "Damn, Smitty, I wish I knew."

We found an inn and rented a room. Chief had wisely decided to search one of the smaller towns, one without any apparent commercial interest in Americans, and we thus got beds and a very satisfying dinner for remarkably little money. The owner had looked on us with a jaundiced eye at first, but after talking in German with Chief for a few minutes he seemed to forget our BDU's and treated us nobly. The only down-side to this was that I didn't get an opportunity to try and wheedle more of his theory out of Chief, because the owner—a secret America-phile, like many Germans—never left us alone, but chatted with Chief all through dinner. I could tell they were talking about the States, and at one point about me. At least, the owner gave me a toothy grin and smacked me several times on the back, laughing gregariously.

He served us beer, which was a mistake for me. After my adventure the night before, only five hours of sleep, and all the long day topped off by a large country meal, I was a helpless prey to sleep. No sooner had I finished eating than I snoozed where I sat.

Chief had some difficulty rousing me when it was time to go, and I was startled to see—once I was awake—that it was completely dark outside. I'd evidently slept for over an hour. He drove us back onto post while I slowly reasserted my awareness of the external world. This became easier when the thumping of tank cannon grew close, and red flashes lit the horizon. We were going to the gunnery range.

"What are we going to do here, Chief?"

"May as well see the fireworks," he said. "This is Charlie Company," he added.

"Captain Worms."

"Mmm."

Soon we were bumping down a muddy and heavily rutted drive. We were brought up short by a line of tanks pulled up on either side of a large concrete platform, where men in t-shirts were shouldering enormous rounds and handing them across to the tank crews, then breaking more out of wooden crates. The tank crews pulled them one at a time down into their hatches, stowed them somewhere inside the turret, and then reached for the next one. It looked laborious, the more so that the men handled the rounds very gingerly, almost as if they were passing around newborn babies. An officer stood in their midst marking on a clipboard, no doubt accounting for each piece of ordnance.

One of the soldiers detached himself and came down to the car. "You might want to back off," he warned, pointing to the tank in front of us, "the exhaust will peel your paint and crack your windshield when he revs up to move."

Chief told him we were looking for the range shack, and at the soldier's direction backed up and turned into a small driveway that wound up through the trees, ending finally in a small parking area at the base of a tower. We got out and walked to the lip of the hill. Below us stretched a long, narrow valley, several hundred yards wide and running a half-mile or more between the tower and a series of high, flat berms. At the near end, just below the tower, a line of tanks were parked side by side. In the valley beyond we could just make out two more tanks leaving dust trails as they careened toward the far end. Suddenly they stopped, and a few seconds later one of them fired. An immense blossom of fire erupted at its muzzle, and a flat orange streak betrayed the path of the round as it flew to its target. The tank's silhouette was swallowed up by the darkness well before the sound reached us, a boom so enormous that one felt it physically, like a slap. A few seconds later it fired again. The pungent smell of cordite was on the wind.

"Well, Smitty?" Chief said.

"It's amazing."

"Yeah. Let's see who's at home."

We climbed the stairs that led up in a square spiral around the outside of the tower. At the top was a large room, about fifteen feet on a side, the top half of which was mostly window, like an airport control tower. A bank of radios and electronic controls on a console, manned by two NCO's, overlooked the range, and the only illumination was from the dull red glow of the console lights. There were two other men in the room, and when they turned to see who had come in I recognized the silver oak-leaf insignia of a lieutenant colonel.

"You must be Colonel Serway," Chief said. "I'm Chief Tobias."

"Ah," the battalion commander said neutrally. "My CO said I

might run into you."

"I've no wish to be in the way, sir. I was hoping to see Captain Worms, actually."

"You just missed him. He's about to go down range. You're welcome to watch."

"Thank you, sir, we will. This is quite a show."

The colonel didn't answer, but turned back to watch the range. The tanks who had just fired were coming off, and he grabbed a radio to congratulate them. Next there was some obscure radio traffic that I gathered had to do with getting Captain Worms's and his wing-man's tanks on the right frequency, and when the previous tanks were off the range these two moved down into position.

"Ready when you are, tower," the radio crackled.

"Roger, Charlie-six. A reinforced mechanized rifle regiment has been reported in your sector. You are to conduct movement to contact, and engage, over."

"Roger, over."

"Move when ready, out."

The two tanks lumbered forward, their gun tubes slowly scanning back and forth across the range. The tanks' radios were kept in the transmitting position, it seemed, for we could hear their crew chatter.

"Load sabot … steady Johnson … keep it about 12 k-p-h … watch our wing-man … "

One of the NCO's flipped a switch on the console, simultaneously starting a stopwatch. On top of one of the berms, a silhouette appeared.

"Gunner! Sabot! Tank! … sabot loaded!"

The NCO hastily started a second stopwatch.

"… target! … FIRE! … HIT!"

"Not bad," Colonel Serway said.

"Eight seconds, sir," one of the NCO's said.

"What's 'say-boh?' " I whispered to Chief, who shrugged his shoulders.

The tanks had never stopped moving, and in a few moments the NCO flipped two console switches.

"Gunner!   Sabot!   One tank, one BMP! Left target first! . . . sabot loaded! . . . target! . . . FIRE! . . . short-line! Reload sabot! . . . loaded! . . . target! . . . FIRE! . . . HIT! Load HEAT! . . . loaded! . . . target! . . . FIRE! . . . HIT!"

"Looks like he picked it up in time, sir. Eighteen seconds on the second target."

"Good. That's a damn-fine loader."

"What's 'heat?' " I whispered.

Chief shrugged again.

"And how can they see the targets in the dark?"

The colonel overheard me. "Here," he said, "look through these." He handed me a heavy contraption made to fit over the head and down over the face.

I put it up to my eyes, and gasped. The range was transformed. It seemed to be bathed with a cold, green light, and I could see every detail: the roads, the grass and shrubs, and especially the tanks and the targets, which glowed brightly. I held my hand in front of my face, and it glowed too.

"Infrared," the colonel explained. "The targets are hot, just like the tanks."

I handed the gadget to Chief.

"The wonder of it all," he said, looking through.

The exercise continued for about fifteen minutes. Sometimes the tanks took up defensive positions behind prepared berms and fired stationary, and once they had to respond to a simulated chemi-cal attack, stopping to put on gas-masks and turn on their vehicle's filtration system. Of forty targets, they missed only two. Often they were firing not only their main gun but three mounted ma-chine guns as well, and the shower of tracers made a horrendous display.

When they were done, Colonel Serway was jubilant. "Thirty-eight! Second highest in the battalion, isn't it sergeant?"

"Yes, sir. Right behind Alpha-six. And even better times to target, I think."

"Beautiful. You doing the range briefing? Tell Captain Worms I said 'good job.'"

"I will sir," the NCO said, gathering up his record sheets and putting cassette tapes of the radio transmissions into his pockets.

Chief and I went down ahead of him, and walked to the tank line as Captain Worms's tank was pulling into position at the near end alongside the others. When it was parked and we approached, I was struck anew by the immensity of it.

"Captain Worms?" Chief called, yelling over the engine noise.

The captain, standing half out of the turret, turned and saw us, but he was apparently still engaged with whatever strange proce-dures are involved in securing a tank. Underlit by blue light from the hatch, he was talking to his crew on his headset, fiddling with equipment, and stacking a notebook and other paraphernalia on the turret beside him. At last he climbed out, jumped from the tur-ret to the hull, thence to the ground, and walked obliquely past us looking the other way.

"Captain Worms," Chief repeated.

The captain stopped. "I've got a briefing to get to," he said, eyeing Chief.

"Of course, sir. I've just got a couple of questions, about Kimberly Merrick."

"I know what it's about," the other man said evenly. "Not now."

"This briefing," Chief said, "er, half-hour?"

"And then I've got to wing-man for my XO. Tonight is out. Come see me in the morn—"

The three of us flinched violently at the sudden explosion of gunfire that pounded the air directly above our heads. It only lasted for a second, and was followed by the heart-rending sound of a man screeching at the top of his lungs. We turned in time to see a soldier stumble off the front slope of Captain Worms's tank, clutching at his leg and screaming in a way I had never heard before—and hope I never may again. Somehow, for some reason, the machine gun on top of the turret had fired and hit one of Captain Worms's men. Chief and I alike were stunned into inaction, but Captain Worms leapt to the fallen man.

"Cease fire! Cease fire! Cease fire!" boomed and echoed from loudspeakers and radios. "Clear all weapons! Cease fire!"

Chief found his legs and rushed over to the front of the tank behind the captain.

"Medic!" Captain Worms screamed, and then, "My first aid kit—it's in the bustle rack. Get it down here!"

Chief leapt agilely onto the tank and yelled at the soldier who was standing half out of the hatch behind the gun that had fired, "Where's the bustle rack?"

The soldier, however, seemed unable to answer, and Chief, after a brief glance in the hatches, went to the back of the turret and found what he was looking for, a large ammunition can with a black cross painted on it.

"Here, Smitty!" he yelled, handing it down to me.

I rushed it to where Captain Worms was crouching over the still screaming soldier. The wounded man was writhing on the ground, and I was stunned to see an immense arc of blood spurt from under the captain's hand where he was pressing it to the soldier's thigh. The blood struck him in the face, but he seemed not to notice. He was trying to calm the man down, and as soon as I arrived with the box he yelled at me to open it and dump it out on the ground, which I did. A mound of bandages and splints tumbled out, followed by clear plastic saline bags and IV kits.

"Can you run an IV?" Captain Worms yelled.

I shook my head.

"Then put your hand here, and press hard."

I looked at the gushing wound, and wanted to comply, but my body seemed disconnected from my mind, somehow.

"Here, Smitty, get up," said Chief behind me, and pulled me up by the arm. He knelt in the spreading puddle next to Captain Worms, grabbed one of the bandages, and took over pressurizing the soldier's thigh. "Go and make sure they're getting the medics," he commanded.

I turned to face a ring of soldiers who had gathered around the tank.

"Where're the medics?" I croaked as loudly as I could.

One of the men pointed back up toward the main drive, and I shouldered my way out through the crowd just as Colonel Serway and several others were shouldering their way in. I ran awkwardly up the road, stumbling and slipping in the mud. I felt I had been running a long time, but I had not yet reached the ammunition platform when an ambulance came roaring towards me, its siren wailing and blue light flashing. In getting out of the way I lost my footing and came down on my face with a mucky splash, and in my panic I somehow found the leisure to wonder if, in the confusion, my squashed body would be noticed lying in the mud. The ambulance driver saw me, however, and careened to a stop. I crawled out of the way, sick and ashamed.

Of course, as I learned later, the battalion had its own medics, who were running up through the crowd of spectators at practically the same instant I was racing away.

At that moment, however, I felt a failure, a disgusting failure, and I huddled by the side of the road with black thoughts, shivering uncontrollably. The spell lasted a few minutes, and then I rose miserably to my feet and headed back towards the range. When I got there the ambulance was pulling away, and in the stroboscopic blue glow I noticed Chief off to one side supporting himself with one arm against the hull of another tank. I thought at first that he was retching, or about to.

"Chief?" I called, approaching him.

He didn't answer, but stood up and motioned me over. Taking a deep breath, he put his hand on my shoulder and looked at me kindly.

"You did a damned fine job, Smitty. I'm proud of you."

"Are you all right, Chief?" He looked drawn, even pale.

"Yes. I'm fine," he said, glancing towards the scene of the accident. "Natural horrors I can handle."

We stood silently side by side, looking at nothing much in particular. I noticed that he held an empty saline bag in his hand.

"This one broke," he explained distantly. "Lucky he had two." He folded it up carefully and put it in his pocket.

"The soldier," I said. "Is he—?"

"He's gonna be okay, Smitty," he reassured me. "It hit a big vessel, but we controlled the bleeding, and there were no other serious injuries. A man can lose a shocking amount of blood, but still make it if he gets fluid quickly enough."

We walked back over to the scene. The spectators were gone, but the colonel and Captain Worms and several others were huddled by the tank, discussing what had happened. Captain Worms looked up at Chief's approach.

"I owe you... that is, I'm grateful for your help, Mister Tobias," he said.

"You're a quick hand with those IV's, Captain," Chief said. "Probably saved that man's life. Where'd you learn to do that?"

Captain Worms made a gesture of fatigue—or was it wariness? "The brigade surgeon gives a class," he said. "All the commanders got certified."

"Colonel," Chief said then, "the range authorities have jurisdiction here—"

Captain Worms shifted uncomfortably.

"—but it might help you later, since Smitty and I are here, if we took down some information on this accident and wrote up a report for you. I have friends in the local office, and they'll trust any evidence I provide."

The colonel hesitated, glancing at his unhappy subordinate, and nodded. "Yes," he said, "I guess you'd better."

For the next several hours, while I took notes, we learned more than we ever wanted to know about range procedures, the proper clearing of weapons when the tanks come off the field, and, incidentally, the politics of duty-related injuries. The accident was clearly the immediate fault of the loader, who responded to his personal disaster by becoming catatonic. He had failed to clear his weapon, and had evidently depressed the trigger by leaning against it when he was getting out of the tank. The wounded man, too, had broken the rules by standing on the hull in front of the weapons. Nevertheless, it was Captain Worms's head that was going to roll, whatever the results of the investigation. He was the senior crew-member as well as the CO, and hence doubly responsible. The crew, flushed with their success on the firing range, had simply failed to follow proper procedure in coming off, and their driver had paid with a grievous—but luckily not a disabling—gunshot wound.

There was, after all, a point to military discipline.

The sky was pale in the east when Chief and I got back to the *gasthaus* and collapsed on our beds.

15   Bringing the Battle Home

Grafenwöhr, West Germany,
Thursday, 3 July 198-, 0830 hrs.

"Wake up, soldier—on your feet!"

I jumped up, momentarily imagining myself back in basic training and about to fall victim to an irate drill-instructor. Then I recognized the room of our *gasthaus* and sank back onto the bed.

"You shouldn't do that, Chief. What time is it?"

"*Um halb neun.* We need to get a move on." He was lacing his boots. "Come on, my friend. We'll grab a pastry on the way."

"Do I have time to brush my teeth?"

"Some of them, maybe."

I put on clean fatigues and loaded our stuff in the car while Chief settled the bill. He drove us back to post while I munched a sweet roll and tried to rub the sleep from my eyes, and wished for coffee. About a gallon of it. Black.

Our first stop was 1st-28th's medical platoon, which set up an aid station for its battalion while the unit was in the field. The platoon was run jointly by a medically trained warrant officer and a (non-medically trained) lieutenant, and its mission in peace-time (aside from training for war-time) was to screen its soldiers who needed medical attention and provide quick first aid when the need arose.

Chief and I found the warrant officer, a round-faced man with a high voice and well-scrubbed appearance, and inquired after the driver of Captain Worms's tank.

"We evacuated him to Nürnberg. After a few weeks' medical leave he'll be back with us. He was lucky—if you want to call it that—ha, ha! We had a man a couple years ago who had to be sent home without a knee."

Chief said he thought the training must be very dangerous.

"Not half so dangerous as when they're *not* in training. I've known a lot of men who got themselves killed, and every one was either a car accident or alcohol related. Choke on their puke, mostly. They're safer on duty than off, by a long shot."

"I have long been of the opinion," Chief said, "that young men should come with a warning label. Er, by the way, what happens if someone needs treatment in the field for—well, for anything, say—and needs to see a doctor?"

"We send them to the clinic here. The Grafenwöhr cadre have a nice setup."

"Have you had to refer anyone to the clinic during this exercise?"

"Oh, sure! This battalion has five hundred men, you know."

"Any officers?"

The warrant officer seemed to hear an internal alarm go off. "Why do you ask?" he said after a pause.

"I'm with CID," Chief said, offering the man his badge, "and I have my reasons. Whom did you refer?"

The warrant officer sat down behind his desk and clasped his hands nervously. "I don't think I should answer that without talking to the colonel," he said finally.

"You do that," Chief said. "I'll be back."

Outside, Chief rocked up and back on the balls of his feet and scanned the nearby buildings. For a man who'd had only four hours of shut-eye he seemed awfully perky, but then, I was on my second day with too little sleep.

"Hey, soldier!" Chief called to a man passing nearby, "where's battalion maintenance?"

"Down here, sir," the man said, pointing along the road, "on the right. About five hundred meters."

"C'mon, Smitty. The walk'll get our circulation going."

We headed down the gravel street, the hot sun warming our shoulders. In a few minutes we felt the ground vibrating, and soon we were regretting the decision to walk; a line of tanks came into view and soon was passing us by in the opposite direction, raising a thick cloud of dry dust that stung our eyes and made us cough.

"Sons a'bitches," Chief said, slapping the dirt from his sleeves when the last one had gone by. "Well, we need to find out where they're going when we're done here."

"Chief?"

"That was Alpha company. Don't you know how to read bumper numbers?"

"They'll be going to the rail-head, Chief. Remember? They're due back in Erlangen tomorrow."

"That's right. Hmm."

The battalion maintenance platoon occupied a cavernous, hangar-like building set up like an out-sized garage. A huge winch, suspended from a track on the ceiling that ran the length of the building, was being used to hoist an engine—itself roughly the size of a Volkswagon—out of the back of an M1.

"Let's just wander around and be nosy," Chief said mischievously.

There were a half dozen tanks in the maintenance bays. Several had their engines removed, and on others components were being lifted in and out of the turrets. We stopped in front of one that had its track broken, and watched the men work. One of them was lifting globs of brown grease out of a five-gallon tin with his hands and stuffing them into a grease gun.

"Ick," Chief said.

Other soldiers were removing cracked and broken segments of the track with large ratchets and attaching new ones.

"How much do those weigh?" I asked one of them.

"Try it," he said.

I reached down and lifted one, and estimated it at about fifty pounds. I wondered if tankers were prone to back injuries. I turned to mention it to Chief, but he had wandered off, and I eventually found him at the far end talking to a staff sergeant.

"Smitty!" he said as I approached. "Look at this!" He handed me a small green tin marked "Grease, cannon, M1A1," and I looked inside.

"Chief...!" I breathed, looking up at him open-mouthed. His eyes glinted. The grease in the can was scarlet.

He walked fast back up the road, me struggling to keep up as I worked out the implications of this find.

"Okay," I said, "I get it now. It had to be ... had to be...."

"Yes—?"

"Captain Worms!"

"Careful, Smitty. Remember how sure you were about Buttenheimer."

"Yeah, all right. But look—it had to be! The red grease

clinches it. He was in Erlangen that night, and he was checking on his tanks—we have Mrs. Worms's testimony on that—so he must've had the grease on his hands or something and wiped it off on that paper towel in her apartment! We just have to check if they were doing maintenance that night." It was all falling into place for me. "He wrote that letter, and when she didn't show up at the rendezvous he went back home—but then he saw her going into her apartment probably, or maybe he saw the lights on, and he knocked and went in. Mrs. Worms wouldn't necessarily have seen him, or she might be lying to protect him. Anyway, he confronts Kimberly, and finds out he's been a fool. He goes into a rage, and kills her."

"How?" Chief said calmly.

"I don't know, but I bet we can find out now. He might even confess. Or maybe—" I stopped and tried hard to create a picture in my mind of what he might have done. "—or maybe she just died, Chief," I said, remembering that there had been no sign of a fight. "Maybe she just passed out and stopped breathing. Then he gets scared, stages everything, and runs upstairs to his wife, pretending he just got home."

We were back at the scarab, and Chief put his hand on my shoulder.

"You might make a detective," he said. "Wait here. Start the car."

He hurried into the headquarters building, and emerged a minute later.

"Wash rack," he said, getting in. "Left, and then right."

Chief directed us to a place where Alpha Company's tanks were pulled up around an artificial pond encased in concrete. There was a pumping station, and the crews were washing down their tanks with big hoses.

"There's the CO," Chief said. "Pull alongside." He rolled his window down. "Captain Merrick! Heading home?"

"What do you want?" the captain said sharply.

"Just wanted to ask you a favor. I've gotta send Smitty back early, and I thought you might let me ride down with you later."

"We don't stop in Nürnberg, Mister Tobias."

"That's fine. You can drop me anywhere—thanks!" Chief said, rolling up his window, and gestured at me to drive off before Captain Merrick could reply.

"You're going back with him?" I said, incredulous.

"Good heavens, no. Actually, I'm going back with the mail truck. It seems a shame to pick on him—but dammit, he shouldn't have pissed me off. Turn here."

"You mean I *am* going back early?"

"Smitty, you're dead tired—"

"I'm fine Chief—"

"—but I need you to do some things for me. I want you to go back to battalion and get all our evidence and lab reports together, especially the physical and medical evidence, and all the witness statements. Can you do that for me?"

I nodded.

"When you've got everything together, put the scarab away and go home. Try to sleep. I'm going to need you alert and ready when I get back, okay?"

"All right, Chief. But what—"

"Turn here. I want you to drop me at the clinic. Okay, now left."

We pulled into a parking area and stopped.

"Now, Smitty, for God's sake drive carefully. Stop first and drink some coffee. If you fall asleep on the road and kill yourself, I'll fire you."

"Okay, Chief. What are you—"

"No time," he said. "Trust me. Get everything together, then get some sleep and wait for my call. I'm counting on you. You gonna be okay?"

I took a deep breath and nodded.

"Good man," he said, and was gone.

Before I was in the Army I had thought it fun and rather worldly to stay up all night, reading or talking with friends, and enjoying the warm, lethargic wakefulness that envelops the mind in the small hours. Then I enlisted, and found out what it is really like to be deprived of rest. The Army prides itself on its ability to conduct operations 24 hours a day, but what that means for the soldier—especially during field exercises—is anything from three to five days functioning on only a handful of three and four-hour naps. Under those conditions a completely different kind of consciousness is experienced; a grim, uncomfortable state of mind under which time distorts and the simplest tasks take on an absurd level of difficulty. One's awareness thins and narrows, until only the present and immediate can safely occupy the attention.

My drive back to Nürnberg was thus a mere registering of miles, my eyes fixed on the road and my mind otherwise lifeless. The trip was neither long nor short; eternal while it lasted, it was over quickly. Mechanically I put the scarab away, gathered the evidence logs and lab reports, and got in my own car. Then I was home.

Maggie recognized the symptoms and didn't pester me with

questions. She had a customer in any event, but took time to pre-
pare a meal of soup and sandwiches for me and make me comfortable in our own room. When I was done eating and her customer
was gone she came in and rubbed my shoulders.

"Tired?"

"Mmm."

"You should take a shower."

"That would feel good."

"Did you solve it, the murder?"

"I think so."

"Who?"

"Uh...I'm not sure. Chief is still in Graf.—he's going to call
me when he comes down."

"You're not going out again—? You need to sleep."

"I'm not sleepy." I was like a child who has been allowed to
stay up late, and feels wrongly accused when told it is tired and
needs to go to bed.

"Take your boots off," she said. "I'll get a clean towel for you."

By the time I got out of the shower it was late in the afternoon,
and I was determined, despite Chief's instructions, to wait for his
call, which I felt should come soon. I sat up in bed wrapped in
a robe, with a cup of coffee on the nightstand and the documents
from our investigation spread out on the covers.

I was determined to piece it all together. Flipping open the
medical report and propping it on my knees, I took a large sip of
coffee and began scanning the evidence. Lividity—what did that
mean? Oh yes, blotchiness from the blood settling, due to gravity, in the lowest parts of the body. That meant she hadn't been
moved postmortem. Multiple hypodermic punctures on the feet,
indicating drug use ... rigor advanced ... body temperature—neat

how Chief could use that to fix the time of death... that bruise, now; what could that mean? Why hit somebody who's dead? Strange... nicotine stains... fingers... that was the first thing that tipped us off... she'd urinated... do people always pee when they die?... its gross... gross to die... so young, too... her eyes....

I didn't notice sleep when it caught me. If someone had said, "Are you asleep now?" I'd have shaken my head no.

I would have been forced to admit, however, that it was odd to be standing in the nave of the St. Lawrence cathedral in my bathrobe. Standing on a pew, no less, and staring up at the tortured figure on the great cross, watching freshets of blood trickle down the cheeks and gather in the eye sockets. That horrid wound in the feet where the spike pinned them dripped onto the stone flags beneath, making irregular splashes.

Looking up again, I saw fiery explosions erupt beyond the stained glass of the choir, bathing the church with a fearsome light, and great booms rocked and echoed in the vaults.

Alarmed, I ran outside. The medieval door let out onto the hillock overlooking the gunnery range. Below, the tanks were firing their great cannons in furious succession, and from across the range other tanks fired back. Tracers filled the air. Between them, in the wasted valley, a group of women huddled in terror. They wore silks and lace, but their hair was matted and their faces and bodies were caked with dirt, while their clothing hung in wretched tatters. Aching with fear and pity I bolted down the shallow slope, calling out to them to flee, to come to me and escape. I tripped and rolled in the dirt and loose stones, and came up next to Captain Worms's tank where it had been when its crewman was shot through the thigh. Staggering to my feet, I saw the women coming toward me out of the valley in a straggling line, like a pilgrimage of wraiths. Despite the deafening noise, I heard their weeping. At the front of the line I recognized Heidi, the little blond girl, cowering and shivering, and I extended my robe around her to protect and comfort her. When we had gone only a few steps, however, she cried out in alarm. Looking up, I saw Kimberly Merrick in her great fur coat and red garters standing on top of the tank. Her hair flew in the wind and the orange flashes from the cannons flickered on her face and limbs, reflected from her eyes like a cat's. She grabbed the machine gun and began firing it in all directions, indiscriminately. Then, the silhouette of a man in battle-dress rose up like a huge shadow, and struck her viciously from behind. She gave a cry and staggered, and fell against the trigger of the machine gun—which fired directly at me.

Everything dissolved, and then I was running back up the road, running and slipping, and terrified that I wouldn't find the medics in time. From the distance came the sound of a siren—rising and falling, harsh and atonal—it hurt my ears.

I awoke and jerked upright in my bed.

It was the telephone.

Maggie was answering it. "Hello? Oh, hi... he's still asleep... just a minute."

It was still light outside, but it didn't look right. I looked at the clock in dumb amazement: I had slept for 12 hours, and it was morning. I dashed to the phone.

"Well, Smitty, you ready?" Chief said.

"Sure... um, I gotta get dressed."

"I'm going to Erlangen. Meet me at the rail-head as soon as you can."

"Right—oh!—wait a minute, where is it?"

He gave me directions. I threw on some BDU's, gulped down the glass of orange juice that Maggie handed me, and didn't wait for coffee.

Chief had said to come quickly, but he hadn't said whether to come in the scarab. I changed my mind three times before rushing to post and getting it, and then hurried to the *autobahn*. My head seemed clear for the first time in days, and I felt I might begin to understand what was going on. And, as I drove to Erlangen, I recalled my dream. The figure who had struck down Kimberly Merrick was that of a man, a soldier. I still thought it must be Captain Worms, but it no longer felt right. And, Chief had spent almost all of his time in Grafenwöhr working on Captain Merrick's alibi.

I paused to think about Captain Merrick. One thing in the case that had never made sense to me was the way Chief responded to that man. In the first interview he had completely lost his temper, which was a very un-Chief thing to do. Then he hadn't even bothered with him again until we got to Graf., but there he seemed to be almost obsessed with doing things to annoy him.

Actually, I would have liked for Captain Merrick to be the murderer, if "like" is the right word. At least, there was something about him that seemed alien and unsympathetic. Perhaps it was his brittle, authoritarian manner, or his bland, angular face. I felt it was something deeper, though, and the more I thought about it the more I realized that there was something offensive about him, something about his behavior that was repugnant. But what was it?

I came into Erlangen and had to occupy myself with finding the rail-head. Once I was parked, however, in among Alpha's humvees, and staring at the tanks which were chained down onto a long line of flat cars, I formulated what it was that bothered me: Captain Merrick not only didn't show any grief over his wife's death, he didn't even seem to take it personally. He was untouched by it—as though it didn't matter to him. He took it coolly. Too coolly.

I got out and looked for Chief. I saw his Toyota, but I didn't see him. I went over to the tracks and scanned the line of tanks, and finally saw him climbing onto one of the turrets at the far end in his wool slacks and suspenders. He was climbing down again by the time I caught up with him, and he greeted me warmly.

"Smitty! You look great, like you've had a vacation."

"What's up, Chief?"

"I'm glad you're here. Did you bring the stuff? Good! I think the time has come to—"

"*Chief* Tobias!" It was Captain Merrick, striding towards us.

"Oh, good morning, captain! Sorry I missed you last night, but I got a ride anyway, with the mail truck—very convenient way to travel. Nothing so reliable as the mail—"

"What the hell are you doing here?" Captain Merrick broke in. His face was red, contorted with anger. "I've had all I'm gonna take of your damned bullshit. You've no business disrupting my unit. We're going to go see the colonel, right now, and put an end to this stupid game." He turned and strode away, but stopped after a few seconds and turned back. "I mean now Mister Tobias!"

Chief shrugged, and followed obediently. Captain Merrick called to his driver when we got to the parking area and got into his humvee in a huff of irritation, barking at his driver to get a move on. Chief told me to meet him at the brigade headquarters, and to bring everything from the car when I got there.

When we got to the *kaserne* Captain Merrick's humvee was parked in front of the main doors and we pulled in behind it, ignoring the no-parking zone. Chief jumped out and talked to the captain's driver while I was filling my arms with the reports. The driver, reluctantly it seemed, turned off the humvee and followed us into the building.

We went upstairs and found Colonel Crick's office. It was an impressive room, paneled in dark wood and hung with flags and other military decoration. There were comfortable chairs and a large conference table on one side, and in front of the windows Colonel Crick himself sat behind an expansive antique desk.

Chief told Captain Merrick's driver to wait outside, and we went in, Chief closing the door behind us.

"Sir," Captain Merrick was saying, heatedly but respectfully, "this man has gone too far, and I want him punished. He practically stole one of my vehicles, he's harassed my driver and my first sergeant, embarrassed my family, and tried his damnedest to turn my wife's death into some kind of a scandal."

"All right, Captain."

"I just don't think I should be subjected to this kind of treatment—"

"At ease, Captain Merrick. I was just about to call Colonel Bragg, Mister Tobias's commander." Colonel Crick reached for the phone.

"Before you do that, sir," Chief cut in, "there's something I'd like to say to Captain Merrick."

"Well?" the colonel said.

"You're right, Captain," Chief said. "My behavior has been out of line. I've bent or broken the rules of military courtesy, questioned your subordinates behind your back, and I've made a special point, frankly, since Kimberly's body was found, of making your life uncomfortable." He paused and took the reports from my arms. "Ordinarily, I would be on your side against me—"

"Don't play games with me, Mister Tobias."

"No, really—I'd be the first to help you get me busted back to stripes, if only—"

Chief dropped the stack of papers loudly onto the desk, put his hand on top of them, and leaned forward, looking hard at the captain.

"—if only you hadn't murdered your wife."

16 Confrontation

Matson Barracks, Erlangen, West Germany,
Friday, 4 July 198-, 0830 hrs.

"This is obscene—" Captain Merrick muttered, taking a pace backwards. "I have a company to take care of." He looked at the colonel, clearly wanting to leave but unable to do so without being dismissed. "I don't have time for this man's stupid accus—"

"If you leave now," Chief said evenly, "I will have you arrested at the gate."

"I hope, Mister Tobias," the colonel said, "for your sake, that you can back up this charge with serious evidence. I think it was obvious to everyone how Mrs. Merrick died."

Chief kept his eyes on Captain Merrick. "Obvious—wasn't it though! And damned clever. I think, Colonel, that it will be in everyone's interest if I am given the floor for a few minutes. But first, I would like to use your phone." Here he turned and met the colonel's troubled gaze.

"What for?"

"I need to call the doctor." Without waiting for an answer, Chief reached across and picked up the receiver, and punched the buttons. "Major Suarez, please—tell him it's Chief Tobias. Major? It's time. I'm in Colonel Crick's office." He hung up.

"Start talking, Tobias," the colonel said grimly. "I hope your

264

story's a good one."

"It is not, sir." Chief took a deep breath, put his hands on his hips, and stared at the ceiling. "It is a bad story, with a bad ending." He paced slowly then, gesturing with his hands as he spoke like an actor in a one-act play. "It begins with a young officer, newly commissioned and very ambitious, who finds himself attracted to a wealthy young socialite. She has looks and charm, and our young officer is quickly hooked and landed—not because he is smitten, perhaps, but because he is eager to be a rising star, and a smart wife with money and manners is a great asset to an officer determined to make a successful career.

"And successful he is, getting his captain's bars in almost record time. He is polished, efficient, and quick to take on the most prestigious assignment offered. He makes sure he gets noticed often, and his superiors are impressed. After all, Colonel, there must be forty captains in this brigade; how many of them are you really familiar with? No matter. He is given a company command, in one of your armored battalions, and runs a crack outfit.

"But there is trouble behind the scenes. The pretty wife turns out to be ugly beneath the surface. She is disturbed—what the textbooks call borderline—and far from being an asset she quickly becomes an embarrassment. She alienates the other wives, flirts with other officers, and runs hot and cold with her husband—mostly cold. She makes ugly scenes with him, threatens to ruin him, then suddenly goes nymphy and jealous. It wears him down, until finally in this nightmare of a relationship it is hard to say which is the more hellish—the senseless, vicious attacks, or the insidious, sickening demands for sex and intimacy."

Captain Merrick was staring at Chief with frank astonishment.

"How—?" he began.

I think he was going to say, "How do you know all this?" But Chief cut him off.

"I'd prefer you to just listen, Captain. I haven't read you your rights, yet." Chief cleared his throat and ran his fingers along the edge of the colonel's desk thoughtfully. "They separated," he continued. "The officer took an apartment in town, and began thinking about divorce. You might think he would try to get professional help for his wife, but it is often not so simple. To begin with, most of us are not trained to recognize mental illness when we see it, and the victims of this kind of affective disorder are typically incensed at the suggestion that there is anything wrong with them. In any event, what mattered to the officer was not that his wife was sick, but that she was nasty and combative and—this is what counted—entirely the wrong woman for his life-plan. He needed a quick, quiet divorce. Naturally, she would make that impossible. Undoubtedly, she would threaten to make a scandal, and to take revenge on her husband."

Captain Merrick's face at this point was a study. I think there were several emotions vying for control of his features, but the only sure sign was the clenched set of his jaws.

Colonel Crick was impassive, staring at his desk.

"I think that is where the matter stood at the beginning of the summer. I suspect, however, that the young commander had already begun to hear the rumors that were being spoken about his estranged wife. They'd been circulating for some time, but he became aware of them only slowly. I believe, though I can't prove it, that he began to keep surveillance on his family quarters, and saw his wife's late-night comings and goings. Possibly, some sympathetic NCO or lieutenant told him that she'd been seen at the wall."

"Is that true?" the colonel demanded, looking at Captain Merrick.

"Please don't ask any questions, sir," Chief said urgently. "Hear me out."

The colonel looked disgruntled, but settled in his chair with his chin in his hand and waited for Chief to continue.

"In any event, his unit was due for a gunnery deployment, and left in mid-June. Shortly after getting to Grafenwöhr, however, our company commander finds himself with a genital infection. He quietly gets a referral from his battalion medical officer, and goes to the local Army clinic for treatment. There, he is told he has syphilis. There can be only one explanation for this, since there is only one way syphilis can be transmitted from one person to another—and although he hasn't slept with his wife, perhaps, for some time, he hasn't slept with anyone else, either. It can take up to three months for symptoms to appear, I'm told—ah!"

There was a knock at the door.

"Come in!" Chief called, winning a sharp look from the colonel. The door opened and Major Suarez looked in. "Come in, doctor. Have you got them? Excellent." Chief took a sealed Manila envelope from the major, together with some other papers. "Please stay, Major. Now these," he continued, throwing the Manila envelope on the desk, "are clinical records on the man in our story; of his visit to the clinic in Graf. They were sent to this brigade to be included in the man's permanent medical file, and arrived just within the last few days. I don't have the authority to open the envelope and look—and neither do you, Colonel," he added hastily, for the colonel had picked it up and looked about to open it, "not yet, anyway."

"Then how do you know what's in it?" Colonel Crick demanded.

"Have you ever been to Siberia, sir?" Chief answered.

"No, but what does—"

"And yet you know it exists," Chief said. "By a similar act of faith, I know what is in that envelope. We live in an ordered universe."

"Ptchaw!" the colonel exclaimed, dropping the envelope in irritation.

"Our man in Grafenwöhr," Chief continued smoothly, "naturally wants to confirm what he already knows, for if his wife has committed adultery it may be possible to have her returned to the States administratively, before she has a chance to make things difficult for him. However, it will not be enough just to make the accusation—he needs proof, and that will be difficult. Medical records are confidential. But he is clever. He thinks that, if he obtains proof, it won't matter much *how* he obtained it."

"I think this has gone far enough," Captain Merrick said.

"Oh, it goes a good deal further, captain. I do urge you not to speak, for your own sake. A week ago last Wednesday, according to his driver—and his first sergeant—our company commander makes an excuse to return to Erlangen. Once here, he dismisses his driver, goes to his garrison orderly room, and prepares fake change-of-station orders. He forges his commander's signature on an outprocessing form—" Chief looked at the papers still in his hands "—Colonel Serway's, in fact, and he even goes to the trouble to initial a few of the less controlled outprocessing stations, such as supply and personnel, to lend the document verisimilitude. Then he takes his form and his fake orders to the brigade clinic, and requests his spouse's medical records. The clerk gives them to him in a sealed envelope, takes three copies of his orders, and stamps his outprocessing form. Unknown to the captain, she also photocopies the outprocessing form for her own files. She is an efficient soldier." Chief sighed. "These documents—the orders and form—are not controlled, but purely administrative." He handed them to Colonel Crick. "Observe the date of the clinic outprocessing stamp—June 25th."

"Christ, Andy," the colonel said when he had looked them over. "What were you thinking? I'd have helped you—"

"Sir—" Chief said.

"Captain Merrick!" the colonel barked, suddenly wrathful, "do you realize this is a court martial offense?"

"Colonel Crick, we're not done yet," Chief said quietly.

The colonel seemed to fully apprehend, at last, where Chief's story was headed. He sat back, and the color drained from his face.

"When the captain takes the records home and opens them he finds what he was looking for—and a good deal more. He wanted evidence of infidelity, and he got that, but he didn't expect what else he found. For now, it is enough to know that what he found was shocking. Indeed, it could be unforgivable."

Captain Merrick, who had been standing throughout all this, reached blindly for a chair and sat down, his face flushed crimson. At first I thought he might be ashamed, but then I realized that what I saw was rage, primitive and consuming. He controlled it—but at such cost! It was frightening to see.

Chief studied him closely for a few seconds. Then, picking up the sealed medical documents and handing them back to Major Suarez, he walked slowly across the floor, eventually placing the sitting man between himself and the colonel's desk. "I think," he said, "that the captain really had planned to go back up with the mail truck, but now—I don't think he knew what he was going to do, but he knew he was going to do something. Something terrible.

He got in his own car and drove back to Grafenwöhr alone. He parked it in the main garrison, where it wouldn't look out of place, and returned to his unit."

"Bullshit," Captain Merrick said.

"I don't know if he returned to Erlangen that night, but I don't think so. No, I think he didn't yet know what he was going to do. But the next day his tank broke down on the range, and had to be taken to battalion maintenance. A problem with the gun re-coil mechanism, or so I understand from one of the maintenance NCO's. By then, he had made a plan."

Chief stopped and pulled a card out of his wallet. I recognized it as a Miranda card, printed with the text of the constitutionally required warning given to criminal suspects. He flicked it with his fingers meditatively. Then he pulled up a chair and put his foot on it, leaning on his knee and looking down on Captain Merrick with the card tucked in his palm.

"It was a hell of a plan, Captain. Your wife was an alcoholic. That must have grated like hell on a sober fellow like you—she'd drink, get bitchy, drink some more, start a fight, then when she was really drunk she'd start coming on to you in that sickening way she had. And you'd wait, knowing that soon she'd pass out and you could have a few hours of peace. But now! Now you could use her drunkenness—use it to finish her." Chief flicked the card again, not taking his eyes off the captain. "You took something from your tank that day. Leaving your driver to help the mechanics, you drove the humvee to your car, put the something in the trunk or the back seat—probably the trunk—and then drove back. That night, with your M1 repaired, you went to the range—"

"This is such total bullshi—" Captain Merrick began.

"—and left the range, Captain Merrick!" Chief could muster

a voice that rocked your bones. "Left it just after midnight, got to your car, and returned to Erlangen! It couldn't be done in a humvee—Smitty and I verified that—but then a man like yourself doesn't drive a clunker. He drives a car with something under the hood—something to take advantage of the damned suicidal highways in this country—something that could cover the distance in an hour—even less."

"And when you got home, there she was... you couldn't have asked for better... gurgling drunk, or passed out cold even... and all you had to do was finish it." Chief's voice had become low. "You stood over the bed, then, looking down at her, at her dead body, and in one final act of righteous retribution you gave her the back of your hand, knocking a drool of spittle onto her cheek." He stood up and said with finality, "You were back in the field in plenty of time."

"But, Chief Tobias," Major Suarez said, bewildered, "how—?"

In answer, Chief reached in his pocket and pulled out a piece of clear plastic, folded neatly into a square. He unfolded it and laid it on the desk. "Recognize that, Major?"

It was a saline bag.

"Oh my God," the doctor said, standing over it and leaning heavily against the desk. "Oh my God...."

Captain Merrick was thunderstruck. "How did you...?" he breathed.

"We're all going to pretend we didn't hear you say that," Chief said. "It isn't the one you used, anyway. It was easy, wasn't it? Just empty out the saline and replace it with the vodka...," Chief mimed each action with his hands. "... then roll down her stocking, slip the needle into the vein on her ankle, and feed in the vodka—drip, drip—slowly, no need to rush... then hold the mirror over her mouth to make sure when she stopped breathing. Then roll the stocking back up—"

"Fuck you," Captain Merrick growled dangerously.

"At ease, soldier!" the colonel said, but his subordinate was beyond respect of rank.

"You can't prove any of this—"

"Where's your car?" Chief broke in. The captain shut his mouth with a snap. "That's right—best if you don't answer that. You were planning on driving it down last night, were you not? Just make up some little fib to your driver about riding with someone else, and then quietly drive home in your own car. But you couldn't, could you? Not after I'd promised to ride with you. I'll bet, if I were to call the MP's in Grafenwöhr, right now, they'd find your car for us—"

"You devil!" Captain Merrick said. "You fucking son of a bitch—!" He leapt up and swung at Chief, a sudden vicious blow.

I'm not sure how it happened, but the next instant Chief had Merrick's wrist in one hand, and with the other he was bringing his head down face-first on the heavy desk, violently enough that some of the colonel's books toppled over. The colonel leapt up and both he and the major stepped back in shock.

"You may not appreciate this," Chief growled, pressing the man's head down firmly and putting his lips to his ear, "but I've been more than fair with you. I've told you most of what I know and haven't asked you a single question yet." Chief's intensity was immense. "That changes now. You have the right to remain silent. If you choose to give up this right, anything you say can and will be used against you in a court of law. You have the right to an attorney...,"

Captain Merrick was perfectly motionless while Chief read him his rights, but his breathing was fitful and ragged.

"... do you understand these rights?"

Captain Merrick didn't answer.

"I said," Chief roared, "do you understand these rights?"

"Yes."

"Now, captain," Chief said finally, "I'm gonna let go of you. Smitty, the tape recorder. And captain, I solemnly promise that the next time you move in a way I don't like—if you even breathe heavy—I'm gonna splash your brains all over the colonel's beautiful desk. You got that?"

The captain nodded as best he could and Chief pushed him back into the chair.

The Colonel recovered himself. "What have you got to say for yourself, Captain Merrick?"

"The bitch," he said, almost inaudibly, "deserved it."

"Mother of God," Major Suarez blurted, scandalized, "is that all?"

The man looked up from his chair and gazed distractedly at each of us in turn. His face was strange. He looked, not like someone who was guilty and had been caught, nor even like a man who has been defeated by his enemy, but rather like someone who despairs of being understood. He was wretched, but it was the wrong sort of wretchedness, and I thought of my impression of Captain Merrick when I had seen him for the first time, just days before: that he was a man whose personal reality was somehow disassociated from the actual world around him.

"You can't prove anything," he finally repeated.

"Can't I?" Chief said. "I said I told you most of what I know. It was a mistake to leave your combat lifesaver's kit in the apartment. Even I can count to two, and I was bound to discover that one of the saline bags was missing—Major Suarez, I'm sure, can vouch for how many are included in each kit." The doctor nodded. "Also, your own crew knew that it had been on your tank when you deployed, and they noticed it missing. Why didn't you take it back to the field with you?"

Captain Merrick didn't answer.

"Also, you'd been working on your tank's gun system that day. There's a very peculiar kind of lubricant used on the M1 main gun. Bright red. You must have had some on your hands and transferred it to the box—I know that you cleaned it off with a wet paper towel after you took it into the apartment. I know because you missed the wastebasket."

Chief leaned against the desk and looked down on the captain. "It's virtually impossible not to make mistakes," he said, almost gently. "I know that you emptied the saline bag in the bathroom sink, and I can guess that you used the fresh roll of toilet paper to mop up the blood that spilled when you were hooking up the bag's tubing. You probably used your wet-weather jacket to shield the bedding. We'll find it—or whatever you used—and unless it's been machine washed we'll find the blood traces.

"Captain Merrick," he coaxed at last, "wouldn't it be simpler to lay it out for us? And more honorable? I understand how you must have felt—what she did to you—what she did to what was yours."

Captain Merrick gave a start, and his jaw set.

"Make a clean breast of it," Chief said. "Fill in the blanks for me, and I'll do what I can for you."

But it didn't work. The captain recovered himself, swallowed his emotions, and said, "I want a lawyer."

Chief stood up. "Yes," he said heavily. "Yes, you certainly do."

Colonel Crick insisted on taking custody personally, which was his prerogative, and, after the MP's arrived, Chief, the Major, and I walked out together. We stood on the steps as they brought the captain out, put him in a green sedan, and drove away.

"Chief Tobias," the major said, "you are an astonishing man."

"No," Chief responded, lighting a cigarette. "You've just never thought about criminal investigation—never been close to it—and had no idea what it meant. No more than I know what's involved in diagnosing cancer, for instance."

"That's true, I guess...." Major Suarez struggled with what he wanted to say. "You've done something, though, that I've never seen anyone do before. This community was ... like a patient being operated on—without anesthetic. You started in with your scalpel ... and we struggled and resisted and attacked you ... but you slipped past every obstacle and carefully separated the tissues, exposing the malignancy."

"That's colorful, doc," Chief said with a weary smile.

Captain Merrick's driver, who had been dismissed ahead of us, came back up the street in his humvee, bringing First Sergeant Frigg and a lieutenant I assumed to be the company XO with him. The first sergeant stared rudely at Chief as they stepped past us and went up to see the colonel.

"You asked me once to look upon you as a fellow scientist," Major Suarez said when they had gone. "I want you to know that I do."

The two men shook hands agreeably, and the Major left.

"Well, Smitty," Chief said then. He stared across the parade field, squinting at the smoke of the cigarette that hung from his lips. "You've had quite an experience."

"What happens now, Chief?"

"To you, or to Captain Merrick?"

"Well," I said, fearing that my stint as junior detective was coming to an end, "I guess to both of us."

"You've both got a tough time ahead of you."

"Oh," I said, and looked at my shoes.

"The captain, if things are handled as they should be, gets to visit Kansas."

"Kansas—?"

"Yep—for a long, long time."

I looked at him without comprehension.

"Leavenworth."

That's right, I remembered; the site of the federal penitentiary.

"And you, Smitty... you're fate is almost as bad. Every job, you see, has its down side. In this one, it's—" he put his hand on my shoulder and looked at me gravely "—preparing reports. Uh, you do type, don't you?"

"Superbly, actually."

"Excellent. We want to get it done quick—you never know when the next case might be going to fall in our laps." He slapped me on the shoulder with a smile. "You want to be ready when it does, don't you?"

He headed down the steps, threw his car keys up, caught them, and said, "Get a move on, boy."

17 Taps

Chief's apartment, Nürnberg, West Germany,
Friday, 4 July 198-, 1900 hrs.

"Well, Smitty, what'd she say? Can you set awhile?"

"I have permission," I said facetiously.

"Good! Here's to understanding wives! Maggie struck me from the first as a generous woman."

"She says she knew all along it was the husband. That reminds me, I owe you five dollars."

"What's this?" he asked staring at the bill.

"The riddle, remember?"

He chuckled long and gloatingly as he opened two bottles of pils and retrieved clean glasses from the cupboard.

I had spent the afternoon at our own battalion headquarters, transcribing all my notebooks. The work was wearisome, the more so that it meant forestalling the task of dealing mentally and emotionally with that morning's scene in the colonel's office. Also, I had a thousand questions for Chief that I was anxious to ask.

Chief had prepared his preliminary reports at home, one for Colonel Crick and another for our own command. At the end of the day he had finally called, inviting me to his apartment. Now, at last, we were seated in the comfortable chairs of his study, and I was able to put the question that tormented me most.

"When did you know, Chief? When did you know it was Captain Merrick?"

"Well," he said, burping discreetly, "that's not an easy question. When did I know—or when did I know that I knew?" He settled back in a ruminative manner. "I thought from the beginning that he was most likely. Then, when I met him on Sunday, there was no question but that his relationship to his wife wasn't right. Remember how he acted?"

"That was a strange scene."

"Yes, well, I erred I suppose. I had an intuition that if I provoked his anger—which he wore like a badge—he would tell us enough either to eliminate him as a suspect, or to allow us to arrest him on the spot. Unfortunately, we were interrupted."

"I wonder how the colonel feels now about throwing you out?"

"May he rot," Chief said sincerely. "But then, it turned out there were scads of other interesting possibilities. Gunther, Sabrina, the Worms's—with Captain Merrick back in the field and no idea at all how the woman had really been done in, there was little else to do but run down the red herrings. At least they were entertaining.…"

"There are lots of things I still don't understand. How'd you know he'd gone to the clinic, for instance?"

"Let's start at the beginning. There were hundreds of details in this case, but only a few were really salient. That's the real trick, you know; separating the accidents from the essentials, as it used to be said.

"From the body, we knew that she had died where she was found. That was the first and most important fact, especially when it became clear that the death was staged. In retrospect, there were only two or three other really telling clues at the scene: the mud on the carpet that Mercy said was there, the paper towel with the grease smear, and the presence of the first aid kit. The mud should have pointed us the right way immediately, because you even pointed out at the time that it hadn't rained for weeks, and the weather's been hot. Still, people do water their lawns, and I didn't make too much of it until you mentioned it again Monday night."

"What about the space-heater?"

"I wish I knew why he did that," Chief said. "Probably some silly reason. People do nutty things, and real crimes are always attended by features that seem to have no rhyme or reason. It's not like books. If you were writing this up as a whodunit, you'd leave it out."

Chief swirled the inch or so of beer at the bottom of his glass thoughtfully, drained it, and cracked open another bottle.

"Anyway, by Tuesday night we had eliminated Gunther and Sabrina—at least, I couldn't get myself behind any workable theory that involved them, and frankly I didn't credit either of them with the brains. That, and the newly revealed Worms connection, turned my attention back to Kimberly herself, and her actual relationships.

"The fact is, Smitty, relative strangers don't often kill one another. In the absence of a financial motive, it takes passion, hatred—and that means a close relationship, preferably of long standing.

"Also, her records weren't turning up. That had to mean something, and the more I meditated on it the more convinced I became that it might be the crux of the matter. I think the idea that Captain Merrick must've finagled them was a long time coming, but when it finally came into full flower all kinds of little meaningless details stood up and demanded to be noticed. I remembered Major

Suarez talking about her abortion, then the mud on the carpet, the greasy stains on the paper towel—even the postmortem bruise on her cheek.

"I guess you could say that's when I knew. Sometime between Tuesday night, laughing my ass off at your misfortune with the immortal Heidi, and Wednesday morning on the way to Graf.

"But, believing you've got the pieces and knowing how to fit them together are two different things. He had stolen her medical records—I was able to confirm that pretty quickly by calling Major Suarez and telling him where to look—but why had he done it? And, all the time, there was still the question of how he had killed her, if killed her he had.

"And then there was that awful, bloody accident."

"It never occurred to me, Chief! I watched you fold up that saline bag, and I thought you were just feeling sick and dazed from the accident."

"I was feeling sick, yes, but not because of the accident. It's funny, how everything can suddenly make a picture, where before it was only a collage of disconnected elements. And it was sickening. I realized all in an instant what had happened. He must've stolen the records because he caught something from her, but once he had them he found out something that would devastate him— that he was a father. That is, he would have been, but she had aborted the fetus. Most men would be affected by that in some way, but some—a man like Captain Merrick, for instance—might be enraged.

"In the space of an instant, I not only knew who, but how—and why."

I sipped my beer, recalling to my mind the ferocious passions the man had shown in the colonel's office that morning. "It makes sense now," I said. "I can just see him standing over her ... having his vengeance."

It was a haunting image. I made a conscious effort to think about something else. Chief sipped his beer in silence.

"What happens to Sabrina?" I asked after a minute. For some reason, I couldn't stop thinking of her as a sympathetic character.

"I called her," he said with a wry grin, "this afternoon. Like a good girl, she was still waiting in her apartment."

"Did you tell her—about Captain Merrick?"

"Eventually, yes. But first I told her what I thought of her. Not a good idea, probably—and I know better—but I picked her apart for a while; told her Kimberly's death presaged her own fate if she didn't grow up." His grin had turned sour. " 'Mister Chief'—camp counselor."

"What about the Worms's?"

"What about 'em?"

"Are you still going to talk to Captain Worms? You said you wanted to kick him—"

"I'd like to kick a lot of people. It's none of my business, Smitty, and none of yours. And Smitty, it won't do anyone any good if his affair becomes generally known."

I nodded. That matter was closed.

"Hungry?" he asked after a pause.

We trooped to the kitchen and Chief dug in his fridge. He took items out, looked at them, and distributed them approximately evenly—either to the garbage, to the kitchen table, or back to the fridge. I wondered if my fridge would get like that if I lived alone. Finally we carried a tray back into the study, laden with blue cheese and cheddar, grapes, cold sausage, a heel of bread, some butter, apples and oranges—a feast.

The phone rang, and Chief conversed with someone for a few minutes, ending by saying, "Tell the damned colonel he gets his report in the morning."

"Damned fools," he said coming back to the table, "think the world revolves around them."

I was finishing my second half-liter bottle (Chief was well into his third) and I felt myself relaxing. I was grateful for Chief's society. I had felt edgy and fragile all through the afternoon, and resisted the thought of going home. I wanted to recover myself, to get balanced or ... or something. I had a sensation that reminded me of the way I sometimes felt when down with the flu or other illness, of not wanting to have to deal with anything.

We munched quietly for a while.

"Where'd you learn to fight like that?" I asked.

"You mean, where'd I learn to *not* fight like that," he said epigrammatically. "Never handle a physical confrontation by trying to fight! It gets you nowhere, and can be messy. It takes years of training to be any good at it anyway. If possible, always walk away from it."

"You didn't."

"I couldn't, of course, so I chose the second-best alternative."

"Which is?"

He leaned forward. "Which is to dominate your opponent absolutely and unexpectedly, and let him believe you are going to kill him. Then offer him the choice of backing down. There are a few simple tricks. I could teach you the one I used today in no time."

"It certainly worked."

The phone rang again, and this time it was the colonel.

"—not there yet?" Chief cried. "Why, I sent it by MP courier an hour ago! I'm sure, sir, it'll be on your desk first thing when you come in tomorrow. Well, if you like to wait... these MP's are an unreliable bunch, not like your brigade, sir. Yes, sir. Goodnight." He hung up. "Idiot." He dug around in a desk drawer looking for "that damned phone key." German phones can't be unplugged, but they come with a key for turning them off. He found it, and used it with satisfaction.

"You feeling okay, Smitty?" he said when he sat down. "You look a little peaked."

I didn't answer, but shrugged my shoulders.

"I'm pretty calloused," he said. "I've been doing this for a long time, and I've developed ways of dealing with the ugliness. But there's no reason to be ashamed if you feel yourself a little knocked on the head by what you've seen and been through the last few days."

"At least it's over," I said.

"Only the fun part. This case'll plague us with a lot of donkey-work, yet. It's one thing to solve the crime, and another to bring the case to court in such a way that you don't lose the conviction. That damned fool of a colonel almost did us out of those medical records today."

"How's that?"

"Evidence that isn't obtained by the rules ceases to be evidence. You can't just go invading a man's privacy because you think he's guilty—you've gotta follow the rules. An improperly obtained document is meat and potatoes to a defense attorney." He settled back into his cushions and put his feet up. "But for now, we relax. Once the colonel gets his precious report—which I'll take to him *in the morning*—so's he can continue to detain Captain Merrick legally, we can kick back 'til Monday. My advice to you is, go home and dance with your wife. Sleep a lot. Get drunk if it suits you."

We sat in silence, me restlessly, Chief with his eyes closed. In a few minutes it was clear he was dozing off. I still didn't want to go home, but after a while longer I got up quietly, collected my hat, and headed for the door as silently as I could.

"Smitty," Chief called.

I turned back.

"You did a very fine job today—all week. Thanks."

"I'm glad you hired me, Chief."

"Say, d'you think Maggie might feed me again? Sunday, say?"

"I'm sure she would."

"You know that's why I hired you, right?"

I grinned. "Goodnight, Chief."

It was dark when I went down to my car, and I drove cautiously, aware that I was tipsy. In the distance I seemed to hear gunfire, and at first I thought my mind must be playing tricks on me—that I was imagining myself back near the gunnery range. But then with a nervous laugh I realized what it was: today was the fourth of July. Somewhere, Americans were setting off fireworks.

I pulled up to my building and parked. We were not the only Americans living in that block, and there were several balconies where people were foolishly shooting off sparkler-fountains and bottle-rockets. I felt it was thoughtless. A sponsored display was scheduled on the *kaserne*—why upset our neighbors? We were guests here, for Christ's sake.

"What do those damned idiots think they're doing?" I barked when Maggie met me at the door.

"They're just having fun—" she began.

"It's stupid," I said. "Where're are the kids?"

"In bed."

I strode to the living room and went out on the balcony. "Hey!" I yelled. "Cut that shit out!" I yelled a few more times, and then returned to the living room.

Maggie was standing in the doorway, looking at me with concern. "It's late," she said, putting her arms around me, "come to bed."

I let her lead me to the bedroom. She took my boots and put my uniform away, and coaxed me into bed. I was fluffing my pillow when someone dropped a string of black-cats past the window, flashing and exploding with a loud rat-a-tat-tat. I jerked involuntarily.

"Sons a'bitches!"

"Mommy!" my youngest called, frightened, from the adjoining room.

Maggie looked at me anxiously before running in to soothe the toddler back to sleep.

I lay on my pillow, listening and resentful. It was not hard to close my eyes, however, and I wasn't aware of it several minutes later when my wife came back to bed.

The sound of the fireworks stayed with me—sometimes close, always in the distance—and in my semiconscious state it was inevitably transformed into the sound of weapons-fire. I resisted the images of the gunnery range that clamored for my attention, but I couldn't shake the sounds. Then one especially loud bang seemed to go off right in my head.

I started and sat up, listening intently. Maggie sat up too and put her hand on my arm.

The phone rang.

"Yes?" I said, answering it. "Oh . . . yes, I—what? Oh . . . oh, God . . . when? . . . yes, I'll tell him."

I depressed the connection, and then dialed Chief. He answered on the eleventh ring—I supposed he must have turned his phone back on before going to bed.

"Chief?"

"Smitty."

"Battalion called. Captain Merrick, he—"

"Yes, Smitty, I know. I'm sorry."

We didn't speak for several seconds, while the phone line hissed gently.

"Tell Maggie," he said then. "I'll call you in the morning."

I hung up.

"What is it?" Maggie said, coming to the bedroom door.

I wanted to speak but my stomach clenched and writhed, and I just made it to the bathroom in time.

When I was done and could breathe again, and could drink the water Maggie gave me, I told her. Captain Merrick, in being transferred to Nürnberg that night, had been allowed to stop at his apartment under MP guard. There, he had taken a pistol from his desk and shot himself in the head before he could be stopped.

"It's just . . . so . . ." I stammered at the end.

She brought me gently back to bed, and we sat leaning against the pillows.

"I don't know how to tell you, Maggie," I groaned miserably. "It's so—"

Another string of firecrackers was set off close by, and I began to tremble. Maggie drew me to her and held me in her arms with my head on her breast.

"Jesus, it's so brutal!"

My wife didn't speak, but stroked her fingers through my hair soothingly, and after a long time I fell asleep.